The Knocking

OTHER TITLES BY
LAURA LEE BAHR

Who Is the Liar

The Knocking

A NOVEL

LAURA LEE BAHR

Little a

Published by Little A, Seattle

www.apub.com

Amazon, the Amazon logo, and Little A are trademarks of Amazon.com, Inc., or its affiliates.

EU product safety contact:
Amazon Media EU S. à r.l.
38, avenue John F. Kennedy, L-1855 Luxembourg
amazonpublishing-gpsr@amazon.com

ISBN-13: 978-1662542220 (hardcover)
ISBN-13: 978-1662537745 (paperback)
ISBN-13: 978-1662537738 (digital)

Cover design by Joanne O'Neill
Cover images: © Artis777, © CSA-Printstock,
© NATALIIA OMELCHENKO / Getty Images; © M_a_r_ii_a, © Mar1kOFF,
© Wanlee Prachyapanapra / Shutterstock

Printed in the United States of America

First Edition

For Ezra, who believes in me

PART I

---·---

**CAN WE SPEAK TO THE DEAD?
ELEVEN-YEAR-OLD GIRL CLAIMS SHE
IS A "SPIRIT-TELEGRAPH"**

Chapter 1

NEWSPAPER WOMAN DIES TRYING TO SAVE
THE SOUL OF AMERICA

A fitting headline or epitaph for the harrowing journey I have endured to get here.

Is this the place?

All the trees move like long warnings, holding out their arms as if to try to slow the storm. I tug my steamer trunk through the mud, up the drive, keeping my mind on typesetting, ink, large printing presses. I am not dwelling on the late hour, that I am utterly alone, or that I am soaked. My integrity and purpose as a journalist burn bright in my mind, lighting my way onward to this destination.

If this is, indeed, the destination.

I hear a branch crack and the groan of wood ripping as a gust of wind threatens to blow me over. I plant myself steady for a moment, turning my face away from the sound. No tree falls, no limb crashes down. I move again.

I am almost to the front door, but the closer I get, the more I doubt I am in the right place.

This house is so deep in the woods that it appears more like the ensorcelled setting of a Grimms' tale than a place for an esteemed man who creates headlines. Yet it gleams white with columns like a Greek temple, a seeming symmetry in the facade. It is the type of construction favored by those who wish to appear as the heirs of Western democracy. It must be the right place. I abandon my trunk and run the rest of the way to the door to avoid drowning.

A Federal Eagle brass ring is an appropriate choice of a door knocker for this great-conscience American representative. I politely knock and wait. It is not a nice time to arrive, I realize, but they must be expecting me.

I drop the brass ring again with three knocks like I mean it. If I need to wake someone up, then so be it, they will be awake now.

I wait. No one is coming.

I steel myself, ready to beat the door with my fists.

There is a sound, a voice on the other side.

"Hello?" I yell, as it is not opening.

A voice calls back something that I cannot make out.

"Hello! It's me, E. A. Howe, I was sent by Mrs. Swisshelm." This is ridiculous, shouting through a heavy door, trying to explain who I am in the middle of the night in a rainstorm. A wind keeps blowing water directly onto me like it has a personal vendetta. "Please! Open the door!"

It doesn't open. Someone on the other side is asking me something. "Are you of flesh or spirit?"

"Flesh! I am flesh!" I yell. "Fully flesh!"

Whoever is on the other side decides it's answer enough, for I'm granted passage out from the dark night, into the dark house.

"*Are* you, then?" she asks in a minor-key Irish dialect. A lamp reveals a woman's face contorted with distress. "Humans don't arrive at hours like this."

"They do after their train breaks down twelve miles from its destination and they are crammed into a stagecoach for a day to get here to Turtle Bay, with men of highly questionable character heading to God-knows-what destinations and a rude, unconscionable driver so worried his wheels will get stuck in the mud that he drops them a half mile from the door in a storm." I am shivering, hoping that fully explaining my dire circumstances will result in compassionate assistance. "I apologize that it's late. Please, I have a trunk and I would love help bringing it in."

"Who are you? What are you doing here?" she demands to know.

"I am E. A. Howe, here at the request of Mrs. Jane Swisshelm to visit Mr. Greeley." I try to speak with the proper pronunciation and tone that is befitting a professional young woman, without my Ohio farm-folk drawl. Whatever the hour and weather conditions, I pull up into full posture to be taken seriously. "I was sent here on a very important assignment."

She moves the lamp close enough to my face for me to feel the heat of it. "We are not expecting you."

"You must be. Mrs. Swisshelm sent a telegraph last week." I start to re-count my days on the train. "At least a week. It has been ten days and many hours. Maybe eleven, the stagecoach ride took forever . . ."

"We are not expecting you, I said."

I can see nothing of the home I'm in, but I can hear a *tock tock* of a pendulum clock, its face gleaming in a reflection of the lamp-light. Somewhere a child's voice is crying. The shadows on the woman's face deepen.

"This is the Greeley residence?" I ask.

"It is." Her reply does nothing to shake the feeling that I've made some terrible mistake.

"Mr. Horace Greeley, of the *New-York Daily Tribune?*"

"It is, and it is the hour of the night when decent people sleep. I was not told to expect any visitors, human or otherwise."

After such a perilous journey—and now, at this final destination, to be so rudely greeted—I do not act with the proper pluck and gravitas that I expect of myself.

Instead, I burst into tears.

"Now, stop it," she chides, pity in her voice. "There's no need for that. I am not going to turn you back out into the rain. We get enough tears in this house without you pouring in more."

She shepherds me through the darkness, a warm hand taking my wet cloak. The *tock tock* of the clock becomes fainter, but the sound of the child crying grows louder. "Come, let's get you dry. Sorry to leave you out there so long in this weather. There's been too many happenings here the past few days. In this house, spirits knock more than people do."

"Are you saying this house is . . . haunted?" I try to maintain a level voice while asking this ridiculous question. This cannot be the right place. I am supposed to be at the Greeley estate, the home of the self-made newspaper titan. Our dialects must have gotten crossed.

"They can't keep help here in this house, miss. But they gravely need it." She stops and puts the lantern to my face again. She looks me in the eye, allowing me to see hers. "That child you hear crying is alive for now, but there are four little graves out back in a family plot with her brothers and sisters that she'll be joining if she doesn't get more care. Are you looking for work?"

It is a difficult question for me to answer properly, especially as I can see she is desperate for me to do what is assumed to be women's work. I am a different type of woman, one who has crafted herself from an ideology of equality, albeit not yet realized in our nation. The times will change, and I will help change them. I stop sniffling and speak with pride.

"I am a newspaper woman."

The woman harrumphs through her nose like a horse. "Women reporters? Well, if anyone would have such a thing, Greeley would."

Finally, a breakthrough. I am in the right place!

"Yes, he would," I say. "He did. Mrs. Jane Grey Swisshelm—I call her 'my Lady Jane' because I am her assistant—and while he has not yet hired me, I have written an editorial of great importance, and I have come all the way from Washington to deliver it." I am speaking very fast, which I always do if I don't remind myself to slow down, and even sometimes when I do.

"Take this," the woman says, handing me a towel and what appears to be a dress made of a flour sack. "So you can change into something and not catch your death. Leave your wet things on the table, and I will put them near the fire to dry in the morning."

"While all the national telegraphs are saying this congressional *Compromise* is a success to save the Union, it is not." Often when I start talking, it is hard for me to stop, especially as this is a matter of life, liberty, and country. "It is a terrible, immoral—"

"You can sleep here for tonight." She cuts me off, pointing me to a pallet of hay near the dead fire in the hearth. "We'll figure out what to do with you in the morning."

It is not a bed fit for any but a dog.

"Ma'am," I say, offended. "This is how you treat a guest?"

"As far as I can tell, you're no guest. You're a stray reporter, and you'll take what I offer, or I can show you back outside."

The woman and the lamp disappear before I can properly reply.

Thus, I find myself naked and shivering, trying to figure out where my head goes in and arms come out of this flour sack.

There are *thump-thump* sounds not too far from me, but I don't know where they're coming from. It's dark, almost as dark with my eyes open as closed, and I don't know the dimensions of this room. Edges of things I can't see creep closer. The shine of something metal stares at me. I can still hear the clock from the entryway if I listen hard enough.

Thump. Thump. Thump. Thump.

Four of them.

"There are four little graves out back," the woman said. Four dead children must weigh heavily on Mr. Greeley's heart. The living one, crying when I arrived, is no longer crying.

Little graves *out back*—wherever that is. How far out back?

I don't much believe in ghosts and haunted houses, but that doesn't scare off my fright. I try to push my mind away from the sense of being swallowed up forever in this darkness and turn it toward my mission here. But my thoughts are becoming jumbled, I can feel sleep fast approaching.

Thump. Thump. Yes, it rather sounds like a knock. I think of a child coming up from the mud, dragging his coffin behind him the way I did my trunk, knocking on the wall to be let in.

"Flesh or spirit?" the woman at the door asked.

In my mind's eye, I am back outside in the storm. I cannot reach high enough for the knocker. But my hands are not mine. They belong to a child.

I am having one of those thoughts that only make sense right before falling asleep.

Something I know can't bear the scrutiny of daylight and reason, but it strikes me as true at this moment:

Oh, the dead children must be the ones knocking.

Chapter 2

I awake to the sounds of women working, chirping like birds at daybreak. A fire in the hearth crackles, warming the room. I open my eyes slowly, discovering the familiar shapes of a kitchen that last night seemed so sinister. The shine of a kettle, the lip of a wide pot, the long edge of a counter table—all, in daylight, are friendly. Two women—one wide, one rail thin—move their bodies in the constant motion of the work of making life anew each morning. Neither seems to have the time to take notice of me. I smell something delicious cooking. Is it gingerbread?

"She says it got out of the attic and means to choke her to death. She says she felt its fingers on her neck last night."

Fully awake, I try to decide whether to stay put or bolt. The women talking seem careless about it, but I am alarmed at the prospect that there is a strangler on the loose in the house.

"Has she had her medicine?"

"No. 'We're trying to poison her,' she says."

"Oh, she's onto that again, is she?"

I relax. It's not a strangler, just bad medicine. Someone here is sick. Both of the women's backs are to me, but I close my eyes and keep still, wanting to seem asleep so I can learn more. A successful reporter is, in some measure, also a spy. Who are they talking about?

"And she puked in the bed."

"Well, you'll need my help getting her out of it to change the sheets. But I can't be four places at once, love."

They quiet their chatter now, as if considering something.

"Is she here to help us?"

"Who?"

Even with my eyes closed, I can feel the weight of expectant gazes. Now they are talking about me.

"Doubtful." A snort. "She's on a high horse, for one arriving on foot. Besides, it was true what she said. He forgot to mention it to anyone, including himself, since it took him an hour to remember this morning."

"Mr. Greeley, you mean? Where is he? When can I see him?" I jump up, relieved and enlivened, pulling hay out of my hair.

There is not a moment to waste. He has no idea how critical the situation is, that a wolf in sheep's clothing just ran through Congress. The Compromise, in its glee to gobble new "free" states and territories into the Union, includes an abominable Fugitive Slave Act, whereby men, women, and children who through superhuman acts have escaped bondage are now to be captured and returned to enslavement, making bounty hunting the new law of the land. The *Tribune* must call this what it is—a deal with the devil where we all burn (also the title of my proposed editorial).

I may have slept in straw, but this morning I will deliver my writing to the man with the most important opinion in America.

Wiping sleep from my eyes, I am still seeing double—the woman who answered the door last night and another smaller, thinner, polished-apple version of her same face. The younger introduces herself as Martha. I stare at the elder, who introduces herself as Martha as well.

"You're both named Martha?"

"I am named after my mother," Young Martha says, as if there should now be no more confusion.

"Mr. Greeley is busy this morning, but he will see you in due time," Martha says. "He has much on his mind." I see my trunk has been pulled into the kitchen. "There's a small washroom you can tidy up in. I expect we will move you into a more hospitable place."

"You mean you might offer me a room instead of the dog's bed?"

"You arrived like a thief in the night, screaming and looking like you were birthed from the mud. Lucky I didn't slam the door in your face." Martha pins me with a look that offers no apology. "Do you want food, or are you going to hold a grudge in your stomach instead?"

"I hold no grudge." My stomach is eating itself, I am so hungry. "I would love some food."

Honestly, I slept pretty well, considering the accommodations. I've had worse. My long-suffering Aunt Clara, who tried her best to raise and tame me, knew that I considered the forest more my home than the rooms beneath her roof. I spent all the time I could in the woods. Many a childhood nap took place on leaf litter and moss.

A bell rings, pulled from some force elsewhere in the house, and Young Martha runs after it.

Martha puts a brown biscuit, a carrot, and a mug of cold water on the table.

"The Greeleys are on the Graham diet, so we all eat the same here. I trust it will restore you to full health." I think she means that in jest. This does not seem like a proper meal.

"The Graham diet?"

"They are very devout, the Greeleys. Apparently, that's where they first met and fell in love, at a boardinghouse for those who wish to follow this way of eating." She squints her bright-blue eyes at me and recites as if she had to say it five times a day. "The Graham diet—keeping people free from sin by eliminating meat and butter, alcohol, and stimulants, and replacing them with fruit, vegetables, and whole grains in the form of these biscuits."

"They don't eat meat?" It is just the type of radical and thrilling behavior I would expect from Mr. Greeley.

"No meat, no butter. Very little milk and eggs. Raw vegetables all the time. Eating like birds, no wonder everyone is cuckoo," she mutters.

"Martha and I escape the Great Famine only to endure this hunger and whatever leftovers I can put together from Mr. Greeley's experiments with farming."

I try a biscuit. It is warm, hearty, made of some type of coarse flour with a tang of molasses.

"It's delicious," I say. A sincere commendation. I could eat twelve.

"I made pie and cider from the bumper crop of apples," she says. "If you like the way I do with these biscuits, you need to taste the pie."

I feel no shame in asking for a large slice, happy my torturous corset is drying on a rack with my dress near the fire. My Lady Jane has trained me to understand that if I wish to become a real newspaper woman, it is important to dress the part. However, I am always pleased to have a breather, especially when food is involved.

"Mama," Young Martha says, returning with a chamber pot and a face drawn tight, "she's starting to look like she does before a fit. She's demanding Pickie."

"Who's Pickie?" I ask between forkfuls of apple filling.

"His given name was Arthur, but everyone called him Pickie," Young Martha whispers, like she's about to tell a secret. "He was Mrs. Greeley's favorite child. He died of cholera last year."

Feeling hands around her neck, complaining of being poisoned, sick and demanding a dead child . . . I realize with a shock the woman they have been speaking of all morning is Mr. Greeley's wife. What I don't understand is why the Marthas now keep talking about whether or not they need to enlist a Miss Fox, and what they could possibly mean about "letting Pickie use her voice."

"Who is Miss Fox?" I ask.

"Cathie Fox, the youngest of the Fox sisters, the family of mediums," Martha says with more pride than she had about her pie. "Mr. Greeley is the family patron, paying for Cathie's education here. The Fox sisters . . . Don't look at me like you haven't heard of them."

"Even back in Ireland we'd heard of them." Young Martha chides me. "They are world-famous mediums."

"Oh, I've heard of them," I say, though I can't remember a thing about them, so perhaps that's a small lie. "What's a medium?"

"Look, miss, we're busy enough without your questions," Martha says. "We don't need another high-and-mighty sort in here when the lowly are suffering."

"Who suffers?" I ask with sincere concern. I am deeply committed to the causes of equality, liberty, and justice for all. I even put down my fork to indicate my full attention.

"They have one living child. A daughter," Young Martha says, dumping the contents of the chamber pot out the window. "We call her Baby Charlotte, but she's not really a baby. She's three and doesn't speak, only screams."

"Well, of course she screams," Martha says. "Who feeds her? Changes her? Holds and rocks her, sings her a lullaby, and teaches her words? The missus is too full of grief and fits, and the master too full of himself, and they can't keep help except that witch of a governess, who only adds more work in any case. They might as well start making a bed for Baby Charlotte out back with the rest."

The beds out back—small graves. The dream I had last night of little hands knocking makes me shiver, even though it's daylight. Mrs. Greeley has lost four children. One is still living, the one I heard crying last night.

Four loud *thumps* like the ones I heard last night rattle the ceiling above us.

"Is that. . . ?"

"That'd be the spirits, talking to Miss Fox."

"*That's* spirits talking?" I say, rapping my knuckles on the table. I suppose the question was in poor taste, for the Marthas give me a quick study of their most disapproving expressions and do not deign to reply.

A sound of wailing begins, it seems four times louder than last night. "That'd be Baby Charlotte?" I ask.

Two heads slowly nod at me. Okay, good. I'm starting to figure things out.

"The last two nursemaids they hired quit," Young Martha says, her chin starting to tremble. "I was hired to help with cleaning and laundry, but someone's got to help *her*."

"All the servants who were here when we arrived four months ago are gone, and the one they hired to help last month walked out two nights back. Even the old dog ran away. I thought when I let you in last night, maybe you'd answered our prayers." Martha uses the kindest tone I've heard from her yet. "I thought maybe you'd come to help that poor child."

Oh no. I see what's happening here. While they may be debating whether or not to enlist Miss Fox to do whatever it is she does, they are already deep in the process of guilting me into duty.

"I would make a terrible nursemaid," I say. This is absolutely true but does nothing to stop the beseeching look of two overworked women. "I am useless with children. Please, I am desperate to speak with Mr. Greeley."

A ringing bell joins the sound of the wailing child.

"You can't speak to Mr. Greeley yet," Martha says, handing me an apron and a baby bottle before I can stop her. "So are you going to be of any use or just sit here and eat pie as we all fall apart? Go and look in on his only living child, and that'll be a service to him and to heaven. Just go change her diaper and get her to eat, that's all."

I beg to be released from this quandary. "You both would do far better comforting a baby than me. I don't make babies stop crying, I make them start."

"You don't need to be better at it than anyone, you are better than no one," Martha says, the bell ringing at what seems to be an increasing pitch as well as frequency. "Tending to Mrs. Greeley when she's in a fit is a two-person job."

"And she is in the way," Young Martha says. "I think that's why she is refusing the medicine."

Martha sighs, long and heavy. The knocks seem to have stopped for the moment, though the wailing and the bell ringing continue their assault.

"In the way?" I ask. "In the way of what?"

Mrs. Greeley—sickly, erratic, and grief-stricken, with four children buried out back and one alive, screaming with neglect—is pregnant again.

I don't want to do it, but I find myself following the two Marthas toward the screams.

Chapter 3

Where is Mr. Greeley?

I know that he's far too busy and important to tend to his own child and sick wife. Better, I suppose, to have an unknown woman put on an apron and try her best to figure out how to pin a diaper without puncturing the skin than ask a man, much less a busy man. Even if he is the father. My forehead puckers trying to account for what doesn't add up. I feel very much like a person pulled from an audience and shoved onto the stage, following the Marthas from the kitchen into the parlor, my arms loaded with linens and a bottle, with biscuits and pins in the pockets of an apron tied around me.

This is my first time seeing the Greeley house in the daytime.

Nine days on a train gave me plenty of opportunity to imagine my destination. I pictured a type of Pemberley estate with wide, lovely grounds and a mansion complete with enormous portraits of the great man himself. Or someplace Gothic, dark, and romantic with a crumbling garden, stained glass, secret passageways, and turrets. While it is indeed dark, there is nothing romantic in here. The curtains are all open this morning, but the sunlight seems to penetrate nothing. Everywhere I look, I am disappointed by the dullness of the surroundings. Aunt Clara's house is far more interesting than this place, and Aunt Clara is a Quaker, *"an extra button on a blouse is a vanity"*–type of Quaker. The walls in Greeley's house are painted in cheerful enough pinks and yellows, reminding me of rouge on a corpse's face.

The wide staircase I ascend has no decoration. No portraits, no needlepoints, no still lifes or landscapes. Nothing feels lived in.

"Go on, then, it's just down the hall," Martha says, shooing me as she and her daughter go to help Mrs. Greeley. As they scurry into her bedroom, I try to catch a glimpse of the woman.

I gasp at what I see through the open door: A writhing figure, black hair plastered to her face, crawls on hands and knees across the floor. Panting, keening—an inhuman animal. She is grief. She is madness. She is familiar in a way that grips my throat in terror. I cannot breathe. I cannot move.

I cannot look away.

Wherever she is crawling to or from, I don't know, but the two Marthas scramble for her.

"Back in bed, ma'am," Martha says, lifting her by the arms.

"Not again, not again," the woman moans, letting her body go slack. "Please, not again."

"Go on, now," Martha hisses at me as I stand gawking and useless. "Go to the little one, we've two of us here."

"My sweet baby boy, why did you leave me?" the woman cries. "Why did you go?"

"Now, no need to start that. Come now, you know he's in Summerland, don't you? You can talk to him anytime, right?"

"And you've got wee Charlotte here for you to love," Young Martha says.

"And another one coming, by grace of God," Martha adds.

Mrs. Greeley lifts her head and her eyes meet mine. "You," she says, as if we know each other from long before.

She raises herself up in Martha's arms as if to testify and vomits.

~

I don't know where the nursery is. The baby has stopped crying, so I can't follow the sound. My thoughts are scrambled, and when I look down and see baby clothes and a bottle in my hand, I feel as if I must be asleep and dreaming. What did I just see? It cannot be that the woman I saw is actually Mrs. Greeley, but must be some awful disturbance in my mind. Am I dozing on the train, still heading toward this destination? Am I still in bed at the Washington hotel where I stay with Mrs. Swisshelm, having one of those nightmares again? And if so, can I wake myself up before I see the thing that always makes me scream?

Stop it, now, I tell myself.

I feel my feet. I feel my fingers.

I am here, I am awake.

No more of these thoughts of dreams, of nightmares. I give myself a good talking-to. Yes, Mrs. Greeley is a sick woman, no need to think any more about it. I direct myself to be practical. I am not here to wonder at how I dream or why. I am here on a mission that has been momentarily diverted by a dirty diaper.

"Oh dear, what can the matter be?" A clear voice, singing. Light from an open door down the hall makes the dust sparkle.

"Dear, dear, what can the matter be?"

A feeling of peace comes over me. How sweet the singing sounds. I move into the open door, seeing the sun shining through a nursery window, illuminating an adolescent girl bouncing a red-faced child, hiccupping. Her *"bonny brown hair,"* like the words she's singing, is plaited into braids. She has gray eyes, so large they seem to take up more than half her face. She's laughing, trying to get the child to laugh, too.

This must be Cathie Fox, then? She looks as guileless as a ewe— angelic, even—in how she's holding a child and comforting her. What a pretty picture they make.

The nursery, unlike every other place I've seen here, looks lived in, with busy print wallpaper and toys tossed about. A wooden doll with no hair sits at a small table with a stuffed-horse stick and a turned-over teacup. A cradle with a drawn lace curtain browning with dust hides in the corner, while one small bed, the covers bunched and knotted, smells of wet urine.

Cathie keeps singing about promises of a blue ribbon. Baby Charlotte turns her wet face to look at me as I wander in slowly, home-sick for a place I've never known, for a home I can't recall, for a sister I've never had.

"Who are you?" a sharp voice rings out behind me.

I pivot to see a woman who looks like a princess, minus the crown. She wears a beautiful dress of blue fabric—oh, I'm no good at identify-ing cloth. Is it damask? Some heavy, shiny, expensive fabric that's all the rage for fancy Washington ladies. She wears it with far better authority. Her skin is as smooth as a porcelain doll, her hair the color of a copper penny, and her eyes . . . I'm not close enough to truly appreciate their facets, but they are piercing. I am struck—I don't know what feature of hers it is; it's not one in particular, but the whole of her—that this is the type of woman whom men write sonnets about. I am utterly cowed and can only stammer. "Oh, I just . . . I heard . . . I came to see—"

"I didn't ask *what* you were doing," she says. "We all heard Charlotte screaming, as she does. The maxim *'Children are best seen and not heard'* has not been properly appreciated in the colonies. I asked *who* you were." Her accent is British and very proper, making me feel simulta-neously low class and rebellious in a 1776 sort of manner.

"E. A. is my name."

"E. A.? Those are vowels, not a name. Is your surname I. O. U.?" Her lip curls up. On a less beautiful face it would be a smirk; on her it looks like it should hang in the Louvre.

"It is Howe. E. A. Howe. E. A. stands for Edith Ann. I am not a fan of the name Edith. For obvious reasons."

"My mother is named Edith," she says.

"Oh, I meant no offense."

"Her mother is also named Edith. I come from a long line of Ediths. I see nothing wrong with the name Edith, except in one's inability to have enough character to own it."

"You can call me Edith, I would be happy to be Edith—"

"I certainly will not call you what you cannot call yourself. E. A., then, you are, and my name is Miss Jessica Elliot. I am the governess for Catherine, here, who is shirking her studies to quiet poor Charlotte since none of the hired help seems to prioritize peace until Mr. Greeley screams for it from his study."

"Pleased to meet you, Jessica."

"'Miss Elliot' is the proper way to address me. We just met."

"Excuse me. Miss Elliot." I take a deep breath. Talking to her is like riding a wild horse, and I am hanging on the best I can.

"I am trying to model what is appropriate for my pupil. I don't mean to be rude," she says, allowing me to appreciate that she is not about to throw me off and trample me. "I know you speak differently in the colonies."

"Oh, and I don't know how to do it properly even here in the colonies, so please instruct me, too," I say before clearing my throat. "I'm an orphan who spent much of her childhood in the woods. I'm still half feral."

Miss Elliot laughs, and it makes me wish to make her do it again and again. "Welcome, Miss Howe, to Castle Doldrum, as Mr. Greeley calls it."

"Castle Doldrum? That's an interesting nickname."

"Indeed, it is an apt title for this home." She lifts her hand in a demonstrative wave at the surroundings. "Even this nursery is depressing."

At this, I remember where I am. Cathie and Baby Charlotte have silently followed our volleys, and my attention opens its borders to include them again.

"So you have answered who you are," she says, "but I have yet to discover what you are doing here. Are you the new nursemaid?"

"Oh, no!" I say with a cough of force. "I am a newspaper woman. Here to see Mr. Greeley on a very important assignment. It's just that my clothes got very wet last night in the storm."

Jessica—Miss Elliot—raises an eyebrow. "Were you the one knocking?"

"Yes, nearly broke my hand—"

"Few living people knock here, you'll come to find out."

The floorboard beneath my feet vibrates with two thumps.

We both look to Cathie, who stands on the other side of the room.

Baby Charlotte coos.

Again, directly beneath my shoeless feet, two thumps as distinct as if someone were hitting the floor beneath with a broom handle.

"It's your mother," Cathie says to me, her voice a whisper. "She has been knocking here before you even arrived. I knew you were coming."

I am not taken with her tricks. She picked up on my saying I was an orphan in my passing joke to Miss Elliot. "I wish you had told Martha," I say, "since she nearly turned me out into the rain." The floor beneath me beats like a timpani.

"She has been waiting an awfully long time to get to talk to you," Cathie insists.

"Well, I suppose she can wait a little longer," I answer. She'd do better saying a felled tree wished to talk to me than my mother. "I am quite busy this morning."

The little teacup that is on the small table shudders itself across to the edge. It hovers there, like a dare. "Quite busy," I say, not taking my eyes off Cathie. How is she doing this? Her arms are still around Baby Charlotte, positioned on the other side of the room. "As I mentioned, I am a newspaper woman here on an important story that has nothing to do with her. Maybe later."

The teacup stops moving.

"Are you here to write about Cathie?" Miss Elliot asks. "Because she already has a full schedule with her studies. If you want to write about the spirit-rappings, you should visit her sisters in Rochester."

"Oh, no. I don't care about the spirits. I'm here to speak with Mr. Greeley about what is happening in Congress." I have never quite learned how to be diplomatic, and my tone is rather lemony. "I wouldn't come all this way to do something as silly as have Miss Fox drum for my mother."

The teacup falls off the table. It's not far enough of a drop to shatter, but a chip flies off the lip.

Baby Charlotte lets out a sharp "Oh!"

"Many important men travel very far to see Cathie," Miss Elliot says, rushing to pick up the broken teacup. "Men who know better than to show up wearing flour sacks and insult her."

"I'm sure Miss Howe didn't mean to insult me," Cathie says in a quiet voice. "If she was insulting anyone, it was her own mother." She smiles at me, a sad smile.

I can't return it; it feels disingenuous.

"I see you have a bottle," Cathie says. "Will you take Baby Charlotte? She's very heavy."

"She said she wasn't a nursemaid, Cathie," Miss Elliot says. "And I daresay neither are you. Just put her down."

Baby Charlotte starts to scream the moment her feet touch the ground.

"Stop that, this instant," Miss Elliot orders Baby Charlotte.

Baby Charlotte obeys, sucking in her cry.

Miss Elliot, while not much taller than Cathie herself and looking no older than I, is the sort of person who gives commands and has them followed. I suppose that is the privilege of the stunningly beautiful. "If you are looking for Mr. Greeley, you certainly won't find him in here," she says. "He never has anything to do in the nursery and is far too important to take much notice of children. So if it's Mr. Greeley you're seeking, I'd suggest you turn around and head to his study. I don't think he takes a bottle, however."

I don't know what to say. I am conscious of how my arms hang, that my hands are coarse and red, my fingers ink-stained, and that my face must not be as pleasant as seeing her own in a mirror. If I were her, I would stare in a mirror as often as I could and smile at myself and say words just to watch how my lips formed them.

She looks back at me with an expression of piqued curiosity. However it is that I am gazing at her, she finds my countenance interesting at the very least. I might even venture that she approves.

"Oh, Miss Fox, please come," Young Martha says, bursting into the room, nearly sliding on the floor in her haste. "She is begging to talk to Pickie. Please, it's the only thing that can help her."

The peel of the wallpaper, the smell of urine, the sun moving behind a cloud—everything in the room seems to have suddenly dampened in despair.

"I can't, I have my studies to do. Right, Miss Elliot?" Cathie pleads to her governess.

"She is a danger to herself and others." Young Martha's lip is quivering, and she holds her own arm tightly. "We don't know what else to do."

"We must remember that you are not only here to get an education but also to provide comfort for Mrs. Greeley," Miss Elliot muses to her pupil, as if balancing an arithmetic problem. "Come on, I will stay with you all the while. It will all be well, as Summerland always is. Stop wringing your hands, Martha, you are making me nervous."

Young Martha is not wringing her hands—she is pulling at her sleeve. Something is wrong with her arm. As Cathie consents to whatever it is she will do for Mrs. Greeley, she hops quickly from the room, and with a rustle of fabric and sighs, Miss Elliot and Cathie follow. Miss Elliot turns just outside the door, leaving them for a moment, saying she forgot something. She comes close enough that I can smell her lilac powder and see that her eyes are the color of honey, encircled in a ring of ebony.

"Actually, I've never known anyone named Edith," she whispers, and winks at me most wickedly. "I would love to call you by your first name, if you'll call me by mine. Yes?"

"Yes, Jessica." I will always say yes to her.

She puts her small hand in mine.

"We will be good friends, Edith."

~

Baby Charlotte and I size each other up, having a staring contest in silence. She sees I am weak and of no use. She starts to cry again. I've told everyone I'm no good at this. Still, I have clean clothes for her, a bottle, and one of those Graham biscuits in my apron pocket, which are so good that if she doesn't want it, I'll eat it. I tell her as much, talking in a torrent of words like I often do. Because I threaten to eat the biscuit, and move it toward my mouth like I'll make good on that threat, she decides to object and take it from me.

"Come now, let's get you out of those cold, wet clothes. That can't be comfortable. I have these that are nice and dry." She squirms as I try to get the nightdress off her, but as soon as I extract her from it, she cheers up a bit and allows me to get a dry nappy on her. She doesn't yell in my ear, even though I can't for the life of me figure out how to fold it properly. When she tries to stand up, it falls right off her.

Standing there, naked, seeing my abject failure to clothe her, she laughs.

"Well, isn't that a nice thing!" I say, making a face that prolongs her reaction. "I just got my first laugh from Baby Charlotte! And isn't that so much better than crying and far less messy, too? Crying is so phlegmy!"

She doesn't talk, but I swear that Baby Charlotte understands every-thing I am saying. Next thing I know, we're having a tea party. I'm speaking at full gallop, telling this captive audience how I've come all the way from Washington to have this important teatime with her and her sad, bald doll. She is drinking milk and eating a biscuit and giggling like I'm the wittiest person in the whole world.

"I didn't ask *what* you were doing, mashing that Graham biscuit with your fist, Baby Charlotte," I say, impersonating the imperious Miss Elliot, holding the chipped teacup with my pinkie out like a lady. "Mashing it is the proper thing to do before eating the crumbs. I come from a long line of biscuit mashers."

I don't bring the chipped cup to my lip.

I hadn't been at all fooled by the antics of Cathie Fox.

What a bad bit of theater! As if my mother's spirit would stoop to knocking on the floor beneath my feet and rattling a piece of china to speak with me. What poor melodrama. I liked Cathie at first impression, watching her kindly comforting Baby Charlotte. It's unfortunate that the teacup nonsense has now soured me toward her.

I will admit there is some skill. I don't know how she made such a racket from across the room while appearing motionless and holding a child. My mother, in actuality, is *not* dead. She has been in an institution since I was about Baby Charlotte's age. Saying I'm an orphan is just easier for everyone to understand, including me. That's what I was told until I turned twelve. At that point, my Aunt Clara thought it best to stop lying—honesty being one of the most important attributes of the Quaker faith—and tell me my mother was in fact alive, if not well. In truth, not well at all.

It wasn't just that my religious Aunt Clara—in her rigorous adherence to the Quaker tenets of Peace, Equality, Simplicity, and Truth— was ashamed of having a sister-in-law in an asylum. It's that my dear mother tried to kill me and my brother. Well, tried to kill *me*. She succeeded in killing my brother.

Suffice it to say that Cathie Fox declaring my mother's spirit wished to speak with me was a misfire on multiple levels. First, my mother is living, and second, I have no desire to speak with her, alive or dead.

Chapter 4

When the Marthas come to save me from the nursery, they are stunned by Baby Charlotte's laughter and the milk and biscuit crumbs painted across her face.

It's not just treasures in heaven, doing a good turn by having pretend tea with a toddler.

My success propels me from the dog bed into a very special room.

"I've never heard her laugh before." Young Martha clucks at my talents, helping me carry my trunk to the top floor, to the first genuinely cheerful room I've seen in this house. A large window opens to the leafy branches of an oak tree. There are shelves upon shelves of books, a writing desk, and a canopy bed. I feel like royalty.

I read the spines of the books. *The Great Lawsuit, Summer on the Lakes, Woman in the Nineteenth Century*—all books by Margaret Fuller.

"Is this the room Mrs. Fuller stayed in when she lived with the Greeleys?" I ask only one question, but I think of twenty. Will I be sleeping in the same bed she slept in? Was this where she lived for the many months before she moved to Italy? Will inspiration, fame, and a friendship with Mr. Greeley be likewise bestowed upon me?

"It was long before my time." Young Martha doesn't seem inspired by the name. "But yes, I believe they mean it as a type of shrine."

"She was the first newspaper woman in America," I say, "writing for a journal put out by Ralph Waldo Emerson, before being hired by Mr. Greeley . . ." I grab Young Martha's old-looking, overworked hands in excitement, feeling it is my duty to educate her about this American hero. I start rhapsodizing about Margaret Fuller's theories on women, on abolition, on transcendence, on her marriage to an Italian man, on her tragic death at sea, clutching her baby.

"Please, my arm—" Blood is soaking through Young Martha's sleeve.

I yelp, releasing her, apologizing. I had no idea I was gripping hard enough to draw blood. Young Martha rolls up her sleeve to show me the bloody bandage on her wrist.

"Oh, carrying the trunk, I suppose it reopened the wound," she says, generously not faulting me. "I'll have Mama help me redress it."

"Did you cut yourself?"

"Oh, no. That's where Mrs. Greeley bit me, before she spoke with Pickie."

"She *bit* you?"

"Mrs. Greeley is a terror with her moods. Sometimes she's sweet, but other times she's wild. We try to get her to take the medicine to calm her, but she says it makes things worse. She hears spirits all over the house. Sees things, too, that make you scared. It's why all the help leaves—can't pay them enough, they say. But we're doing our best to stay, my mum and me. It's good that we get to be here together."

"But she bit you?" I find it quite challenging to fully grasp.

"Oh, it's all right," she says, as if getting bit by Mrs. Greeley is the same as accidentally burning a hand on a cook pot. I suppose in this house, it is. "I feel for her. We buried two of my brothers back home, and I did have a wee . . . a wee mite of a child of my own that . . . also died. I know what it can do to your way of thinking. I used to swear I could hear her crying in the wind."

I am moved by an emotion I can't identify. Young Martha seems barely older than Cathie.

"My milk didn't dry up until we got on the boat to cross here."

"Here you are, then!" Martha comes in, all bustling brightness, holding my traveling dress and a stack of clean linens. "In the Margaret

Fuller remembrance room. Only fitting to have a newspaper woman in here! Wup, is the wound opened again, love?"

Martha lifts the bandages from her namesake's arm, blotting the blood with a salve. I can't look away from the teeth marks on Young Martha's wrist. From them, I can see the shape of Mrs. Greeley's mouth.

"Come, now," Martha says to me over her shoulder, wrapping her daughter's arm. "You'd better get dressed if you want to speak to Mr. Greeley. He won't be here all day."

I open my hastily packed trunk, trying to divine what to wear. While I do have things stored at Aunt Clara's, I could argue that everything I owned that was necessary to my survival (excepting food and a privy) could fit into this one trunk. My little journal, ink pots and quills, my twelve most treasured books, a nightdress, and an evening gown that Mrs. Swisshelm insisted I bring in case of a dance or a dinner. I have a pair of men's boots that I wear for comfort, but Mrs. Swisshelm would murder me if I introduced myself to Greeley in them. I've only one professional dress, and one corset, which Martha has just brought up with my other petticoats from their morning of drying by the fire. I'd hoped maybe the corset might fall in the flames so I'd never have to wear it again, but no such luck.

"Are you going to get dressed or just stand there gawking?" Martha asks.

"I am trying to decide what to wear."

"Just wear what you wore when you arrived last night. It's dry enough."

"But it's mud stained."

"Not as much as it's going to be after you tramp around the muck, trying to speak with Mr. Greeley. He's out back, trimming a tree. Thinks letting a little light into the house might help with the missus's moods." Martha looks toward the window, canopied by an oak. "A little light might do us *all* good—all these dark rooms and whispers in the walls. We don't need any more sad sounds of leaves blowing in the trees."

As a tree lover, I try to find the right quip about how sad sounds are in the ears of the listener, but as I am the only woman in the room who has not lost a child, I have a rare moment of good sense and just let it be.

"You'll be able to get work done in here, as long as you don't go messing around in the attic," Martha says, pointing up. "Don't go up there."

"You know that to tell a reporter *not* to do something is the same thing as telling her she must. What's wrong with the attic?"

They both stare at me as if I have asked a question for which there is no answer.

"Just leave it alone," Martha says, "and go about your business."

She already knows me well enough to warn me again, in a way I'm better to understand.

"You didn't come here for a haunting. You're here to write papers, not exorcise demons."

Chapter 5

I walk outside into the sunlight, brimming with confidence. Why, I am about to meet Horace Greeley himself. I am moments away from changing the course of history for the better. How far I have come in such a short time!

The Humble Origins of E. A. Howe, America's Third Newspaper Woman
By E. A. Howe

I've always loved the newspaper. As a child, I would carve block letters on the ends of carrots, potatoes, and turnips. Yes, I created my own vegetable printing press. No matter that a root vegetable would soon wither, there was always another to pull from the dirt and put to work. I would post things on the old oaks around the Edgemont township where I lived. I had a pen name, "F. Reed," which I thought very clever at the time, and my articles consisted of farm news or neighborhood scandals. **SMITH FAMILY HEIRLOOM MISSING, Memories of a Suspect**. I implied that seventy-eight-year-old Mrs. Smith herself was the culprit of her heirloom thievery, since she often forgot things. Mrs. Smith banned me from her property after reading the story. This was my first introduction to making enemies through my reporting, even though my assumption turned out to be correct.

I was not an easy charge for my dear Aunt Clara. I suspect she half hoped I'd be eaten by wolves in the woods I roamed. By the time I was fifteen, I'd frustrated all attempts to educate me in the ways of being a young lady of any proper manners. Then a divine messenger appeared. When I learned that our new neighbor down and around the way, editor/founder of *The Abolitionist*, was my second cousin (well, second cousin once removed), I did everything but get on my knees to convince her to allow me to be her apprentice.

"I am your blood relative!"

"We have no blood relation," Mrs. Swisshelm replied. "You are the third cousin of my husband's sister-in-law."

"I am an orphan!"

"Well, that is no rare thing. You are lucky to have a doting aunt who makes sure you have a roof over your head and that you don't starve."

"But she's trying to marry me off to a local farmer!"

"There's nothing wrong with being married to a farmer. I am married to a farmer." Well, that tactic backfired. Miserably. "The important thing is not to be of the same mind, in any case, but just to love him."

"But I don't love Frank Jackson. I love the newspaper!"

I then did get on my knees and beg, and not just for one day but for many. My unceasing appeals of handing her old rags with turnip-stained letters reading "Jane Swisshelm Hires Plucky Assistant" finally wore her down. It was not my penmanship or my typesetting she found to be of help, but I did offer her some flashes of insight and rhetorical devices that she found useful. Mostly she considered me a charity case, and a girl worth saving by teaching me how to *be* a girl. She taught me how to cook, clean, milk, and sew (very badly). She taught more talented ladies how to weave lace, but for me, darning a sock was triumph enough. I wore farm dresses, too, for her sake, wherein before I had much preferred to tromp about in trousers. By the time I was seventeen she had taught me, with the patience of a saint, how to do basic womanly things. I did them poorly, but I did them nonetheless. She had used the old carrot-and-stick method, with the carrot being able to help her with the printing press, and the stick being an actual stick.

I began calling Mrs. Jane Swisshelm "my Lady Jane," for she certainly was, in all ways, my "Lady" in the same way that God was, to many, "Lord."

I would do anything for her. When a local mob came to burn down the press house because of her editorial—a statement that the enslaved should be entitled to the same rights as their enslavers—I draped my body over the press and refused to leave. I didn't fear being burned alive with a printing press for my Lady Jane's sake, and she could not talk me out of my martyrdom. Abolitionist editors died such deaths. Elijah Lovejoy was the most famous, murdered with his printing press a few years back, and I was ready to count myself among such esteemed dead. But Jane Swisshelm was not going to let herself or me be burned alive. Instead, she talked her way out of it. She was wonderful at speaking to people and making them change their minds.

I knew only how to persist.

I will never forget her face when morning broke and we had survived the night, with neither of us, nor our press, burned to ash. "There's righteousness in you, E. A.," she said, her eyes shining. "A righteous streak that some may say is stubborn or a wildness to be broken. Don't believe anyone who says that. Don't listen to those who would trample or tame your thirst for justice."

Her reputation grew, and then this year, she received a huge break. It arrived in the form of a letter from Horace Greeley. He offered her the position of the first female Washington correspondent for the *New-York Daily Tribune.*

She of course accepted, bringing her indispensable assistant with her. (As my bags were already packed, and I refused to get out of her carriage.) I was in for quite a shock, seeing how things actually worked in Washington. Most barn floors are cleaner than the halls of the hallowed Congressional chambers. The constant tobacco spit alone that flies from the mouths of so many purportedly enlightened men is enough to quash any idealization, if not the bluster and buffoonery. On my Lady Jane's first day on the job, a brawl broke out on the Senate floor. The senator from Missouri charged the senator from Mississippi, who pulled a pistol on him. My Lady Jane had quite the scoop, and all the other papers were jealous of the immediacy of her prose. Of course, *she* promptly became their news story: Congress was no place for a woman!

I had to admit, with all my "pluck" that I had touted to my Lady Jane, it certainly felt like no place for me. I hated the smell of pipes and powder and gas lamps. I hated the way the men walked and talked and spit. And to be allowed in the hall, I had to wear proper ladies' attire, which was far more torturous than a farm dress. These clothes were heavy, and not just hard to move in but also hard to breathe in. I hated the weight of my skirt and the way it rustled, and the feeling of helplessness that came with these women's clothes in these rooms of male power.

I felt sick with longing for my beloved woods, for wandering about in trousers, foraging for mushrooms and berries. But day by day, night by night, for the sake of those who have no choice, I chose to stay. I learn what I can so that I can write columns with both passion and perspective, like Margaret Fuller. Like my Lady Jane.

Now, five months later, the black-spit-laced floors have been a place for dancing rather than dueling. The Compromise has just passed, and Northern and Southern Congressmen spent the past weekend drunk and celebrating. They had "saved the Union."

Most papers declare the Compromise a victory for the entire Union, but the *Tribune* mustn't follow suit—not on my Lady Jane's watch.

"I think it is a sin to be polite in these times," she said to me. "And I've written the same to Mr. Greeley."

It was a bitterness I'd never known before, hearing the satisfied congratulatory whoops of these powerful men. Fireworks of celebration lit the sky over the Capitol, and abject betrayal at the hands of the representatives we'd counted as friends soured my Lady Jane's sweet featured face. "You, for one, do not know how to be polite when you are outraged, E. A. You barely know how to be polite in the best of moods. I need you to do something very important."

I was ready to do anything for her, the more important the better.

"I am sending you to speak with Mr. Greeley. You must let him know that this is no compromise. He tends so much to favor measured approaches. He has, in the past, called out abolitionists as too rash, but it is because he has never lived in Ohio or Kentucky. You have been here in Washington the same as him, same as me. But your tongue is sharper than both of ours. Use it, and cut through all niceties. Wear Mr. Greeley down until he has to call the Compromise like it is."

"A deal with the devil that will make us all burn," I said.

"Yes," she said. "Use those exact words."

A Deal with the Devil Where We All Burn may be my first published work, but I know it won't be the last. I will never forget where I came from, nor the causes that—

~

My autobiography is broken as a loud *CRACK* alerts me to stop. A giant limb crashes down.

Someone is high in the branches, sawing.

Why, that must be Horace Greeley himself, up a tree.

Chapter 6

It must be a hundred years old if it's a day, the hemlock tree that he is in the process of maiming, if not slowly murdering. I hear his voice before I see his body. He operatically sings ballads from the Revolutionary War. I think he's about halfway through the fifty-five verses of "American Taxation":

> "We have a bold commander, who fears not sword or gun,
> A second Alexander, his name is Washington."

The great American opinion-maker, founder and editor of the *New-York Daily Tribune*, is twenty feet up a tree, hacking away—and as happy a person as I've ever seen, grunting, swinging, and singing.

"Mr. Greeley, sir?" I call, waving my arms, then hop back several feet to avoid a falling branch.

I am inspected from porcine eyes blinking behind little round glasses. He has a ruddy face, a tow-colored neckbeard, and a white, battered top hat that curiously remains firmly on his head even as he bends down from the bough.

"Mr. Greeley, I am E. A. Howe, assistant to Mrs. Swisshelm!"

"I'd forgotten the telegram last night," he says. "This morning I remembered."

"Thank you for remembering!"

"Well, then, carry on." He begins hacking at a branch once again. I can see he does not aim to come down.

Fine. I will give my full oratory right here and now to God, Greeley, and the whole of the woods.

"Sir, I have been sent here by Mrs. Swisshelm for the sole purpose of relating to you my firsthand account of the chicanery of the Compromise that was just passed and—"

"Is this some filibuster to impede my tree trimming?" he roars from above.

"If a filibuster is required, I will oblige."

The tree branches rustle with their occupant's contemplation. "Stand back, then."

I move just in time.

First comes the hatchet, then the man—hand over leg, leg over arm—with surprising dexterity for his middle age. He drops beside me like a nimble spider, sweating in his unkempt clothes like it's summer, before turning his full invaluable attention to my humble person. I stagger a bit in the wake of the heft of Horace Greeley, both physically and mythically.

"You are only trimming . . . You would not cut down such a tree, I hope?" I will plead for the tree's life by appealing to his patriotism. "It is older than this nation."

"Oh, I wouldn't cut down a hemlock. Now, the old apple trees here that were never grafted, I take down remorselessly, for they are a wormy nuisance. In their place, I have planted such *new* apple trees that even now are beginning to fruit . . ."

Thus he begins talking about his apple orchard, how to best trim a hemlock, explaining that witch hazels must be axed immediately on sight, and declaring why the world would do better if everyone kept their cows fenced in and planted hickory, white pine, chestnut.

"May this world unitedly cease to do evil and learn to do well in relation to trees," he says, and I offer a hearty "Amen." What a joy to find that Greeley and I have this in common—we are both unapologetic dendrophiles. "I should have been a farmer."

"But, sir, your work as the editor of the most popular paper in America is a moral duty. Especially now."

"Yes, maybe so," he says. He stops abruptly, looking at me as if I'd suddenly transfigured into a witch hazel tree. "What did Mrs. Swisshelm mean in sending you here? That was a presumptuous action on her part. It is hard on Mother's nerves to have visitors unless they are expressly invited."

"I do not think Mrs. Swisshelm meant to cause any anxiety by sending me here," I lie. She certainly sent me to provoke him. "She thought I might be an influence—"

"I do not need influence. My discernment is my sacred duty to the people of America. I am not a person who can be lobbied by anyone, Miss Howe."

"Yes, indeed. I am not here to convince you so much as bear witness to you, sir."

"Bear witness, influence," he grumbles. "Six of one, half a dozen of the other. My household can be a difficult place for me to think properly, and I am quite certain you will not add to my mental clarity. My thrift, humility, hard work, and above all my attunement to the laws of nature have yielded this bounty of wisdom that must be carefully harvested. Mine is not a position that any other can fulfill. I am the conscience of this country."

He pauses to take a breath, and I seize the opportunity. "Indeed, your opinion is even more important than President Millard Fillmore's, since Fillmore wasn't elected but obtained the position due to President Taylor's death."

He nods. "Yes, I helped get President Taylor elected. He did appoint me to the Thirtieth Congress as Representative to New York when the seat was vacated. I accomplished much in my year there, but I did not win enough friends to seek reelection."

I've heard of Greeley's time in Congress. It seems that all he accomplished while there was alienating wide swaths of influential people. I can see that he is not good at making friends.

However, I will win him as mine.

"Most of Congress are old, wormy apples," I offer. "We need new plantings."

"Yes," he says. "Apt metaphor."

We start walking again, seemingly without a destination.

"You should know I am prepared to think well of this Compromise," he states. "It will put an end to the slavery issue and will keep our states united."

I am looking for an appropriate tree-killing metaphor to interject how it will do quite the opposite, but he changes the subject.

"I think we should be called the United States of *Columbia*, rather than America. In my brief time in Congress, this was my proposal, which I had neither the grift nor corruption nor political power to push through. But I do, privately, still think of her as Columbia rather than America. We should be named after Columbus, not Amerigo Vespucci. The United States of Columbia. Do you not think it a more appropriate name?"

"Isn't Columbia already a country?"

"Was. It has been disbanded and is no longer in use. Looking out on these lands, hear how the word seems to echo back to you?"

"Columbia!" I call out to the fields with throaty conviction. They don't echo back. But my commitment makes him eye me as a coconspirator.

"Well, state the case, then, for which you have made this journey."

Ah, at last! I reach into the pocket of my skirt and pull out the best draft of my well-worked editorial. My penmanship and last night's rain render it barely legible, but I know it well enough to imagine the words that are now but ink spots. I read:

"*The Compromise of 1850 is a deal with the devil, and as such no good can come of it. The United States . . . of* America, *which would have been* better named Columbia"—I say it as if I had written it just like that. He is smiling—*"is in a fight for her very soul, and as this government expands farther west, the debate between states being Free or Slave begs the question: How can any administration professing to love freedom compromise with those who enslave their fellow men? But this question is not even allowed to be uttered with the current gag rule. Northerners are not allowed to talk about the morality of slavery or question it as an institution. What kind of world is it when one cannot discuss what is moral, what is good and evil? To compromise with evil is to participate in it—"*

"Stop there," he mumbles.

I pretend to not hear his request. *"To compromise is to be complicit—"*

"Enough!"

I stop reading, cowed by the force in his voice.

"This is all very radical," he states calmly. "Compromise is the very fabric of our nationhood and of the political system. You are speaking like a schoolgirl. Surely Mrs. Swisshelm's opinion shows more restraint."

"She says, *'It is a sin to be polite in these times,'* sir."

His mouth widens, and I see both rows of teeth, and where there are gaps. "Yes, she did write that to me. That is quite a quote. We could use that. But you have nothing so elegant thus far."

"May I continue? There may be something you find useful or elegant." My face burns in shame.

He doesn't say no, so I press on, quickly reading, feeling like I might faint, skipping over the continued moralizing and getting to the most damning bit of the legislation:

"Moreover, pressed upon this Compromise like a bloated tick is the Fugitive Slave Act, which criminalizes those in the Free States who would act both as their conscience and as God demands, forcing those—who have against all odds escaped—back into the chains of their oppressors, and those who've assisted them in their pursuit of freedom to be prosecuted and jailed. How is it a compromise to condemn a person of conscience and character to be a criminal?"

I look up at him with all the conviction of my beliefs and the surety of my knowledge. *"This Compromise is an affront to the very ideals of this nation. It makes the blood of the martyrs boil."*

He removes his hat and begins scratching the large bald spot at the top of his head.

"Mrs. Swisshelm herself could be prosecuted and jailed for her work on the Underground Railroad," I say, with enough gravity to root us both to the reality of what this means to his personal empire. "Though I'm sure she could write some very good editorials from behind bars."

He sighs heavily. "Who from the North approved this Fugitive Slave Act? They would need Northern votes to pass it."

"Sir, the Northerners all hid out in the library when it came to vote on the Fugitive Slave Act . . . so they would not be on record. None of them voted for it. Or against it. And this is how the Compromise came to pass."

He looks up into the sky, as if searching for something, then back to his shoes.

"You do not know how politics work," he says finally.

"You are in a position, sir, by God, to change how politics work."

He nods with such a serious expression that I know I've polished his pride to the best light.

"Yes, indeed . . . indeed."

He starts walking again, so I follow. He stops to stare up at a tree and makes an observation about how to properly prune it. We walk again and he points to a cow, noting some milking technique that I've not heard of in practice. I understand that I am being given a rare tour, and although pruning and milking are low on my list of interests, I am doing my best to appear otherwise. "I do often wish I could just be a farmer," he says again.

I nod, even though I truly cannot sympathize with his sadness over having obtained so much power that he could shape the beliefs of much of the population of America instead of spending all his time thinking about inventive ways to press apples.

"What a time it is to be alive!" he says with a burst of excitement. "Experiments are showing us that there is magnetism, electricity— forces that have never been known before. We can use a telegraph and talk to people hundreds of miles away. Get on a locomotive and travel distances at speeds only imagined previously. Why, look at you—a week ago you were in Washington!"

It is best to let powerful men rhapsodize when they're inclined to do so. A harmonious "Mm-hmm" should be the only response if one wishes to influence them, so I make no interruption.

"These Fox sisters have discovered something, sure as the telegram." He raps his fist on a wooden fence post. "It was Cathie who first had the genius to devise a system for talking back to a spirit. Like Morse code. So simple only a child could think of it."

I try to get back to the point at hand. "Sir, Mrs. Swisshelm thought you might wish to publish my opinion on the Compromise."

He faces the pasture as if the grazing cows themselves are rapping out Morse code. "These girls have harnessed a new technology, as sure as Benjamin Franklin discovered electricity with his kite and his key. They have found a way to talk to the dead."

"Sir, I write as E. A. Howe. No one will assume it is a woman, so we need not fear that the opinion will be derided because of my sex, as happened with Mrs. Swisshelm."

He blinks at me from behind those round little glasses. "No, no. That will not do. I must make my own judgment. I am the voice of the *Tribune*, not a . . ." He motions with his hand like the word he had omitted to say were some manner of flying insect.

It is my turn to look out to the cows for a message. My cheeks are hot with shame, disappointment, anger. My first published article, my importance with my pen, my mission here, my Lady Jane's faith in me, my purpose in life . . . All have just been waved away like may-flies. I audibly whelp with sorrow, and he pats my shoulder, consoling, patriarchal.

"Mrs. Swisshelm has requested I give you an assignment for an opinion piece. The Compromise is too important, but since you have come all this way, I can give you a way to prove your mettle."

Oh, Lord. Will he conscript me into being Baby Charlotte's nursemaid?

"Now, Cathie is very young, and she needs an education, so I am paying for her governess as she develops and refines the techniques that she has for this line of communication. I don't think she understands her gift, but the spirits have chosen her and her sisters to talk through, so we have to be patient as the girls mature. Already, people all over the country are doing their best to create the same scientific conditions, but with mixed results. I have been in contact with Dr. Jules Vincent, the world-renowned mesmerist and inventor, who is eager to witness Cathie's abilities. He believes it is possible, with some time and experimentation, to create a patent around the knocking."

"That all sounds very interesting, sir." Does he not realize that we are losing time, that as we speak, bounty hunters are tracking those brave souls who've escaped to freedom in the North? "I am not sure how I figure into this process."

"I would like you to write about the science of Cathie's abilities. You should interview Dr. Vincent once he has studied the knocking, and his ideas of the good this new technology can bring to the world. Write an editorial about the benefits of speaking with the dead. We must be timely. There are detractors, as there always are against progress. Those who wish to silence these voices. I want you to utilize, to harness the same passion you have for abolition and direct it toward something you are better able to grasp."

"Sir, I am very gratified by this opportunity," I begin, swallowing the intensity of this insult. I would rather be conscripted into being Baby Charlotte's nursemaid. "But I know nothing of the technology of which you speak."

"All the better. Why, just last weekend after a sold-out perfor mance, I spoke with a certain celebrity songstress. As busy as her touring schedule may be, she could not pass up the opportunity to witness this amazing phenomenon herself. I hereby invite you to the most exclusive engagement of the decade. I'll be hosting a séance this weekend with"— he pauses for dramatic effect, and heaven help me, he's as pleased as if seeing the first bud on one of his new trees—"the Swedish Nightingale herself, Miss Jenny Lind!"

I suppose my response is not enthusiastic enough.

"Come, now, you must have heard of her."

"Yes, of course." I know of her, but I don't care for the constant stories of her talent. And I am sure I have better things to do than attend a dance—or whatever a séance is, I have no idea—even if she is there. Everyone these days is swooning over the tour of the songstress instead of attending to earth-shaking injustices. I only skim the arts sections of papers. "But, sir, as we are speaking, the fate of the soul of this country—"

"I will consult the spirits! I will request that we have the company of Benjamin Franklin. We will see if he will attend."

"But, sir, Benjamin Franklin is, uh . . ."

"Dead, yes. I know. Perhaps Miss Fox can persuade him to speak with us on these matters of great importance. Surely no one cared more for these colonies and their unity than he. He has shown up for the Fox sisters before, using the code of the knocks to proclaim this new technology, allowing the living to make contact to Summerland, where the spirits reside. I have many children who reside there, in Summerland."

It's his first mention of his children. A melancholy key change in his last sentence makes me realize the music of his oration has stopped. He says no more, continuing to walk the length of the field, frequently kicking a grounded fruit here and there, at times picking up and examining an apple for bruises. He walks us toward that original hemlock. He's going back up in the tree.

"Congratulations. You may have just lucked into the scoop of a lifetime." He grabs his axe, pats my shoulder in farewell, and starts to climb up. "The spirit-telegraph could be bigger than the cotton gin!"

He disappears up the trunk, and I hear it screaming as he whacks its limbs, starting anew the whole long ballad of "American Taxation" from the first line:

> "While I relate my story, Americans give ear, of Britain's
> fading glory you presently shall hear . . ."

I walk away slowly, my shoulders drooping in defeat. I have not just failed myself and my Lady Jane.

I have failed my country.

Chapter 7

Stinging with rejection, mind racing with Greeley's words, I walk as if I have somewhere important to be, which I do. I need to be out of these fields and into the woods. Insects hum cheery tunes and birds call that yesterday's storm is over, but my thoughts continue to thunder. The picture of what has just happened paints itself in my mind. I see red with rage. How can you convince someone of what is true if they refuse to see it? How can you stand for freedom on the backs of the enslaved? How can it be tolerated by any thinking person?

My hero—or should I say former hero—Horace Greeley insulted me for having morals and ethics *like a schoolgirl.* He has prohibited me from writing about what is truly important. He insulted me *and* schoolgirls, as if we are both so foolish when we speak that we are better off silent. Yet this exact silence is what breeds complicity and produces a world for us that exists on nothing but a surface of manners.

There are the Southern men in Congress who take the matter of simply broaching the morality of slavery as justification for a duel. As such, they reduce talk of reality to tiny islands of safe topics among men of honor. I am no man. I have no honor. May the *schoolgirls* take over this Earth, if they are the only ones who will speak the plain truth.

I stop where I am. My editorial, in which I have poured so much of my heart, soul, and time composing each word, I tear in half.

I tear it into quarters.

I tear it beyond even fractions, into tinier and tinier pieces that flutter away from me.

Gone.

Words of a schoolgirl, now torn into nothing amid a childish tantrum.

Good.

I pull an apple from a tree and take big enough mouthfuls to eat the entirety in three bites. I start to walk again, pulling more apples from trees, munching as I walk. I can nearly eat my weight in apples, I remind myself, like a dare. I eat them hard and fast, flinging the cores with half-said prayers of them making another tree.

Lady Jane said I was righteous, but what does that even mean if not knowing right from wrong, knowing the truth, and being able to speak it, write it? To give my life, if need be, to write the truth.

But as Pontius Pilate asked Jesus, *"What is truth?"*

To this, the Lord gave him silence.

I know the weight of silence.

Aunt Clara dragged me to Quaker meetings each Sunday in her Sisyphean attempt to give me religion. There have been years when I knew no torture greater than being forced to sit still in silence and "wait on the spirit" for an hour. A spirit certainly moved in me, but not the one that would speak with a message from the Light. Aunt Clara's hand would clasp my kneecap, trying to get my foot to stop its constant up and down, up and down.

"Ye Shall Know the Truth and the Truth Shall Make You Free" is a needlepoint she stitched and framed as the creed of her household and of her life—that old crone of a spinster. I think of her wrinkled, age-spotted hands and how she would pat and hold mine, especially after I'd had "a temper" as a child. I am a talker, she is a listener. I would talk on and on about something, and she would have two or three words in reply that would usually smash all my conceptions. Her white hair. Her knitted shawl. Old, creaky, smelling of the ointment she applied to her joints. That she, at age sixty-two, saved me from the orphanage to raise me, best she could. Trying to impart wisdom to me with a religion whose idea of worship meant sitting with nothing but my own thoughts.

I look up. I am at last out of the orchard and submerged into the trees. A cathedral of canopy, still wet from last night's storm, branches like spires to heaven. Light dapples down upon me. My thoughts rest for a moment.

So it has started to work on me. All those hours upon hours sitting with the Friends in silence, sometimes punctuated with their messages from the Light, along with my own experiences—watching a spider weave her web, climbing a tree as high as I could go to see out on the patchwork of farms, fanning turkey-tail mushrooms sprouting from dead logs, the soft of moss—have made me believe that something of God exists in all of life.

I am not a Quaker, but I know that what is Truth is obvious. People avoid it, hide it, lie about it for self-interest to deny another fundamental human truth—Equality. And now, here we are as a country. What is the obvious Truth becomes far more murky when you are trying to get things done in the world of politics.

"The Truth Shall Make You Free."

I wish I could ask Aunt Clara for advice right now.

I tilt my head and sigh up toward the tops of the trees.

Now that I'm calmer and full of apples, I do understand that there is wisdom to Mr. Greeley's logic: He cannot let something as important as the Compromise be a topic anyone less than he himself tackles. I must not let my pride stand in the way of seeing facts. Even if it were assumed that E. A. Howe was a man, as an unpublished and unknown writer, I couldn't cause a shift in public opinion. He has offered me an olive branch and a kindness. He doesn't mean it to be an insult. It is a break to be given any assignment that could be published in the *New-York Daily Tribune*, even if he thinks that I have the opinions of a schoolgirl and thus should write about one.

A woodpecker *tap tap taps* a tree somewhere.

My first published piece is not the point of my being here, in any case. It is a heroic charge, but it is not the battle that must be won. Mrs. Swisshelm has sent me to convince him, through my dogged persistence, of the way that his opinion, his paper, must go. I must *influence* him. And to that purpose, I must not give up. But that doesn't change the truth:

Mr. Greeley will not listen to me.

Tap tap tap, says the woodpecker, working.

A lightning bolt to a kite and key illuminates my mind, and I know my path forward.

Mr. Greeley will not listen to me, but he will listen to the knocking of Benjamin Franklin. He has given me the perfect assignment to be bent to a double purpose.

I accept this challenge. I will write an editorial about thumping ghosts, but I will make sure they tell no idle tales. Let's see what sabers spirits may rattle from the other side, what drums the dead beat for freedom. I'll rally every storied Founding Father, plus Betsy Ross for good measure, through this so-called spirit-telegraph. If I can only figure out how it works.

I must make a fast friend of Cathie Fox.

Chapter 8

I don't need to wait. As if Providence affirms my redirection with opportunity, I walk past the tree line of the woods and see little Cathie Fox, her back to me, at the bottom of a small hill where she sits with her governess. My eyes narrow like a hawk spying a sparrow. They are having a picnic, I believe. While the weather is pleasant enough, considering yesterday's downpour, the ground is muddy, and only one with a fever or a delusion could call the air warm. I suppose the sunshine must have drawn them out with that feeling of optimism and promise that only happens after the rain.

Idyllic as a painting, they are seated on a large checkered cloth with a wicker basket between them. Cathie, from this distance, is small as a wren; Jessica's bright dress and large white hat with yellow feathers make her look like an exotic nesting partridge. Jessica sees me, acknowledging me with a wave of her hand, and Cathie's head turns in my direction. I pull my mouth into my most winning smile, telling myself that befriending a child should be a simple undertaking, even as my stomach lurches as it always does whenever I have had the task of facing down children with the purpose of teaching them something. But this will be different. This is just one child, not a schoolhouse full of them.

This is a sneaky purpose—to influence. It is a very different thing from trying to help children learn how to read or spell. I do not need to make the comparison in my head of those terrible two months when I was a disastrous failure of a schoolteacher.

I failed Lady Jane, who had insisted even the most successful newspaper women need additional skills and a way to make their own income. She taught lace making. Surely I could teach children how to read, write, and do basic arithmetic.

No, I couldn't. How could I keep up the charade of being more interested in slate arithmetic than in getting outdoors to look at the geometry in the faces of sunflowers? I had no discipline with the students, and they ran amok while I was distracted with questions I did not know how to answer: Why do one hundred pennies make a dollar but only sixty minutes make an hour? I would lose myself wondering how any of it made any sense in the first place. What *is* zero? How is nothing also something?

Jessica is effortless in her instruction. "Dans l'ouvrage intitulé *Essai sur les mœurs et l'esprit des nations et sur les principaux faits de l'histoire depuis Charlemagne jusqu'à Louis XIII*, Voltaire écrit."

I think she is referring to a famous Voltaire essay. Typical of an English governess, acting like it is better to be speaking in French.

"Hello," I say, a caricature of a gigglemug.

"Et qui est là? C'est Mademoiselle Howe, n'est-ce pas? Bonjour, Mademoiselle! Écoute et répète: Bonjour, Mademoiselle Howe."

"Bonjour, Mademoiselle Howe," Cathie repeats.

Oh no. Jessica is using me as a subject for instruction.

"Comment allez-vous?"

"Comment allez-vous?"

They both await my response.

"Yes, hello, Miss Elliot, Miss Fox." I know French only well enough to know not to reply in it if I don't want to be mocked. "I am fine. May I sit?"

"Bien sûr!" Jessica pats the patchwork quilt. She continues speaking to Cathie, best I am piecing together, about the mud on my dress, the look on my face . . . something about the theater? Jessica speaks French beautifully. Everything about her is beautiful. It is difficult to think about anything else.

Cathie replies, haltingly, quietly, but still far better than I could do.

"Vous comprenez?" Jessica says to me.

"Non. Je ne comprends pas." Best to not be entrapped into more.

"Miss Howe, why are you traipsing through the orchards with mud on your skirts?"

"Is this a day for a picnic?" I answer her question with my own.

"Touché." She laughs lightly. "We do often prefer to do our schooling outside. Inside, it is so damp and dark, and there is a screaming toddler and other disturbances. Being outdoors is healthful, whenever possible. Mr. Greeley agrees. In fact, he suggests it when the weather permits."

There is something in the way she says *"Mr. Greeley"* that gives it an extra shine of importance. She points to their basket. "Would you like a little refreshment?"

I am not sure what food is laid out before them, but it looks like something far better than wheat biscuits and carrots. However many apples I ate, it only whet my appetite, and I am neither dainty nor coy in gobbling what she offers me: Tea! Little cakes! Cheese!

"But aren't they . . . Isn't there some strict diet of gruel and cabbage?" I say, gulping my tea, which has the decency to be warm but not hot. It is fascinating . . . By what invention did she transport warm tea to this spot? I need to ask her, but not when my mouth is full.

"We suffer with them on their diet when necessary, but there are exceptions made as part of my position here and Cathie's education."

Cathie hums to herself a tune I don't know. She lies down on the picnic blanket, seeming distracted, bored. I don't blame her. Learning French is boring.

A bird lands on the grass close to us. He's black, with shiny wings, a puffy little fellow. He lets out a melodious chirping song.

"It's a starling," Cathie says. "There's a nest up there in that tree." She motions to a beautiful oak not too far away.

"Yes, and they like coming after our crumbs," Jessica says.

"I love watching the different birds fly around here," Cathie says, now perking up.

Suddenly, I cough out a bit of tea, ruining the serene moment. I am eating and drinking too quickly. And of course, I spill a bit on my dress. Cathie laughs, seemingly amused by my lack of grace.

"I was saying to Cathie, en français, that every time we see you, your clothing becomes more ridiculous. You seem rather like a character in a play. First appearing in the scene as a maid, now as a bedraggled lady from the Northern colonies, though your accent is all wrong for a Northerner. Where are you from, Miss Howe?"

"Ohio." Her manner is as imperious as when we'd first met, if a little more friendly. I'd thought we were on a first-name basis. She said she would call me Edith, and I would call her Jessica. But I suppose that was a whisper, a secret between us—not in front of Cathie Fox.

"What a strange place to be from. I know nothing about Ohio."

"Where are *you* from?"

She ignores me like she didn't hear. "When I said you looked like a character from a play, Cathie said she has never seen a play. Certainly you have seen a play, yes, Miss Howe?"

"Yes," I say, mouth full again. "In fact, I did a number of reenactments for various church and social clubs in Ohio, in particular, Shakespeare soliloquies. My favorite is *Hamlet*. What is the fruit in this biscuit?" It is a thick jam of perfection.

"Currant," Jessica says, pinching in her eyes and pursing her lips at my manners. I know better. I am eating with abandon, distracting from her lesson, and jam is a digression from the topic at hand. "Cathie, you must have at least *read Hamlet*?"

"No." Cathie shakes her head.

"Oh, we must rectify this situation immediately. I am certain Mr. Greeley must have a *Complete Works of Shakespeare* in his library. Miss Howe, surely you can spare some moments for us. You must join us in reading *Hamlet*. You can read all the soliloquies aloud. Shakespeare is wonderful when read but meant to be spoken."

"To be, or not to be, that is the question," I begin, with the musicality of a tenor. I rise to standing, like I used to in the parlors and drawing rooms of the Women's Clubs, forgetting my surroundings with the shape of the words, the pulse of my heart with the rhythm. I know it like my own breath, this soliloquy. *"Who would fardels bear to grunt and sweat under a weary life, but that the dread of something after death, the undiscover'd country, from whose bourn no traveller returns . . ."*

My voice builds to a crescendo, my eyes on the horizon, feeling the story as my own—the ghost of Hamlet's father walking the night, days spent in fire. What might my own father say to me? I've never known his face, though Aunt Clara says I look like him. How well do I even know my own face?

"Thus conscience does make cowards of us all." A horse kicked my father in the stomach, and a few days later he was dead. Leaving my mother alone in the middle of nowhere with two children, including me, an infant. What words could his ghost say that could ever change what she did next?

My breath seeps from the soliloquy and finishes: *". . . and lose the name of action."*

The hill, the sky, the trees come back to my eyes. I have half forgotten where I am.

Cathie and Jessica honor me with applause, but I sit down quickly.

"You are a strange sort of person, Miss Howe. I believe you could be an actor if you were a man." It is hard to tell whether Jessica means it as a compliment or just an observation. "You bring much emotion to the words without any provocation."

"I liked that very much, Miss Howe." Cathie is still clapping. "So very much."

"*Hamlet* is an excellent study for us, Cathie," Jessica says. Nowhere in this statement are the words for Cathie to cease applauding, but somehow it's understood, and Cathie's hands fold into her lap. "Miss Howe certainly seems to find him inspiring, and could assist us, if she can spare a moment from her all-important mission." Again, I cannot tell whether she disdains or approves. It is like a riddle between her words and expression. "Did you find Mr. Greeley?"

"Yes. He is still out here, somewhere." I motion to the woods. "Hacking limbs off a tree."

"Oh, wonderful. I told him that a little light would do Mrs. Greeley good, and I hope he takes down that tree right outside her window. She needs some sun."

Cathie frowns and hums again. A bit of a minor key, in the same song as before.

"Have you met Mrs. Greeley yet?" Jessica asks.

I am unsure how to answer. Locking eyes with her while she was in a fit does not count.

"We haven't been formally introduced, though I know she was sick this morning." This seems the most polite way to put it.

"Yes, she is often sickly," Jessica says.

"Yes, because she is often pregnant," I say.

"That is a vulgar way to speak," Jessica says. "Especially in front of a child."

"Apologies," I say to Cathie, who barely seems interested.

"Her sickness may be compounded by being with child, yes," Jessica continues primly. "But she often refuses to take her medicine, and that is the root of her maladies."

"Well, if you ask me, a lot of those medicines cause more problems than they cure. I remember this talk in one of the Women's Clubs about mercury poisoning—"

"Are you a doctor now, as well as a newspaperman?"

"Newspaper *woman*, and as such, I know enough to know that women's issues are often completely misreported and misunderstood. The root of her maladies is probably the root belonging to Mr. Greeley."

Jessica looks shocked. I do not believe "root" is considered a curse word, for Shakespeare uses it.

"I need the privy," Cathie says. "Miss Howe, will you accompany me?"

"I think that's appropriate since that's where her mind is at," Jessica says. "And perhaps then Miss Howe will continue with her business so we can continue with our lesson."

"Oh, yes. Certainly," I say.

I have been dismissed to the outhouse.

There I go again, saying things without thinking and offending sensibilities. But then, here I am, walking alone with Cathie, a perfect opportunity to try to understand what is possible with her as the subject of my to-be-written editorial. When we are out of hearing distance from her governess, I begin my questioning.

"When you use the spirit-telegraph, Cathie, can you ask to speak to anyone? For example, if I wished to speak with a Founding Father—"

"Help me, Miss Howe," Cathie interrupts me, grabbing my arm with a desperate tug, like we should run. "I love Miss Elliot, and I know it's important for me to get an education, but I do not like it here. I want to leave. I do not want to knock for Mrs. Greeley anymore."

"Why not?"

"I hate her." She says it softly, so softly I'm not sure I heard her right. She says it again, loud enough that there is no doubt. "I hate her!"

"Oh." It is hard to find an appropriate reply. I mentally sort through phrases people said to me when I was a child, but aphorisms about walking miles in someone else's shoes or God making no mistakes do not fit this situation.

"I miss my mother!" Cathie bursts into tears.

I kneel and hug her. It isn't some tactic to win her affection; anyone with a heart would try to comfort her. She sobs the way children do— coughing, hiccupping, complaining between wails. "Why do I have to get an education?" and "My sister Maggie gets to stay in the city with my mother, why do I have to be here?" and "Mr. Greeley says my studies here will be for two years! Two whole years!"

I find myself saying things just to say them, and because I am a failure as a teacher, I do my best to match the tone and reasoning of Miss Elliot. "When you are special, sometimes you have to make sacrifices.

Mr. Greeley is convinced you have a gift. Maybe you can use it to help persuade people of what is right and moral."

"It frightens me!" Her tear-filled eyes tug on mine, pulling me underneath to where something unfathomable drags its chains on the bottom of the ocean. "It frightens me! It frightens me!"

"The knocking?" I whisper.

"The house!" Her upturned face contorts. "This house is eating me alive!"

"Well, I . . ." She presses her head into my chest, and I feel the wetness of her tears soaking through my dress, the heat of her breath, and her body shaking in its sorrow. "I think you should go home, then."

"But Mr. Greeley is protecting our family, advising us at every turn, recommending us to celebrities and artists, and making sure we aren't hurt . . . There are many people who want to hurt us." She is through the worst of it. She tells me it must be that she is so nervous for the séance this weekend, hoping the spirits show up for Miss Jenny Lind. She wipes her nose on her sleeve, for some reason apologizing, saying how sorry she is for her behavior, and asking me not to tell Miss Elliot of her childish outburst.

"You don't need to apologize, and I won't tell."

A wind picks up, blowing leaves across the grass.

Cathie stares over my shoulder, her eyes widening, as if something or someone just appeared there.

I feel a prickling on my neck, which I am sure is just the breeze.

Still, I can't stop myself from turning to see what Cathie is looking at.

It is nothing, of course. Wind is invisible. It blows cold in my face.

I don't want her to say it. So why do I ask? "Do you see something?"

"It's her, again. You don't have to talk to her if you don't want to." Cathie's gaze moves from over my shoulder back to my face.

"I don't," I say. "And if you are seeing a ghost, I assure you, it isn't my mother." My breath gives out on the last word. I guess I've been holding it. I gasp, trying to fill my lungs again. It must be a trick. But why is she trying to trick me? Maybe she thinks it would be a comfort to me, as apparently the dead are to others. I don't want to tell her that my mother is alive, a murderess, and terrifying to me.

"If you don't want to talk to her—"

"I said I didn't. I do not."

"Then I won't, either," she says. "Let's change the subject." She straightens herself, and we start walking back the way we came. She asks me how I remember all those Shakespeare lines I had spoken, and what I think about when I recite them, and if I would rather be an actor or a newspaper woman.

I am suspicious now of the cloud that moves over the sun, the way the leaves keep blowing. I say something about acting and performance, and my connection with the emotions of *Hamlet*. My mind is not fully in my mouth, but still outside my body, fearing what might be there that I cannot see. I don't even know what I say, but she is nodding as if we have come to an agreement.

"It's the same with me and the spirits," she says.

I suddenly forget to be afraid, because I am curious about what she means.

"*What* is the same?" I ask.

The wind picks up again, and Cathie doesn't answer. The strangeness of this girl, of this place, of all the torturous days and nights it has taken for me to get here, and the weight of my disappointment, weary me to my bones. I must rest.

In the distance, Jessica, in her blue, shiny puff of skirts and red hair, sits awaiting her pupil.

"I will let you get back to your French lessons," I say, turning around.

"Miss Howe, there is something stuck to your skirt."

Somehow the wind has blown a piece of my torn and scattered editorial all across the orchard and back onto me. Ink blotted but still clear are these words I had written:

"a fight for her very soul"

I stare at my own handwriting like it is a threat from a stranger. Each word loses its meaning and takes on a more sinister shadow. Is it a warning?

I need to get away from Cathie, from Jessica. Put distance between us. I cannot run in these shoes. As I clutch my skirts, the scrap of paper seems to burn into my palm. I look for the coincidence, the logical explanation. Perhaps it hadn't flown across the orchard on the breeze; maybe it had dropped onto my skirt and been stuck to me all along, unseen. I don't need to find a sign or a symbol where there is none.

I am walking fast—too fast, I suppose. I cannot get my breath.

My corset is always as loose as I can make it, but it is still too tight, and the skirt feels too heavy. The bodice is damp from Cathie's tears.

I miss my mother!

What must it be like to have a mother one could miss?

Chapter 9

"I will *not* be a lady!" I was twelve years old, having a tantrum like a child half my age. I had hacked my hair off with sewing scissors to punish Aunt Clara for having the temerity to try to teach me some proper manners.

"You look like you don't have a mother," Aunt Clara said. It was one of those phrases people said around our part of Ohio. No one thought about what it meant or took offense, even those of us without mothers. At that moment, however, I decided to buck the norm and do both.

"I *don't* have a mother! She's dead!" I screamed. "I am an orphan, and I will look like an orphan!" I think I threw something at her. Probably my dress. I do remember I was stark naked.

"Your mother is alive in a lunatic asylum, where you'll end up if you don't learn to control your temper!" she yelled back at me, in a voice I had never heard from her. She clapped her hands over her mouth, as if to prevent the devil from escaping.

Perhaps not Aunt Clara's finest moment. But she was, after all, at that point seventy years old and had spent her whole adulthood with the rare privilege of being a self-sufficient spinster until she made the terrible decision of trying to raise me rather than sending me to an orphanage.

"She's alive . . . ?"

Stoic Aunt Clara, with lines that showed pursed lips and narrowed eyes that were her most consistent expression, let loose the hell of my history, begging my forgiveness that she had kept it secret for so long.

My father and Aunt Clara were as close as brother and sister could be growing up. Then he took up with a woman who had episodes of melancholia and no family, and against all the advice of loved ones, decided to marry her.

"I loved Ned, but a sister's love is nothing if his wife won't have it, and she was jealous of everyone. So, close as we were, when they married, that was the end of it." Aunt Clara was still bitter, however many years had passed.

They had moved to the outskirts of nowhere with a young child, my brother. Aunt Clara heard almost nothing for two years, until she received a letter from my father that another child was on the way, that being me. She supposed my parents continued to eke out a life on that little farm until an accident killed my father.

"I heard that Ned was dead—mind you, no word from her on that. I heard it from a friend that lived in the nearest town over. I sent your mother a letter saying that she should come stay here with me until she could sort things out. As I said, we never got along, but I was worried about her lack of good reason in the best of times. Never mind after burying a husband and all alone out there with two young mouths to feed. She did not reply, and I was unwilling to show up unannounced. That was a mistake. I should have just made the journey. I should have braved her temper and swallowed my pride."

She showed me a clipping, yellowed and cracking where it had been folded: **WIDOW DERANGED—DID SHE TRY TO DROWN HER CHILDREN?** The article's writer was not listed with a byline name, thus giving the appearance that *The Ohio Star* birthed the article of its own intelligence. Whoever wrote it made it seem no question at all that my mother went mad as a hatter and dragged me and my five-year-old brother to the lake with the intention of *"drowning them like kittens."* It could not be an accident, as my brother was fully clothed and *"the infant* *was placed in her bassinet."* My brother died, but the bassinet saved my life as I floated like Moses, alive and screaming, nearly two miles downstream to where a neighbor was washing her clothes. They could not prove murder, however. *"It is unlikely that Grace Howe will stand trial or hang, as she seems incapable of speech and insensible to inquiry."*

This newspaper article revealed not just awful truths but also unforgivable lies and omissions from Aunt Clara. Her story was that my father had died in a farm accident and that my mother died from grief afterward. Aunt Clara had never even told me I had a brother before, much less a murdered, drowned one.

My mother is a murderess!

I must admit, at age twelve I found this a terribly romantic concept. I knew I was too wild for the constraints of society, and my famous, wicked mother proved my dangerous and rebellious lineage. I could not have been more excited if I had learned she was actually a queen, placing me in line for the throne.

I wanted to see her. I couldn't imagine *not* seeing her, no matter what she had done. I didn't have to insist much; Aunt Clara said it was my right to try to reach her, to do what good could be done for her, even now. We rode in a buggy for a day, a night, and another day, my leg going up and down with the *clop clop clop* of the horses, my mouth constantly talking, and Aunt Clara likely praying for the patience to refrain from killing me herself.

I imagined my mother as some terrible and beautiful force of nature, her eyes boiling with the rage of volcanos, her mind a hurricane of the injustices of life, creator and destroyer. She escaped hanging by only her madness, or her pretense to madness. Perhaps it was all a calculation. Knowing my own tendency toward the dramatic, I figured it could be an act. I fantasized that when I would meet her, she would see the *me* in her, the her in me, and she would tell me a secret that would reveal my wonderful destiny, even though her own fate was sealed. I would fall into her arms, weeping. She would pet my hair and call me her "darling." She would scream in protest when her jailers told us it was time to part.

Even now, remembering, I had imagined it in such detail it feels like a story I'd read, memorized.

The reality turned out to be quite different—as dull and painful as a rotting tooth.

The asylum itself was far from horrific. A Georgian mansion with meticulously cultivated grounds where inmates stood or sat outside, taking in the sun. I found it rather lovely. "Maybe I can move in here with my mother instead of being a canker to you," I said in the cold way I'd acquired when speaking to Aunt Clara.

"I'm sure you would be most welcome," she replied with those pursed lips and narrowed eyes.

I looked at the manicured hedges and how the bushes had been sculpted and tamed. I started thinking of how I could help all the mad ones find their reason, of the happy little press I would start with all the inmates' stories, and how delighted all would be with my cleverness and unbreakable spunk. Yes, I thought with the innocence of a child, the mad people are the only ones of us who are still wild, untamed, free.

The inside was less cheerful. Someone kept singing the same three pitch-poor notes again and again for the entire time I was there. Another kept arguing with herself violently. And someone sat facing the window, looking out, still as a wax figure.

I don't remember the nurse. I can't recall whether she was fat or thin, old or young, I only remember her voice and how she rotated the wax figure of the woman toward me, claiming this was my mother.

"It's your child, the one who is still alive," the nurse said.

Her hair was colorless, matted. Eyes cloudy, her lips moving with no sound. I would like to say that tears ran down her face, even though her eyes seemed barely able to function. I would like to say there was something in her that acknowledged my presence in the slightest. But there was nothing. She was not reachable. There was no one there.

I stared at this woman—dead while alive—and tried to find any thread of connection between us. I felt more alike to the chair she sat in than the person in it.

"She sometimes will talk," the nurse said. "But I suppose it's not today."

"What does she say when she talks?" I must have asked. Or maybe Aunt Clara asked it. I don't recall if I'd found my voice at the moment.

"Nothing but gibberish. Talks of buttons, missing buttons, losing buttons. Never heard so much talk about buttons. Makes me want to go mad myself."

I touched her hand—it reminded me of when I'd touched the skin of a toad.

I did not like looking at her.

"Button," my mother said in a sad croak. She did not see me, even though I was right there. "Button eyes."

Something about those words stopped my breath. The words, somehow, connected my mind to a picture of her toad hands pressing my face underwater. I saw a memory with those words that I didn't want to see.

"I want to go," I said to the nurse, to Aunt Clara.

"Well, we came all this way, you might as well sit and spend a moment—"

I screamed that I would *not!*

It is a wonder Aunt Clara didn't leave me there, and instead took my hand and walked me out.

Neither of us said anything about it, ever again. I cried of a broken heart as we rode the buggy back home, and she held me in her arms, rocking me like a baby.

I try not to think about my mother. Alive in her body, dead in her mind, speaking nonsense. She is not bumping the floor in a nursery in New York, chipping a teacup. She is not over my shoulder, insisting a child intercede for her. She is not the wind, blowing my own words back at me.

She is still there today, in that chair, staring out the window at a world she no longer knows. She is worse than dead.

Chapter 10

"This house is eating me alive!"

It frightens Cathie, but I can see nothing hungry in its humble facade. It's the type of house an important person like Greeley could say befits a modest man with a modest family, neither inviting nor demanding. While it had loomed before me like a mistaken path in a storm, here in the daylight it is a forgettable structure. The trees that surround it are far more impressive and stately. My head hurts and I need to lie down. I've slept peacefully in barns that look more haunted. The need to rest pulls me inside, and the outside of the house does nothing to make me hesitate.

I let myself in the large front door—why give Martha extra work?

I choke on my first breath. It smells like two dozen biscuits are burning. My eyes hold a blinding imprint of the sunlit sky as I walk into the dark house. I am unable to see for a moment. The regular *tock tock* of the clock here in the front parlor cannot find rhythm with the clanking from the kitchen. The shrill voice of a woman commands, "Each dish must be scrubbed with vinegar and salt. No lye. No soap. Do you understand? No more poison!"

Beneath it all, the usual sound of a child crying upstairs. Poor Baby Charlotte.

I need to walk by the kitchen to get to the stairs. There's a vignette through the open doorway of the Marthas surrounded by stacks of dishes, and Mary Greeley, head cocked, holding up a plate for interrogation. This is the first time I've seen her upright.

I creep as softly as I can, trying to keep my skirts from whooshing, my shoes from clip-clopping. They don't yet see me, and if I can just get upstairs without being noticed . . .

"But there is still this spot." Mary Greeley scrubs the plate like Lady Macbeth. "This spot, it—"

The dish breaks in her hand.

The Marthas look to her for their cue. Is she hurt? Upset?

"And now what, will you bleed me like another phony physician?" she says, laughing, speaking to the plate.

I am almost past the open doorway of the kitchen to the steps when a floorboard beneath me creaks, and Mary Greeley turns to me.

"Oh, hello," she says. Her black hair is pulled back tight. Large, dark eyes seem to bulge directly from her skull, glittering. Yet her face is young, freckled, sweet. She is very pretty, if not for the troubling intensity of her gaze.

The Marthas have stopped their scrubbing, as if ordered to freeze in place and watch.

"You are the newspaper woman?" Mary Greeley asks brightly.

"Yes," I say, standing with straight posture and purpose, like I had intended to be seen and was not skulking upstairs to hide from her.

She dries her palms on her apron, leaving a small smear of blood from the fresh cut on her hand. She walks over to me, her gaze moving all over the top of my head, around my face, like looking for will-o'-the-wisps. "You have a very high vibration. I am glad you are here."

"Thank you," I say, unsure how else to reply to that observation.

She snaps her head toward Martha, who has left her position in the scrubbing line. "Why are you stopping?"

Martha doesn't answer but pats a roll of bandage into my palm. "Can you help Mrs. Greeley wrap her cut?"

"Everything must be washed," Mary tells me. "The wheat flour was poisoned."

"Poison?" Oh, dear, I had at least three biscuits, and . . . what about Baby Charlotte? I made her eat one, too.

"We all ate the wheat and feel fine," Martha calls out, back to scrubbing with a forced cheer. "Mrs. Greeley is just very sensitive and had a dream."

"It wasn't a dream," Mary corrects her. "I looked into the wheat and there were weevils."

"There weren't weevils when I baked this morning."

"Well, you didn't look! White, maggoty weevils were crawling when I looked in there—so maybe you like to eat weevils, but I don't!"

She turns back to me with a conspiratorial whisper. "Did you know that it's rotted rye that made medieval peasants see demons and burn with Saint Anthony's fire?"

"No, I had not heard." I have this bandage in my hand, so I hold it out. "Shall we?"

"We shall." She puts her arm in mine and starts to walk me. "Weevils in the wheat carry a fungus, and it has contaminated the entire kitchen. It is why I have been so terribly sick these past days and unable to keep any food down. So it is a chore, but it must be done, yes, it must be done. The flour, with the weevils, we already set that in the fire, didn't we? But we do need to have someone go now, into town, yes, and get more flour, and I must have a tincture of rhubarb for my stomach. Where are you headed?"

"Oh, I was just going to my room to write to my employer, Mrs. Swisshelm." I hold the edge of a doorframe to keep myself steady. "I am on an important assignment to—"

"Mrs. Swisshelm? You mean Mrs. Jane Grey Swisshelm? You work for her?"

"Yes," I say. "Yes, I do. She sent me here to—"

"She must have a very high vibration, don't you think? Mrs. Swisshelm's words vibrate and elevate, yes?"

"I could not agree more. I adore her. In fact, I call her my Lady Jane."

"Lady Jane! Yes, she *is* a lady of the most important sort, not some inbred royalist. I have not met her in person, only I have met her in her writing, which is a true way of meeting someone, even spirits you can meet in writing, and really meet them, really, truly meet them . . . here." She presses a hand to her heart, leaving a red smudge.

"Let's wrap that cut," I say.

"I told Father to hire her, just like I insisted he hire Margaret Fuller—oh, I can never call her by her married name." It doesn't seem as if she is intentionally ignoring the bandage, just that her thoughts are too consuming to stop for such a small consideration. "She and I were friends, Margaret Fuller. Very good friends. I met her first at a number of events. I am crazy for learning, just crazy for it. I wish I could go to school and be surrounded by all the books like old friends, but all my old friends—well, they left me for Father's library, just like Margaret Fuller. She was my friend, but then she became Father's friend more especially, the letters they wrote to each other, letter upon letter, yes. She did disdain women, really, Margaret Fuller, but I heard her first, and I was the one who insisted to Father that he hire her. I insisted. I do miss her. Miss Fuller, I mean. I do think . . ." She wipes tears away quickly, the comma of blood from her cut mixing with the tears on her cheek. She does not seem aware of the red smear. "I do think if she had decided not to get married, to not have a child, she would still be with us."

I would agree with her, but I am caught in the downpour of her words, and she continues before I can.

"Oh, what am I saying? Of course she is still with us. Everyone is still with us! We need only ask and we can talk to them. No one ever really dies. But you do still . . ." She wipes her eyes again, and at last, noting that she is still bleeding, wipes her hand on her apron. "You do still miss them."

"I have a bandage," I say. "For that cut."

"Oh, yes, thank you," she says. But she does not take the bandage or give me her hand. "I often get lost in the details. I forget things, and it gets worse with the poison they call medicine. It has been hard for me to be a wife and mother. How can I keep a house? When we first married, I couldn't keep a fire lit. I told him I was leaving because I couldn't keep the fire lit, but then I didn't know where to go."

Her moods pivot quickly, but we stroll slowly. Arm in arm, we promenade about the main level of her home, making no mention of each room but merely moving as if there's an invisible path and nothing of note to look at. Which, truth be told, there isn't. I have never been in an inhabited home that holds so little decoration. No rugs, no pictures, no bric-a-brac figurines. Even furniture is scarce. Whether it's still the imprint of the outdoor light in my eyes or Cathie's cry about this house trying to eat her, the bright spots and shadows move just outside the corners of my vision with sharp, jagged edges. Or maybe there really were weevils in the wheat.

"I am crazy for learning, but not about properly ironing shirts."

"I completely understand," I say quickly, dreading her saying *"crazy for learning"* again. "But you are studying, now that you have help, and you can go to events?"

"Yes, I can. I did. But now, oh, I have been sick. So sick. This whole year, ever since Pickie . . ." She stops talking for a moment, staring out into nothingness.

I feel it—the house as something alive. Air pregnant with burned weevil wheat and who knows how many months of endless tears. The walls bend beneath the weight of Baby Charlotte's cries and the echoes of the children who are gone. The momentary suspension of Mary Greeley's keening is the eye of a storm.

It is not a hungry house. It is a house that has been gorged in grief.

"May I please have your hand?" I ask.

"Oh, are you going to read my palm?"

"Yes," I say.

She offers me a small hand, with nails chewed down.

"The other one, please."

"Oh, but don't you read the opposite of the favored?" Still, she places the bleeding hand in mine.

The cut is not deep, and evidently doesn't hurt enough for her to notice.

"Have you heard of the works of Dr. Jules Vincent?" she asks.

"I'm not sure." I have wound bandages before, but I am no expert. It's just a matter of getting it around her thumb, below the fingers.

"He is a most famous mesmerist." She watches the poor job I am doing here. "A doctor, an inventor. A real scientist. Father says he may visit in the near future to meet with Cathie."

Ah, this is the man Mr. Greeley said I should interview.

I need to unwrap the wound and start again. Lights taking over portions of my vision make it a more difficult task.

"He works wonders. I am sure he could cure me of these headaches and stomachaches. He is a real doctor, not these local bleeders. Not like Dr. . . . I can't even remember his last name. I blot it out. Dr. Bug, I call him. What a quack. Leeches and laudanum—that's all he knows. And yet everyone here says, 'Take the medicine, Mary! Take the medicine!' What is that sound?"

"Baby Charlotte is crying."

She looks up as if hearing her daughter for the first time. Her face twists down.

"Yes, yes, she is always crying. By this age, Pickie was talking, walking—Pickie is a medium, born that way. As a baby, he could see spirits, he could talk to the other side, he saw Summerland. Very special. Oh, he has these blue eyes and hair the color of dandelions."

"There we are," I say, having made a far bigger mitten than is warranted for the wound. Teeth seem to have bitten into the side of my skull, as more of my vision disappears into ovals of white. A migraine is coming.

"It's not just Charlotte crying, that noise—" Mrs. Greeley's arm lifts out of my grasp, boasting a well-swaddled hand.

"Why not fetch Baby Charlotte and bring her in here?" I ask. The sound is throbbing into my brain. Diamond halos block my sight. How long do I have before the pain completely knocks me down? I know from experience that once the light takes over the center, it isn't long before I'm no longer able to stand.

"Oh, I don't think Baby Charlotte should be exposed to the dangers of the kitchen. Especially not with the weevils." Her voice is sharp in my ear.

We have circled back to where the Marthas continue the clanking business of cleaning each dish.

"Mrs. Swisshelm always has her children in the kitchen with her," I say. "She thinks it is good for children to learn early about the heat of the hearth and how to be safe around the bustle." I try to focus my eyes to look toward Mary's. "Plus, Baby Charlotte has such an exceptionally high magnetism that it will help to battle whatever evil spirits are in the weevils."

The Marthas look up at me at the same time.

"Charlotte barely speaks, but"—Mrs. Greeley's enormous eyes move around my head—"she recovered from the cholera that killed Pickie. She is a hale little thing, and her magnetism, I never really thought about it, but it is—"

"Exceptionally high," I say, as if I have always been in the business of assessing magnetism.

"*Exceptionally* high," she agrees, nodding to me. "Go get Charlotte and the bassinet," she screeches at Martha before turning her head back toward me, shaking it. "But the sound of her crying, that's not the sound I mean. It's *that* sound—"

"Mr. Greeley is trimming a tree," I say. I hadn't heard it—I had been overcome in her gale of talk, Baby Charlotte's cries, the shadows and light, and the vise tightening around my head—but I hear it now, the back-and-forth of the saw against the rings of time in the wood.

"But which tree is he trimming? Surely not the one that hangs right over my window?" she asks me. "That is *my* tree he is trimming."

"Perhaps he thought it would do you good to have more light in here," I say diplomatically.

"Oh no, oh no! He must be stopped." She's outside before I can even quite comprehend that her voice is no longer next to me.

I turn to look at the Marthas. We survived a squall, but the storm isn't over.

"My head is killing me," I say. "I'm going to hide in my room."

"We are green with envy," Martha replies.

~

I find my way to the bed where Margaret Fuller slept, but it is too late. My closed eyes are blinded with light.

(Sew them shut. It's too bright in here for baby's eyes.)

Whose voice is that?

(It's your mother's voice. You always know your mother's voice.)

No, it's just a thought in my head. A thought in my head doesn't have sound. But it does have pain. A terrible, sharp shooting pain, breaking open my head with a scream.

I hear her screaming out the window.

It is not my mother—it is this house that is screaming.

No, it is *her*, Mary Greeley. That is the voice outside. Screaming at Mr. Greeley.

That is not my mother's voice, pressing my face under water.

Will I—

(to be or not to be your mother)

Will I go mad—

This house is haunted.

It knocks.

It frightens me!

It is eating me alive!

(The dead wood of the house holds the spirits of her dead children.)

Will I go mad like her?

(That is the question.)

Too late to stop the thought, *to think or not to think.*

This is not my mind, these are not my thoughts.

Will I go mad like my mother?

Chapter 11

"Edith?" A prayer of a voice with a soft knock.

I open my eyes with a gasp, gulping air like I have been drowning.

"I didn't mean to frighten you."

Jessica glides toward me, angelic, restoring my vision. The blind spots of white have faded. I don't know what time it is or how long I've been in this state. I can see out the window that it is still daytime.

I've experienced migraines before, but none has ever come on so suddenly or painfully. This is the first time I've experienced thoughts seeming to make sounds both in and outside my head. The thought that I could lose my mind, as my mother did . . . I press this idea away, far away. The worst is over. I am here, and so is Jessica. She orients me back to the Greeley home, in the room that is also a shrine to my hero. Material objects, real things. A row of books, a writing desk, walls painted robin's-egg blue. A cheerful room, after all.

"Good that you are getting some sleep, as there's no supper. The wheat was all burned. Mary Greeley had a fit about the stupid tree and ordered Mr. Greeley away." She speaks like we are both old, practiced gossips. "Now he's at the Rookery for who knows how long, and there is nothing to eat. Luckily, my cousin sent for me, so I'm going to head into town. I suppose I will have to pick up some supplies. Not to mention more of her precious tincture of rhubarb, the only medicine she'll take, and it's not medicine at all. Whatever the *root* of it, watch out. There's no protection from her as long as he's at the Rookery."

I do my best to sit up, though it feels like an anvil is sitting atop my head.

"What is the Rookery?"

"That's what he calls the *Tribune* offices. He has a stupid name for everything. I told you what he calls this place. 'Castle Doldrum.' Or alternatively, 'Castle Doleful.' Either of those titles are far too kind." She sits on the bed next to me. "'Castle Dreadful' is more apt."

I laugh, even though it takes its measure in the pain in my head.

"And here Mr. Greeley plans to host the most famous singer in the world, I shudder to think of it. Although I suppose one could argue the only thing that's appropriate to host in this place is a séance."

"Is it a type of dance?"

"A type of dance?" She laughs. "I suppose in a way. Dancing with spirits. Why are you hiding up here?"

"I got very sick. I've a terrible headache."

She places a hand to my forehead. "You don't have a fever."

"It was a migraine. I get them sometimes. I see these blinding lights, but this one, this was worse. It was a nightmare—I had a horrible nightmare." I take her hand and press it to my face. It is cool, beloved, a dear friend. A refuge.

"Why all this with my hand?" She says it like I am insufferably silly. "Are you so taken with me?"

I suppose I am. I feel so unreasonably happy at this moment that she has come to comfort me. I cannot account for how glad I feel. She is blushing as if it pleases her, too, to have the delicate pink and white moons of her fingernails clasped between my rough, ink-stained fingers. Her red hair has fallen out in wisps around her face, her lips curl up on both ends in a smile. I press my mouth to the small knobs of her knuckles, and my lips brush the back of her palm. She squeals with an expression of surprise and delight.

"Now, don't pretend you are some gentleman, kissing my hand!" She moves closer, maneuvering the layers of flounce in her skirts, progressing in pieces with her corset and stays, finally plopping herself next to me with a whoosh of fabric. If lying down is such a production, it is going to be that much harder for her to get up again.

We face each other like open and closed parentheses.

"I am sorry about your migraine," she says.

"It is better now. I'm through the worst of it."

"The house *is* haunted." Her eyebrows arch. "It affects us each differently."

"I don't believe in that sort of thing," I say, with far more assurance than I feel. "Do you?"

"Of course I do. It's not a matter of belief, for me. I know it's real. The house calls to me like a wounded creature under a bad spell. When I first arrived I had the strangest sense of it, like a living thing. A sad and starved place. All the poor children who died here of sickness and neglect, those feelings warped into the wood. It is hungry for beauty and people."

"*There is nothing either good or bad, but thinking makes it so,*" I quote *Hamlet*. Jessica sees it as a house to pity, Cathie feels it's eating her alive, and it gives me a blinding headache. "I suppose if you think it's haunted, it is."

"Oh, Edith, there are ghosts, spirits, a whole invisible kingdom one only needs to open your heart to see. I'm an orphan, too, Edith. I lived in an orphanage with so many ghosts it was hard to ever sleep. But as much as there are spirits that would harm you, there are even more that would help. I know I have a powerful destiny. The spirits helped me, and help me still. They led me to my education, to my position as a governess, they guided me across the ocean to a cousin I'd never known I had—then they guided me to Cathie."

She speaks with such sincerity it's impossible not to believe her. Or at least, I believe that *she* believes it. In the same way that as a child, I knew I could talk to animals and felt I could whisper secrets into trees. She is clearly charmed—one can see that simply in the sight of her. I know I can see and feel things that other people refuse to allow. I believe in things other people say are impossible—even my own equality in this country.

"The spirits don't knock for me yet, like they do for her, but I am learning. I have premonitions. I see things." Her fingers walk across the white coverlet to touch mine. "Things about you, too."

I don't ask her what she sees about me. That doesn't keep her from offering.

"You broke some boy's heart," she says with great seriousness. "There is someone pining for you."

I snort hard enough to make my head throb again. The idea of Frank Jackson pining for me is laughable. He is the most practical, rude sort of fellow, not capable of pining for anyone or anything.

"You wouldn't marry him, even though you do, in some way, love him," she says with an ethereal glint in her eyes, like one would playact seeing Hamlet's ghost.

"I don't love him," I say. "And I don't believe in second sight or other powers." I immediately wish I hadn't said that. Even if it is true, it isn't nice to say it, especially when she is here comforting me after a terrible nightmare.

"Well, maybe it doesn't matter what you say you believe," she says matter-of-factly, "if it helps you when you are afraid and lost in a dream."

We stare at each other. She is daring me to deny that she has read my mind.

I won't deny it. I lace my fingers through hers.

"So who is he?" she asks.

I really don't want to think about Frank Jackson when I could just look at Jessica Elliot. I suppose I should tell her something about him since she is so curious.

They—Aunt Clara, his family—always threatened that Frank and I would end up married since we were around the same age, lived next door, and spent a fair amount of our lives arguing with each other. He didn't like that I seemed to be able to do whatever, whenever I wanted, when he had to work tirelessly on the family farm. He was always trying to trick me into helping him, which, well, most of the time I did because he'd rile me up by saying I wasn't as strong or as fast or as able.

"He's just a neighbor in Ohio," I tell Jessica. Frank Jackson is no one I could marry. "He's a good, hardworking sort, but my only love for him is as a friend."

She watches my face, and I watch her. Can she read my mind? If so, she will see the story of me and Frank is no romance.

"And I don't want to get married. I am a newspaper woman."

"Not yet, you're not," she says. "Isn't that why you're here?"

"No. I mean, maybe, but that isn't the *purpose* of my being here. I am an apprentice to a newspaper woman—"

"Oh, who needs newspaper women anyway?" The spell she has cast is in danger of breaking into a squabble. "Isn't it terrible enough that there are newspaper *men*, scribbling their lurid, low-class stories? You colonists . . ."

The dull pain in my head fuels my indignation. "I am sorry if this offends you, but a vibrant fourth estate provides the necessary checks and balances for our government. Without a free press, there is no freedom of the people. And we will be a free people. All of us."

She laughs at me as if I told a great joke. "Oh, E. A. I. O. U. and sometimes Y. You truly are half feral. Especially in your opinions."

I close my eyes and let her win. It is better for the slow throbbing in my skull. Better to just feel her next to me, anyway, than to talk. I am glad for her presence. She smells of the orchard and her lilac powder. She's here to comfort me and bring me back to my wits and purpose. Why argue?

"I like this bed," she says. "I would sleep better in here, I think, with you."

I feel her hand on my chest, her breath against my skin. My eyes open to watch her trace a line around my heart with her finger.

"I will listen, and know where you have hidden your love," she says, placing her ear on my breast.

My heart knocks a code against the bones of my chest, spelling out for her the secrets I have yet to know.

Chapter 12

The sound of a child laughing wakes me. Jessica is gone. I don't know how long I've slept. The imprint of the curl of her body on the bed and the scent of her powder prove she wasn't a dream. I hear the laugh again. It sounds like Baby Charlotte.

I sit up too quickly. My head still hurts, though it's nothing compared to what it was. I am frustrated with myself that I have wasted today's hours when I have so much to do. This is no time or place for my head to be taking me out of my mission. I pull myself up from the bed and open the door, making my way downstairs, dull pain returning with each step and the smell of burned wheat getting stronger.

A woman screams.

I jump back, trip, and fall down three steps of the staircase. I might have just broken my leg, or at least I yell loud enough to justify something broken.

"Oh, good Lord, is that you, Miss Howe?" Martha's face comes toward me.

"Yes . . . Ow."

It's a dangerous time of day before the sun is down and lamps are lit, and we are lulled into thinking that we still have enough light to see. We don't. The dark is taking over.

"You were knocking like a ghost there on the steps," Martha says. "Scared me half to death."

"I wasn't knocking, I was walking. Walking down the steps. Of course, now I may never walk again." I think I may just have a bruise, truth be told.

"Miss Cathie is at the table and would love your company," she says, as if whether I broke my leg is of no matter to her.

I follow her down, groaning loudly about my leg even though I am fine. A little sympathy for me wouldn't hurt.

Young Martha continues to clean and stack dishes while Cathie sits at the table, eating an apple. The near-constant sound of crying that has been a given for most of my time in this house is finally absent. I recall the laugh that awakened me. "Where is Baby Charlotte?"

"Baby Charlotte's in the room with her ma," Young Martha says, smiling widely. "Apparently now Missus thinks Charlotte is magnetized for some higher purpose and doesn't want to let her too far from her sight."

"So much the worse for Charlotte," Cathie says with a mouth full of apple.

"Now, Miss Cathie, it must be good for a mother to tend to her child." Martha pats her head.

"Not with a mother like her." Cathie makes a disgusted face. "Why do you think all her babies die? And now Baby Charlotte is stuck there with her in that horrible room with the portraits of her dead children and their halos made with hair cut from their dead heads. Ugh . . ." She pulls a chewed piece of apple out of her mouth. "There's a worm in this one." She throws it into the fire. It takes a moment to catch, and then it explodes in the hearth with a pop.

"What do you mean?" I ask, confused about how there are portraits with hair. "What kind of portraits?"

"In her room," Cathie says. "She had pictures painted of all her dead children by these spirit-painters who see to the other side. They use the actual locks of hair that she cut from their heads after they died. Dead children with dead hair."

"Now, Miss Cathie, don't say that," Young Martha murmurs, as if the children could hear our conversation. "They are still alive in Summerland."

"I know that," Cathie snaps at her. "I know that better than anyone else."

She doesn't seem a sainted child right now. More like a young girl on the edge of a temper.

"Where is Jessica?" I ask. My tone is perhaps too warm and familiar, from the look on Martha's face. "I mean, Miss Elliot?"

"She's doing some business in town, staying with her cousin," Martha says curtly. "She'll be back tomorrow."

"I guess we aren't all prisoners here." Cathie's face puckers with misery. "Just me. But I won't do it much longer. I took your advice, Miss Howe."

Advice? What advice did I give her? I struggle to remember.

"I told Mrs. Greeley that I will leave after this quarter. I told her that, and she said nothing, but fixed me with that ugly look of hers. I don't care. I will be home for Christmas and never return here. C'est juste."

"That was *your* idea?" Martha accuses me. I might find myself back in the dog bed tonight.

"Well, I . . ." Was that my advice? When she had cried, yes, I had said perhaps she should go home. Oh, this is not good. How will Mr. Greeley feel about the fact that I've sabotaged his two-year lease on the spirit-telegraph in the form of Cathie Fox?

I rest my head on the table—not a ladylike thing to do, but it seems to weigh too much to hold up.

"You've still a headache, Miss Howe?" Young Martha asks, finishing what seems to be the last dish of today's ordeal. The clank as she stacks that dish affirms a *yes* answer to her question, but I don't say it. It must have taken them hours upon hours to clean all the dishes and everything in the kitchen. And still everything smells like burned flour.

"Is it always like this?" I ask instead of answering. Shadows of despair, futility, and suffocating boredom seem to contract the room in a slow squeeze, despite anyone's best efforts.

"Like what?" Martha puts her hands on her hips.

"Yes," Cathie said. "It is always like this. Or worse."

There's a *crash* of something breaking upstairs. Mary Greeley wails so loud the walls shake with it. Baby Charlotte now adds her own wailing.

I press my hands to my ears and wish I were anywhere else but here.

Young Martha races up the steps and starts yelling down to her mother something I cannot understand.

Martha runs up after her daughter, and then every other word I am hearing is about blood.

Oh no.

"We have to help her," Cathie says. "I hate her, but I don't wish her dead."

~

Lighting lamps, boiling water, preparing bandages, compresses, rushing up and down the steps—I do none of these things.

Instead, I sit useless in a room with children. The Marthas are doing their best with trying to help Mary Greeley through a miscarriage, while I am back in the nursery, attempting to put Baby Charlotte to bed with every possible trick in the book. Cathie helps by singing every verse of "Oh Dear, What Can the Matter Be?" On and on she sings with all the things Johnny promised.

"No wonder 'Johnny's so long at the fair,'" I snap. "He might as well just stay there." But I should be grateful.

Baby Charlotte has, at last, fallen asleep.

"Mrs. Greeley was pregnant when I first arrived here and lost that one, too," Cathie whispers. "It was awful."

My knowledge of pregnancy and birthing are pretty much limited to farm animals, but of course I know, as everyone does, that when a woman has a baby or a miscarriage, there is always a good chance that it will take the mother's life.

"Well, let's pray that she recovers quickly," I say. "From what I gather, this was very early in the time of pregnancy, so her chances of being just fine are very good." I am absolutely bluffing. I sure hope that's true.

"Cathie!" Mary's voice wails from down the hall.

Young Martha beckons us from the nursery with the same plea she made this morning.

"She's asking for you, Miss Cathie," she says, face swollen with crying. "You'll let her talk to Pickie, won't you?"

"I can't get the bleeding to stop," Martha says, emerging from the room where Mary calls out Cathie's name, summoning her.

Martha huddles her daughter into a discussion that results in an alarming decision.

I am to watch over Mary, Cathie, and Baby Charlotte while Martha walks the mile in the dark night to bring the doctor back here. Her daughter will ride the old horse to fetch Mr. Greeley at the Rookery.

I protest that I have no business tending to a woman in such a state, not to mention that I scarcely can be of any assistance when I barely know the layout of the house or the people in it. The Marthas are too busy preparing to leave to care what I say.

I cannot stop the selfish thought that it will be very difficult to be a positive influence on Mr. Greeley if his wife dies on my watch.

"Cathie!" Mary's voice is insistent.

"Come, Miss Howe," Cathie says, pulling my hand. "We have to help her."

We pass the threshold from the safety of the hallway into the room where Mary is wedged upright in her bed, brown-red stains soaking through the coverlet.

"I need to speak with my son," she says, as if Cathie holds him hostage. "However much you wish to leave this place, you will do that for me now."

Fire sputters in the fireplace, light flickering on the only pictures I have seen in this house. They are portraits of children's faces, painted in the manner of cherubs, floating over a field of flowers. The portraits have no brushstrokes—the children are nearly without features, eyes set in pale faces with no expressions. The hair has texture, however.

Dead children with dead hair. That's what Cathie said about them.

Mary has ordered Cathie to contact her dead son, and the Marthas are gone.

I am trapped here, at this moment, like Cathie.

"I feel I can almost see him and almost speak to him, even without you," Mary's voice trembles. "Miss Howe, look there . . . Do you see him?"

I do! From the corner of my eye, just outside my direct vision. A child stands at the foot of Mrs. Greeley's bed!

I turn from the pictures on the wall to look directly, but now see nothing but the empty space.

My eyes are playing tricks on me. Staring at the portraits with the light, leaving an impression, perhaps, of a floating face. See, there's no one there. Mrs. Greeley, Cathie, and I—we are the only living beings in this room. Mary stares at the space in front of her.

"Stay," she says in jagged breaths. "Please, my angel, my baby, stay. Come," she says to no one. "Sit in the bed with me, hold on to me like you used to, comfort your poor mother."

She beckons the air toward her, lifting her arm to wrap around nothing—and then drops her arm. She turns to me in supplication.

"He cannot come to my side, for he has no body. And all I can get from her"—she flings her fingers at Cathie—"are his raps on the floor. One for yes, two for no, spelling out words. It is not enough, a telegraph from Summerland, it is not enough, no."

Small taps on the window, then the wall, then the floor increase in a steady pace and volume until they crescendo around Cathie's chair, which rocks violently back and forth, then suddenly stops.

"He wants to use my voice," Cathie says.

Mary stops crying, pressing her hands to her face, wiping tears away. "Oh, will you? Will you let him? Oh, please let him use your voice. I will be so grateful, and whatever you wish, you dear child, you dear special child, you will have from me." She straightens herself, sitting up on the bed, her face contorting between grief and expectation.

"Don't be afraid, Miss Howe," Cathie whispers.

She squeezes my hand as if we are about to drop off a cliff. She releases her grip and then goes to a place where I cannot follow. The white of her throat curves like a serpent's, and I can see a bubble of breath move up and escape her mouth in a high pitch with no discernible word.

"Pickie, my dear boy, is it you?" Mary asks. "Is it you coming through?"

"It is me, Mother." It is not Cathie's voice. It is a little boy's. "I am here."

"I am bleeding, my sweetheart. I am bleeding and I may die. I may come to you soon, yet. Will you come and take me with you to Summerland?"

"It is not your time yet. You need to be brave, Mother. We are all here, we are all watching you. This is all part of your soul's lesson." Not Cathie's voice. Not Cathie's face. Her visage seems to have retreated, and what is pushed forward is a death mask.

"Oh, but I don't want to live anymore without you. Why did you have to die, Pickie? You said you wouldn't go. When Irene was born, do you remember? Dead before she could even talk. She never cried. She never made a sound. Yet still you did not like her. Do you remember how you said you did not like her eyes?"

"I was sorry to see her die."

"But you weren't. Don't you remember what you said?"

"It is different here, in Summerland. We learn together, we grow together, we *play* together, all of us." I cannot bear to look at Cathie, and yet I cannot look away. The voice laughs, the hands move as if catching a golden ball thrown by a playmate.

"You said I could not take care of both of you. That it was her, or you. Yes, you were sorry, in your way, but you said—Oh, that little determined look on your face!—'You could not take care of both of us.' You needed me, all of me that I could give and then more."

"Stop, Mother. This isn't helping you, and I don't like to remember." The voice is no longer happy. The child's voice is shaking.

"Poor little Irene, never made a sound! I just found her dead in her crib!"

"You couldn't take care of both of us because you wouldn't leave me alone for even a moment."

"I couldn't. I couldn't let you out of my sight. In every corner, you saw a spirit, and you became wild. You wouldn't obey and you would run and—"

"Don't put me in the attic!" Cathie's head tosses back and forth, rocking the chair, thumping the floor in a relentless rhythm. "Oh, you hateful creature! No! No! No!" The child behind Cathie's face begins to cry.

"Forgive me, forgive me . . . but I had to! You would run, you weren't scared of the switch, you'd gone wild and Irene was dead and Charlotte just born—"

"No more, Mother! No more!"

"And when Charlotte got cholera, I thought she would die, too, and you'd come back to me because you wanted me all to yourself, didn't you? That's why you went so wild . . ."

"But I died instead."

"You died instead."

The child's cries subside. "No more of that, Mother. No more. I am in Summerland now, and all is well with my soul "

The chair rocks back and forth, forth and back. On the wall, four pale, painted faces make no accusations. They float as silent as mist. One still holds Cathie by her throat, breathing with her lungs, speaking with her mouth.

"There is no need to mourn, Mother. We are all growing up together here, even if we did not live to grow up there. Charlotte is meant to live. You will see—she is very special and will become a great comfort to you."

"It is hard for me to love her as I loved you."

"You will learn to."

"Or maybe I will bleed to death tonight and join you there." Hope in her voice, she's asking for permission. "Maybe I can learn everything I need to learn with you, there in Summerland."

"No, Mother. You won't die. You will be alive for many years, now. You will go across the oceans and see beautiful things. You will meet many wonderful people. And you will join the cause—you will make a difference."

"Yes!" Mary is crying again, but this time, it is not a despairing sound. "Yes, there are things here I want to learn. Things for which I must fight. Yes, that is right."

"The blood you are bleeding was never a spirit. It was never a baby. That's what my teacher here is telling me. Don't worry. He says . . ." Now a different voice, a deep sound that no child could make comes through Cathie's mouth. "This is the blood that washes you clean."

I shove my fist into my mouth to keep from screaming.

That was a man's voice!

That was a grown man's voice coming from inside Cathie Fox.

It has the opposite effect on Mary. She is completely calm and still. "Thank you, Uncle John. Thank you for that wisdom and for teaching Pickie and for being there for my children."

"You must rest now, Mother." Pickie's voice, again. "You must rest."

Cathie's head pushes back. She gulps, her throat moving like a fish's gills as it tries to breathe on land, dying.

Her hands grip the chair's arms, and her head rocks forward. Back and forth the chair goes, so fast she could be thrown from it. Raps on the floor sputter all around it, like a hundred little spirits, knocking.

The knocking stops.

The rocking stops.

Cathie's face is slack. She looks like a sleepwalker. "They have gone." Her voice is without emotion.

A quiet descends that makes the other noises—the embers in the fireplace, Mary's breaths, my pounding heart—seem loud. What have I just seen? What have I just heard?

This is madness, a horror, and yet neither Cathie nor Mary make any comment of it being unusual. They both settle into the silence as if it were bought and paid for.

"Thank you," Mary says, exhausted.

"I am merely a vessel for the spirits," Cathie replies. "I must go to bed now. I am tired."

"Yes, I also must, I must . . ." My voice stammers, atonal, shocking me in its volume.

"Honor me a moment longer, Miss Howe," Mary says. "Woman to woman."

"Oh, then, I . . ." What can she want from me? I cannot conjure anything for her.

Cathie's hand reaches for me, and I help pull her up from the chair. Her body seems a limp rag, wrung out.

"Little Miss Fox," Mary says, eyes closed. "I will not allow you to leave at the end of this quarter, as you requested. Your education and your family's protection depend on your remaining here."

If Cathie hears her, she makes no acknowledgment of it.

"I'll never let you take my son from me."

Chapter 13

"I am so glad you've come here, Miss Howe." Mary Greeley's intensity is gone, bled out on the coverlet. We are alone in this room, and I do not want to be here. "It's as if I have known you forever, even though you just arrived." Her bulging brown eyes are dim. This is what it looks like to die.

I feel as if there are ghosts all around me, prickling every pore of my skin from the tip of my head to the cramp in my foot. She will become one of them soon. Her ghost will follow me, trying to put her arm through mine, speaking ceaselessly but with no lungs, no mouth.

"I will stay alive," she says, contradicting her appearance. "My child tells me I will join the cause. I can help you, as I helped Margaret Fuller and Jane Swisshelm . . ." She laughs weakly into a cough. "Your Lady Jane."

"Thank you, I . . ." I wish to say nothing. I need to get out of this room.

"Father does not believe we should have suffrage, but he believes we are capable of higher thought and reason." She is quickening with her words. Despite the miscarriage, the continued bleeding, and whatever it is that just happened between her and Cathie, she seems more lucid than ever. "Be my friend. Help me to be a servant to the cause, and I will convince Father that he must listen to you."

I swallow, trying to find words again. I'm shaking all over. I will myself to stop. My mind races to try to remember my righteousness. All the words I've worked so hard to put together for just a moment such as this. They pour from me, in comforting familiarity. "I am here in particular because the *Tribune* must come out against the Compromise that just passed and—"

Voices. Stomping. Something is here, coming this way.

"You must stop them," Mary says, sitting up. "They mean me harm."

"Who?" Louder now, the voices and the thumping.

"Can't you hear the insect scuttle? It's Dr. Bug!" She grabs my arm in terror.

A cloaked, gray-haired man lumbers through the door, carrying a satchel large enough to make him walk crooked. Martha trails behind him, making a clucking noise meant to comfort, though she seems like a hen chasing a giant beetle-man. "I will not submit to Dr. Bug!" Mary yells.

It means nothing to the man, who drops his satchel on the bureau and goes about his business, now pulling out a dark-brown vial of liquid.

"She must be sedated before she is bled," he says calmly to us.

"No, I will *not*! None of your poison!" Mary twists in her bed as if to get up.

"Hold her down!" he instructs us.

A man of authority, giving orders, seems to be all that's needed to override Mary's violent protestations, even for two women as head-strong as me and Martha. Martha grapples to restrain Mary's legs, while Dr. Bug presses one arm down with his full weight on her chest, his other arm holding out a vial of liquid. "He is here to help you, let him help you," I say.

She rocks her head back and forth, still gripping my arm.

"Make yourself useful and hold her head!" Dr. Bug barks at me.

She screams vile curses at Martha and Dr. Bug. I don't want to wrestle my arm loose to grab her head, but I find myself doing it, as if this doctor knows better than I do. Knows better than *she* does, as though Mary's opinion in the matters of her own health are beyond her understanding. I reach my hands out and grip both sides of her skull.

Her hair is wet with sweat, her skin cool. I apply pressure, keeping her face still, her eyes swimming up in their sockets to try to catch mine and tug on my conscience. She says something to me, but I can't make out the words. Something in a different language. Is it French?

Dr. Bug pries her lips open, placing a full dropper of liquid on her gums—her teeth remaining clamped.

"Keep holding her," he orders.

Fascination takes hold of me as I watch the medicine take effect. Her tension seeps out through my hands slowly, so slowly. First, her eyes roam around in circles, losing speed until they flutter, then close. Her clamped jaw softens, loosens, slacks. I don't need to hold on anymore.

She is unconscious.

"Now," Dr. Bug says, "she is calm enough so that we can help her." He pulls his weight off her body and begins methodically unpacking his satchel. "You women are no longer needed."

"I'll stay on just the same," Martha says. "Until my daughter returns with Mr. Greeley. He will want me here."

I stare at the motionless figure on the bed. What did he give her that knocked her out so completely, so quickly?

"What is that medicine?" I ask.

Dr. Bug's head twists to regard me, the lamplight reflecting in his eyes. It's his body that resembles a bug. His face is more birdlike.

"A tincture of laudanum and mercury. I had to give her a double dose. She is supposed to be taking a half dropper three times daily. The mercury aids her melancholy, the laudanum is to calm her nerves. It only works in aggregate. Your top priority must be to make sure she takes this regularly, or we will never get anywhere with her."

"*I* must? Why me?"

"Are you not her maid?"

"No, I am not her maid."

Martha starts in with introductions, which go about as awkwardly as I could possibly imagine with Dr. *Bing* (though "Bug" is more apt, to Mary's credit) pulling something goopy and slimy from a jar of dark floating globs, ordering Martha to lift up the patient's nightdress so he can apply it to her skin.

It is a leech.

Martha pulls down the coverlet and pulls up Mary's undergarments. Seeing her belly exposed while she is drugged asleep, pale above where blood has soaked, seems a criminal violation.

He presses the leech onto her flesh. It makes a sucking *squooch* as it attaches.

I have completely lost interest in explaining to the doctor who I am and what I am doing here. What he is doing to her is far too distressing. It looks medieval.

I realize suddenly what it was that Mary said to me as I held her head.

It was Shakespeare. *Julius Caesar.*

"Et tu, Brute?"

Chapter 14

"If the disease doesn't kill you, the doctor will."

I remember sitting in a hot Ohio parlor, stuffing myself with sticky pawpaws as Aunt Clara and her peers complained loudly about all their ailments, extolling the virtues of their own particular homemade ointments over the medicines suggested by their doctors. Mrs. DeWitt, a most hardy crone who had a family history in midwifery, made it her practice to blame doctors for every death they happened upon.

I felt it was unfair and puppy-headed logic—since someone was only very sick when a doctor was called in—to tie every patient's death to their treatment and every patient's recovery to Providence. I considered it my duty to debate Mrs. DeWitt and did so with such tenacity that she pointed a finger and cursed me. "You will eat these words like rotten fruit, child. And when you do, don't you run to me to cure your collywobbles!"

If I could run to her right now and beg her forgiveness, I would. What do I know about medicine? Nothing! But I do know I want nothing more to do with Dr. Bug/Bing.

I step out into the dark hallway, abandoning Mary to Martha and her compresses and the doctor's leeches.

A ghost! I am startled, seeing an apparition at the end of the hall. A little phantom in a nightgown with a head made of tapered glowing glass, like an oil lamp.

It approaches slowly on bare feet that touch the ground.

"Miss Howe?"

If only I felt relief that it is Cathie Fox, after all, and not a ghost. Truthfully, she's more frightening to me at the moment.

"Miss Howe, will you sleep with me? I'm scared. Aren't you scared, too?"

Of course I'm scared—of her. Of whatever I saw come over her in that rocking chair. I would rather sleep with one of the copperhead snakes I used to find in the woods. I saw what I saw: the bones of her throat jutting against her skin, her eyes glazed and unseeing. I heard what I heard: two voices, a child's and a grown man's, coming from that throat. And I felt what I felt, no matter the strength of my denial that such things could not be real: that the dead boy's spirit was alive.

"I must sleep alone," I say. "I have a habit of punching in the night, and I wouldn't want you to be on the receiving end." This is a terrible lie.

"Please, Miss Howe." She is not at all fooled. "I've never had to sleep alone here. Miss Elliot always stays with me."

"It's important to learn to be comfortable alone."

"We can talk politics, if you like."

I tell myself to settle down. I am here on a mission. What I've seen tonight is nothing compared to the horrors that people are experiencing every day due to our own government.

"I will tuck you in," I say, swallowing my reservations. I am here for the cause of abolition and human dignity; I must not drown in the grief and abuse of this domestic drama. "Does Benjamin Franklin knock, or do you need to let him use your voice, too?"

She stops at the room that she and Jessica share. I can't tell whether she's offended, hurt, or merely considering the question. The flame in the lamp is leaping and smoking. She has the wick too high.

"He knocks," she answers finally. "The knocking is enough for everyone else, but Mrs. Greeley always wants more. She wants the knocks and then to let him use my voice. Soon she'll want me to let him use my whole body and parade around all day as Pickie. It's never enough for her. Mrs. Greeley should be named Mrs. Greedy."

She pushes against the door, and I follow her in. Black smoke and a hot-yellow light reveal her room in the flickering ellipses of her unsteady hands. Every surface seems a clotheshorse of gowns, petticoats, bows, further complicated by a rug sprouting stacks of shoes, stockings. I move just in time for me to trip, but not topple over, my tongue falling into curses.

"Miss Elliot is desperate for a proper maid," she says. "She is very messy."

"Why does she not have her own room?" There are plenty of closed doors and open ones with nothing inside them but emptiness.

"Mrs. Greeley said we needed to share. I am sure she meant it as a punishment, but I am glad. I am so lonely without my sister; she and I have always shared a bed. My mother, father, me, and Maggie all shared a room half this size in Hydesville."

"Yes," I say, thinking of where my Lady Jane and her family lived. "I know of places where up to twelve people share a room. Cramped, but good for keeping warm in the winter. All of those bodies are the best way to heat a space, don't you think? And cheerful. As an orphan, I was often lonely and would fantasize I had a huge family."

I am thinking about those I lost before I really knew them. A father, a brother. No sisters. A mother—lost, if not dead.

"You *had* a family, though. Something happened to them . . ."

"Yes, but I don't want to talk about it right now. Come on, get back in bed." I take the lamp from her, turning down the wick and placing it on the vanity, where the reflection casts light around the room. I cannot help but linger.

Here is where Jessica sits; what pleasure she must have in seeing herself in the mirror. It's as if the glass has treasured away her reflection somewhere, and the light dances with it. The glow of all her things casts a charm. It's unbearable here without her, but with her . . . Yes, this room holds her effects like a protective amulet. I touch the glass perfume bottle of rose water. I can see the red of her hair caught in the silver hairbrush.

The tin of her pearl powder was left open. These embellishments hold her scent like scattered petals in a carefully cultivated garden.

"It's so cold." Cathie's reflection in the mirror startles me. "Will you make a fire? The Marthas never have time to do it, even when Miss Elliot asks them directly."

"You'll be fine once you're under the covers." I certainly will not remain in here long enough to make a fire for her. "I am sure they will find more help by the time winter comes."

"Won't you just stay in here with me until I fall asleep? The bed is freezing."

"Well, don't you have one of those bed warmers?"

"Yes, silly. But the bed warmer is no good without a fire," she says, kicking at the metal canister on the long metal rod. "Why won't you start one for me? I know how to start one, but I promised my mother I wouldn't until I was older. Her aunt died from a kitchen fire. Someone died in this house from a fire, too—"

"Yes, lots of people die from fire." I will suffer no more ghosts. "So we'll just leave it alone for tonight. Maybe an extra blanket. Come on, get in bed now. I will tell you my tales from Congress—they are sure to put you right to sleep."

She gets under her covers, and I sit at the edge of her bed, keeping my distance. I will stay with her no longer than strictly necessary. If I hear any strange voices coming out of her throat, I will make a fast run out of here and not look back.

Now, what would be the most instructive story to tell her of the goings-on in Washington? My mind goes straight to Daniel Webster, who up until this year, I had looked upon as a hero. I think of how to phrase the betrayal I felt at his oratory in favor of the Compromise. I will tell no idle tales. I need to make sure this child properly understands how people in power flatter and cajole each other, and how even those we abolitionists lauded the most seemed to buckle and sway beneath the tyranny of institutionalized evil when their pocketbooks were at stake.

"What is that?" Cathie grabs my hand.

"What?"

"That knocking!"

"This knocking?" My foot is jiggling, as it does whenever I'm trying to sit still. I know it is annoying to others, but now it strikes me as funny that she mistakes my toe-tapping for spirit-rapping.

"Oh, it must be a ghost," I joke, smiling broadly. I'm not actually trying to fool her, simply lightening the mood. "Is it a spirit? Once for yes, twice for no."

I tap my foot on the floor and then again. "Not a spirit? Then what is it?" I am clearly jesting. "Is it my foot on the floor?"

I tap once.

"Be careful." Cathie turns her face away from me. "That's how you call the devil."

"That's just what my Aunt Clara used to say. That my foot was the part of me that was owned by the devil. I have never been able to tame it."

Cathie keeps her back to me. I suppose I should be more sensitive to my toe-tapping around someone who claims that the spirits of the dead communicate by rapping floors. It could be considered as mocking. I never expected that it would make her frightened.

Wood conducts sound in the most incredible of ways. Truly, a knock can seem to come from anywhere, no matter where it started from. Once, during the silence of a Quaker meeting, my foot bumped so loudly that everyone turned as if there were someone banging on the meeting-house door.

Aunt Clara knew better. She brought her palm down with a slap on my knee.

"Mr. Splitfoot," Cathie murmurs. "That's another name for the devil."

"Yes," I say. "So I've heard."

"It's true," she says, turning her face back to me. "Don't you know about me and my sister and Mr. Splitfoot?"

I don't.

The lamp sputters and smokes as Cathie begins.

Chapter 15

**PEDDLER TELLS OF HIS OWN MURDER
THROUGH "SPIRIT-TELEGRAPH" CATHIE FOX**
—as told to and interpreted by E. A. Howe

Hell is no place to win justice.

While Charles Rosna hadn't gone to the typical version of hell, there's endless suffering in hanging around where he'd been killed, outside his body. He had not yet made his way to Summerland, so bitter was his spirit and so vocal his protestations.

Charles Rosna did not deserve to die. He had fled violence in a place across the ocean called Odessa to come and make his fortune in America as a peddler. He was a good peddler, young enough to easily bear the load of his trunk, old enough to discern the difference between need and want. He knew that to have a little something of beauty—even something as small as a thimble—was not a luxury but a necessity.

He had bright-red hair, a giant set of easy-smiling teeth, and blue winking eyes, but his most winning quality was his voice. He spoke in a pleasing, deep, and vibrant tone, his accent slight enough to charm instead of confuse. He couldn't help but often break into songs of his old country and songs of the new while showing off his wares, singing phrases and notes that stuck in people's heads and made them want to sing, too. He made customers feel that each object he sold had a bit of enchantment.

Most of the other peddlers kept to the cities, but Charles knew it was the outskirts where the mothers most needed a ribbon of an unusual color, a pin with a butterfly, a special spoon for their toddler.

In 1843, he was trudging up north on his way to Rochester when a little hamlet called Hydesville took his fancy, and he stopped at a small saltbox home where the Bell family lived. Mrs. Bell fell in love with his thimble. She just had to have it. Sadly, she didn't have the money, though her husband would be back soon. Would Charles Rosna, with his smiling mouth, shiny eyes, and singing voice, come back this way another day?

In 1848, Cathie and Maggie Fox, ages nine and eleven, moved with their parents from Rochester to Hydesville. Since they'd moved that past fall, none of them had been granted a proper night's rest. The house that they rented from Mr. Bell, who'd left town some five years past, thudded and bumped, knocked and moaned. No one could sleep. Mrs. Fox cried upon waking, she was so exhausted. One particularly noisy night, the whole family unable to sleep, Cathie jumped out of bed and talked back to that which refused to rest in peace.

"Mr. Splitfoot," she said, snapping her fingers, "do as I do."

The wood beneath their feet knocked back in the same rhythm.

"Mr. Splitfoot," she said, "are you a spirit? Rap once for yes, twice for no."

The wood knocked back one bump.

"Mr. Splitfoot, did you once live in this house? Once for yes, twice for no."

Two knocks, no.

"Did you die here?"

One knock. Yes.

Cathie suggested to her family that it must be a joke, a trick someone was playing on them all. It was the wee hours of the early morning of April 1—April Fools' Day, after all.

Mrs. Fox started asking questions. Mr. Splitfoot knew all about the history of the Fox family. It knew about the adult children the Fox parents had, and about the decade-long separation of Mr. and Mrs. Fox due to Mr. Fox's fondness for drink, and that Maggie and Cathie were children of their second-chance reunion. It knew the number and ages of all their children, including the one who had died stillborn. Mrs. Fox was familiar with second sight, having such powers herself, but Mr. Splitfoot had insight that only comes from the other side of the earthly veil. Terrified of the knocking ghost, Mrs. Fox sent her husband for the neighbors both east and west, north and south, and soon, there in the middle of the night, a small town meeting was taking place in the haunted house, talking to Mr. Splitfoot, who told the lurid details of his death—right where the neighbors stood.

Mr. Splitfoot was not his proper name, of course. He spelled it out for Cathie in raps on the floor as she spoke out letters of the alphabet. Long into the night, letter by letter, knock by knock, he told his sad tale.

His name was Charles Rosna, and he'd been murdered by the Fox family's landlord, Mr. Bell. When he had returned that fateful day to Hydesville bearing the thimble, Mr. Bell invited him in. Mr. Bell was no fool, and he didn't like to be taken for one. He was suspicious of the peddler and his ribbons and bows, thimbles and threads. He didn't like how he heard Mrs. Bell singing bits of songs from a place he had never seen, or the look in her eye when she talked about the man who came and would return. Most of all, he didn't like the pretty tenor of the peddler's voice. What he did like was catching sight of all the money this peddler kept in his trunk (for Mr. Rosna had been a big hit in Rochester). When Rosna was bent over in front of him, singing about a missing bobbin, Mr. Bell crept up behind him with a knife and slit his throat.

The knocks stopped there, and Cathie panicked, for she felt the spirit coming into her body. She gurgled, grabbing at her neck.

All the neighbors were horrified at the sight and sound of Charles Rosna trying to breathe and scream through the mouth and body of Cathie Fox.

Maggie Fox, two years older and twenty years wiser, ordered the spirit out of her sister, instructing him to behave better. He did not need to take her sister's voice, for she had given him the chance to tell his story now, unburdening his spirit through the knocking. Subdued raps on the floor confirmed that Rosna accepted this offer, and Cathie's own voice returned. It was up to Maggie now to finish helping him drum out the rest of the story.

Mr. Bell had placed a bowl beneath the man he had murdered to catch his blood so as not to stain the floor, though one could still see, in the light, the places on the wood where dark drops had set into the grain. And so this was how poor Charles Rosna, who'd escaped the murdering mobs across the ocean, who'd come to America full of promise and songs, was killed.

When Mrs. Bell discovered what Mr. Bell had done, he promised worse for her. She vowed to keep silent. She helped him take the body down into the cellar, where Mr. Bell buried Mr. Rosna's body ten feet deep in the dirt floor, along with the bowl that held his blood and the trunk that held his dream—minus the money and a single memento: Mrs. Bell would have her thimble.

~

Cathie presses upon her thumb, speaking of Mrs. Bell's prize.

"That's how it all started, all of this. We taught Mr. Splitfoot how to use the knocking, and soon, all over this country, spirits were knocking in places we'd never even heard of. For people we've never known."

It has been two years since Cathie and her sister Maggie began speaking for spirits in their humble Hydesville home. They are now ages eleven and thirteen. In the past two years, they've been simultaneously hailed as witches, frauds, prophetesses, inventors. They've been run out of towns, feted by luminaries, pursued by mobs, and the stars of sold-out shows where the spirits demonstrated secret knowledge to hundreds of people. They've transitioned from playing local halls and exhibitions to being put up by America's original showman, P.T. Barnum, in his hotel, to knocking for more money than they had ever dreamed of for the biggest celebrities of the world.

Yet Cathie insists they are nothing special.

"It's just that the spirits know us now. And trust us. It is like a telegraph. Me and my sisters know the code. But anyone can do it. You could do it, too. You would need to learn to control your leg tapping, or all the critics who think it's humbug would swear that was how you were doing it, and then they would make you undress so they could hold your legs while they say, 'What do the spirits say now?'"

"It's not something I would like to learn," I say.

"But don't you see, Miss Howe? If you learned how to do it, you wouldn't need *me* to talk to Benjamin Franklin for you. You could do it yourself. That's what you want, right?"

"I don't want to talk to Benjamin Franklin. Mr. Greeley does."

"But what does that have to do with you, then? Why are you always talking about it?"

"Look, Cathie . . ." How can I explain this without seeming like a horse's rear? "Mr. Greeley doesn't care about what I know. He doesn't care about what I've seen or about my opinion. I need famous spirits to help me convince people to do what is right."

She closes her eyes and curls into me like a cat.

"It is literally a matter of life or death," I say. "If you can reach Ben Franklin—what he might say about all this. Life or death, for many, many people. Do you understand, Cathie Fox?"

"I just want to go home." She isn't listening. She is falling asleep, in that way children do, as quickly as kittens. She puts her thumb in her mouth. "Home."

"What—back to your haunted house and the ghost of a peddler?"

"Not there, not anymore. Just back to my mother. My mother is my home."

She falls asleep, sucking her thumb.

Chapter 16

It's quiet this morning in Castle Doldrum. Cathie refuses to get out of bed until Jessica returns. The Marthas are working in the kitchen and tending to Baby Charlotte. Mary Greeley has not yet awakened. The longcase clock in the parlor seems to have stopped. I think it is the type that needs to be rewound, but I won't mention it. I don't miss the endless *tock tock.*

Martha informs me that there is no breakfast but yesterday's pie, and that Mr. Greeley has summoned me to his study.

Summoned by Mr. Greeley!

My journey to that room takes on the weight of a pilgrimage to the holy of holies. Indeed, I walk with the epic poets toward the open door at the end of the second-floor hall, *where I have ne'er yet tread, but in a dream,* as one might say.

Ah, this is not just any study. Every square inch of it boasts that it belongs to a peerless bibliophile autodidact. Shelves buckle under the weight of important words, revolutionary ideas. The keys to world civilizations to be turned open in encyclopedias, dictionaries, histories. I cannot help but let my fingers touch the smooth spines of Aristotle, Cicero, Diderot, Voltaire—their names alone point to a promised land of learning. A blast of the morning sun casts light across opened pages, tempting my eyes to try to peek, as if at a wizard's incantations. Horace Greeley sits at his desk, blinking at me amid stacks of books and letters, moving his hand in the backward wave of "come, come closer."

"Miss Howe," he says, "can you do something for me?"

I nod before I even know what it is. I hope it is a mission, and the more important, the better.

He tells me in many long words that he sleeps most of his nights at the Rookery. Being editor in chief for the *Tribune* demands such devotion from him, and he is happy to give his lifeblood to the conscience of the country. It is a sacrifice he makes, being unable to spend much time here at home. It is difficult for him to work here. Mother keeps the home the way she likes it. He finds it dark and damp.

"I do call it," he admits like he is the prince of wit, "Castle Doldrum."

I laugh like I don't already know his nicknames from Jessica's gossip.

"It is sheer coincidence I was here yesterday to receive you," he says, forgetting that he did everything he could to avoid it. "I was only here because Mother has been so sick. As you may well now have gleaned, Mother's sickness is not just of the body but also of the spirit."

"Yes, I have observed it." Of all the nicknames, I find his calling his wife "Mother" the least agreeable.

"She is still sleeping and needs the rest. But when she wakes, I am sure she will talk of her nightmares. Dr. Bing is a prized physician in these parts, but I think he may be out of his element with her. Cathie's knockings have been more healing for her than any of Dr. Bing's medicines. I don't know what we would do without her."

I keep my expression even. I will not let it slip that it was I who advised Cathie to go home, or that I still think it best for her to get away from his wife—Mrs. Greedy, as Cathie said.

"Of course, for many of us who are so attuned, we start to see that there are no coincidences. I now believe that your presence here is part of how this divine tapestry weaves together. You came here thinking it was for one purpose, and I saw you fit for another. And now . . ." He looks at the floor. Clears his throat. "I daren't leave while Mother is in this state. I had thought to make proper introductions between you and Dr. Vincent at some point. Now it is imperative that you go and bring him here for Mother."

He holds out his hands toward me, as if to give me a blessing.

"Of course, sir." I wish to kneel like a knight. "Where do I go?"

"I will write you a letter of introduction to bring with you. The horses need to be rested from last night's late journey. So you will need to walk—some may consider five miles a long walk for a lady."

"I often walk five miles before breakfast." True. Though not in these shoes.

"Good for you! In my younger days, I made up to forty miles in one day. We don't need so many horses, cabs, or railroads when we have a working pair of legs."

"Hear! Hear!"

"Fine, then." He beams at me.

I am as pleased with myself as he is of me. I knew he was a kindred soul. Why, I could be the next Margaret Fuller, writing him long familiar letters that will be treasured and published ages after I am gone. He gives me directions—the circuitous walk to Odellville, the trick of catching the stagecoach into New York City, and where to find Lovejoy's Hotel, where Dr. Vincent is a guest.

He takes his pen and begins writing the letter for me to give to Dr. Vincent. This missive, he claims, will make the good doctor drop everything there and return with me at once. I let my eyes wander the expanse of his desk. Oh, to snoop the disarray of papers! Letters upon letters stacked hither and yon. Letters *to* him—he publishes them sometimes, like he did with the letters of Margaret Fuller and Frederick Douglass. Letters *from* him—he publishes them sometimes, eye-stinging criticisms to detractors and fans alike. My gaze falls upon the names of senators. Henry Clay, Daniel Webster—that sellout! As Greeley is still scribbling, I take advantage to turn Webster's letter just enough that I can surreptitiously read.

> Dear Friend,
> You well know how our discourse has served as a torch in our many days in the hallowed halls of our nation's Capitol—

"I beg your pardon!" Greeley's weather-beaten hand pulls the letter from my view with a quick swipe. He then begins organizing the entire stack out from under my ability to spy. "These are not public letters."

He hands me the one he has just written. His handwriting is terrible. What does that even say? *"Toad Vacant?"*

Oh, wait, maybe that is *"To Dr. Vincent."*

"Be on your way, then." He sniffs. I will not apologize for snooping, but I am sorry I didn't do a better job of it. I would very much like to know why he is rereading old letters from senators who helped engineer this Compromise. He must not find reason to find them reasonable.

"Sir, I know you must be consulting friends in Congress, including the senator from New Hampshire. Know that there is no greater betrayal of a cause than that of a man who was once its friend."

"Daniel Webster is the most principled senator to have ever—"

"To have ever stabbed us in the back," I say. He was once one of my heroes. The most skilled orator, a man of great defiance against the tyranny of the expansion of slavery. But it was his capitulation in the midnight hour that allowed this Fugitive Slave Act to pass. We must obey "the law of the land," he'd said. Once my hero. Now I would refuse to shake his hand.

"Miss Howe, I am trying to—" Greeley suddenly breaks down, coughing into his fist, wiping tears from his eyes. "I am trying to do the right thing. Please. I need your help. Go."

I turn and quickly leave this beautiful room, this shrine to learning, knowing that this room is as empty as any of the others in this house if the man who worships in it cannot find the truth.

PART II

MESMERIST CLAIMS "SCIENCE OF
THE MIND" IS SOON TO REPLACE
MODERN MEDICINE, CHALLENGING
THE STATUS QUO

Chapter 17

These streets are a thousand loud, dirty ways to get run over. I need at least four more sets of eyes to see all the things I've never seen before and continue to stay alive. I have almost died three times already, nearly killed by a milk truck, an ice wagon, and a horsebus.

It's my first time in New York City, and my neck hurts from craning it upward, my jaw aches from dropping it. Heaven and hell compete for the same inhale. The potpourri of everything good to eat—baking, roasting; served fresh, spiced, and sweetened—comes into my nostrils, along with coal smoke. I see fine black particles dusting everything into a fog. Or maybe it is actual fog peppered with soot. Whatever it is, it's giving me a coughing fit. And yet, after the days I have spent at Castle Doldrum, it's a breath of fresh air. There's no time to think or feel sad or be haunted when everything is moving this quickly.

Horses snorting, clopping, dropping their manure as if they play their own target game for human shoes. Looming brick boxes, brownstones, and minipalaces that may be hotels or industrialists' homes, where gargoyles and graces are sculpted into stone and secret society symbols promise covens of wizards behind marble facades. All the buildings claim their right to grow as tall and wide as the will of men, stopped only by the natural law of how much ambition can occupy finite space. People hustling every business invented and imagined. This is what a city is meant to be!

Of course, the only other city I know is Washington, which is an ugly place where Greco-Roman buildings mushroom on a river of mud. The only truly notable thing about the whole of Washington is the sludge and the smell of decay, rot, and every living thing's excrement.

New York is clearly the true capital city of our young nation. Brimming with life, industry, aesthetics, and adaptability. And everywhere, newspapers!

A pinched-faced newsboy right out of *Oliver Twist* screams the headline off the front page:

"SWEDISH NIGHTINGALE JENNY LIND GREETED BY 30,000 FANS! ALL NEW YORK SHOWS SOLD OUT! LINDMANIA EVERYWHERE!"

I want to see the news from turgid Washington. This illegible letter from Greeley has served to provide the credit I need to get myself a large noontime dinner in a local tavern and a proper clopping ride in a stagecoach, but I don't have any actual money. Ironically, since I've arrived at the newspaper magnate's estate, I've had none of my usual daily papers. The cobbler's children have no shoes.

"Any other headlines?" I ask the urchin, making my way to the street corner, speaking to him as an equal in our shared work for the fourth estate. "News from Washington?"

"It's a penny," he says, covering the papers with his arms. "You look like an empty pocket."

"How rude. I'm a newspaper woman, newsboy."

"Never heard of her. Move along if you don't have coin."

"Look here, I'm on a mission from Horace Greeley. I don't need money. I know the most famous newspaper man in this city."

"Don't gimme that soap. Greeley's a humbugger. This is a *Herald* corner."

"Fine. It's a *Herald* corner. Look, what news from Washington? I don't care about music."

"You're the gump, then, lady," he says, sticking out his chest like I've started a fight. "Jenny Lind is the voice of the 'progress of civilization.'"

"Says who?"

"Says the *Herald.*"

"Gimme that." I wrestle it from him. He is, after all, a third of my size. I break open the paper and scan the articles. The headline story is about sold-out shows, the staggering number of fans trying to get a peek at this modest, philanthropic Swede with the voice of an angel. Then a long, unctuous editorial about Jenny Lind that compares the sublimity of her voice to Eli Whitney's genius invention of the cotton gin, her "superiority" to her competitors as Whitney's is to cotton pickers. What rubbish.

Oh, this article lays it on thick about her modesty, how she spurns glamour for simplicity. She inspired Hans Christian Andersen's story "The Nightingale"—about a sweet little bird with a life-giving song. How magnificent to hear the music of this Swedish Nightingale, here to bring life and culture all the more rare for its humility, et cetera, and more puff and fluff. Another article quotes her, upon arrival, saying how the American flag stands for freedom everywhere in the world, and how she has found her voice here in the States like nowhere else. She is touring all of America, including the South, where her popularity before even performing there promises to eclipse her reception in New York . . . et cetera.

What cow pies for news!

Where is the important news? What of the free people in this city who have endured death-defying acts of heroism to escape bondage and are now being stolen from their homes, their businesses, off the public street? Where are these stories? Where is the conscience of this country?

Not here. Competing newsboys yell insipid Lind tales across corners. A horsebus makes a sharp turn, and a crowd in the street scatters to avoid being run over. A cart pushes toward me, offering chestnuts. No one here cares about congressional policy. The news is strictly bread and circuses. I look all around me at this city that stops for nothing. I feel useless, inept, and this paper is equally useless with its stupid headlines.

A brilliant idea occurs to me. Why, I am to meet Jenny Lind at the séance this weekend, and as she proclaims she is so impressed with American freedom . . . I need only to get her on record speaking of anything having to do with supporting abolition.

Now here's something that is actually important, in the advertisements section: Frederick Douglass will be speaking at the Broadway Tabernacle Church this Saturday! In my pantheon of heroes, he sits at the apex. His autobiography is one of the twelve books I pack in my trunk to take with me on any journey. I have never heard him speak in person, though I know his words better than the Lord's Prayer. If I have to walk my way there, camp overnight, I must get to the Broadway Tabernacle Church.

"Hey, you owe me." The kid shoves me from my reverie. He is popping mad. "I get almost nothing just standing here, and you're stealing from me."

"Oh, keep it." I push the paper back to him. "This rag is trash anyhow."

"You *still* owe me." OW! He's kicking my shins. "You read what's in it, you owe for what you know."

"Look, I don't have any money." I push my hand against his head to keep him from kicking me again and try to find my compassion. Probably an orphan, a victim of child-labor exploitation. "I have something better than money, and that is opportunity. Maybe I can get you a better job, kid, selling for the *Tribune* instead of this sensationalist horse manure."

The kid answers me by picking up a rock, and a decent-size one at that.

Well! I quickly make a getaway, but a gentleman brushing past me gets it square in the chest. The gentleman sprints after the kid, promising him a beating, not knowing that it was nothing personal to him. That rock was meant for the back of my head.

Now nearly killed *four* times!

$$Chapter\ 18$$

"THE FUTURE OF MESMERISM IS IN HIS MACHINE!"

Lovejoy's Hotel looks more like a theater than a place of residence, with this clapboard advertisement out front in large lettering. A giant poster proclaims exhibition times with an illustration of a woman, eyes closed, arms outstretched, and an imposing man with a piercing stare, a finger raised up to the heavens, holding an instrument that looks like a wheel attached to a scale in his other arm, wavy lines like ripples of water between them. DR. JULES VINCENT & THE REVOLUTION IN MEDICINE.

Should I count myself lucky to be allowed into Lovejoy's Hotel? Pointed gazes of disdain toward my dress and footwear from staff and patrons alike say so.

I told Greeley that I love to walk, and I do, but not in a corset and ladies' shoes. I did not wear trousers, as I would have preferred. Lady Jane would send me packing back to the woods immediately if I'd done so. She specifically forbids me from wearing trousers at any point when I am working. I am careful to wear enough of a dress for it to still be considered one, but a mission that involves brisk walking would be jeopardized by layers and layers of skirts, a binding corset, and ridiculously shaped footwear. I had no choice but to leave the layers and the corset, and to wear the men's boots I treasure—the sole inheritance from my father. Two years ago, they started to fit as if cobbled just for me. I do know that they are scuffed, worn, and were probably out of step with the popular style even when he wore them in the 1830s. I don't care. I love them, and when I walk in them, I feel a sense of his gait with mine, almost like we are walking hand in hand.

I suppose fashion is more important in New York City than in Ohio. A concierge leaves his post to try to stop me from making my way to the front desk. I brandish my letter like a weapon. "I have been sent here with an urgent message for Dr. Vincent by Horace Greeley."

He glances at it and immediately apologizes.

Soon a pocket of people surround me, aiming to assist. Just showing them the scratchings on the envelope provides a magic admission— Greeley's bad handwriting is famous. As if with a finger snap, I am instantly transformed from Ohio hayseed to a piece of that man's eccentric collection. I am directed to an exhibition space in the hotel where Dr. Vincent is concluding an "open demonstration."

The exhibition hall is a room large enough for dancing but currently set up to resemble a makeshift theater. There are rows of chairs facing a raised platform. Red velvet curtains are drawn against the enormous windows to prevent too much daylight leaking in. Instead, the room is lit by gas lamps on the walls and candles that are ensconced about the perimeter of the stage. It seems a waste of daylight, but I have no experience with how to properly witness a medical breakthrough.

A young woman sits in a high-back chair on the platform, eyes half open. She wears a device on her head that looks like a hat made of wires.

Dr. Jules Vincent, I presume, stands center stage. He has one hand raised and his eyes closed, standing behind a table holding a machine that must be the inspiration for the poster's illustration. It appears to be a box made of wood and metal, with a large circular wheel attached to the top and a coil reaching out the back, attached to the vibrating wire hat on the young woman in the chair.

About twenty properly dressed men sit in the audience, watching the two onstage.

Watching them do what, exactly, I don't know.

No one is moving. Those who sit in the audience are all tipping slightly forward, as if to see something hidden. I follow suit and bend forward as well.

I notice now that the chair in which the woman sits is a wheelchair, and that while most of the audience are men, there is one back of a head in the front that belongs to a silver-haired woman. The machine makes a slight whirring noise, and the circular dial rotates back and forth. Dr. Vincent's hand and fingers gesture ever so slightly. The woman in the chair breathes deeply enough that I feel the room itself expand and contract.

It is like seeing a play frozen in time, slowly thawing.

My leg starts to tap.

I press it to stop, in honor of Aunt Clara. The demonstration seems as serious as a Quaker meeting.

How much longer will this go on?

The machine makes a *whir-tic* sound as the wheel now spins in a full revolution. It stops with a hiss, like steam releasing from a kettle, and a bell rings.

Dr. Vincent opens his eyes with a fiery gaze at an unseen horizon above our heads.

The woman slowly, as if sleepwalking, rises from her chair as a gasp moves through the audience. "It's a miracle," the woman in front murmurs.

Dr. Vincent seems to pull the sleepwalker with an invisible string as she walks across the stage. He suddenly claps his hands together violently, and her eyes open wide.

"Vera Smith, whose feet have been paralyzed since birth . . ." His voice resonates from all corners of the room with his medical authority. "See now, you walk."

The woman looks down at herself, standing, like she has just realized where she is. Then slowly, like a newborn colt, she begins to walk again. She stares out at the silver-haired woman in the front row. "Momma, I'm walking! I'm walking!"

I have to stifle the urge to laugh. It all just seems so ridiculous, like the climax of one of those revival meetings that would blow through Ohio on its way to somewhere else. She keeps walking slowly to Dr. Vincent, grasps his outstretched hands, and weeps. "It's a miracle!" she cries out. "A miracle!"

"No, Vera Smith," he crows. "It is science!"

Yes, concluding just like one of those fly-by-night revivals, except instead of everyone hollering out hallelujahs, the buttoned men fall over each other to offer congratulations to Dr. Vincent.

Chapter 19

"Would people commit murder if they knew they would be caught? If the victim could tell every grisly detail of their death?"

Dr. Vincent cuts slowly into a piece of possum. It is swimming in a sauce of candied red jelly, so that the body is hard to recognize as belonging to an animal. The head remains attached, however, with its bald face, closed eyes, and long snout. I wonder whether the possum could tell of the grisly details that led it to this plate. I think of the possums of my woods back home, a mother with the babies gripping her back. How they waddle along with those pink, humanlike faces.

Why did the chef leave the head on?

It certainly doesn't seem to bother Dr. Vincent, who continues to wax on about his interest in Cathie Fox and unsolved murders.

"Perhaps it would make no difference in matters of war . . . But then, if we were all assured a comfortable hereafter, would wars even exist? This spirit-telegraph . . . What possibilities it has for all human conditions. What is more fascinating than developing a method for talking to spirits, and in a way that may be, like all science, observable, predictable, and replicable? Of course, that is, provided it is a genuine phenomenon. There are plenty of scientists who think this is all a hoax. Especially some of my peers on the medical board in Rochester, who have examined the other sister. Did the girls actually solve a murder? As of yet, they still have not found a body."

"Whose body?"

"The peddler who they claimed was killed in their home."

Oh, yes. Rosna was his name.

Dr. Vincent scolds me for not having researched the Fox sisters, especially as I have been assigned to write a story on Cathie. He lists papers, points of view, and tells me that even though it has been only two years since the first rappings, there has already been a book written about it. The author is a scientist who traveled to Hydesville to interview the neighbors, who went into the basement to search for the murdered remains of Charles Rosna. They dug three feet into the dirt floor and hit water, which flooded the area and prevented the continuation of the search. Dr. Vincent has a copy of the book. He will loan it to me.

"Thank you," I say, attempting politeness.

Dr. Vincent, I understand, sees himself as being very gracious, educating me on my own assignment, dining with me at his hotel. This restaurant feels macabre and disturbing, with its dark patterned wallpaper, Lovejoy's uniform red curtains, and lamplit glow. The women here look like they are competing over who can wear more feathers on their head, while the men sport smug expressions. The violinist plays a high whine of strings that grates on my every nerve. Everyone here knows Dr. Vincent, and he is continually approached both by doctors huzzahing his demonstrations and by pretty women with health complaints.

I am made to understand by these visitations that I am in the presence of celebrity, if not divinity.

"I am not Christ," he says to a man who attended the exhibition, now stammering, on the verge of kneeling in worship.

"And yet you make the lame walk!" the man says.

Yes, there is something otherworldly about Dr. Vincent. He has a European accent, but I don't know enough about the world to place it. Is it German? Russian? At times, I would swear it is French, and then just as undeniably British. He has a long equine face, slightly pocked, deep-set eyes whose color I can't settle. He has a large black mustache, making it difficult for me to determine his age. He appears to be somewhere between thirty and fifty, but from the way he speaks of the history of his life, he could be two hundred. He has the quality of being many different people at once, depending on who is speaking to him. Whatever his accent or eye color, wherever he is from, however old he is, he is a master at wasting my time. He keeps talking of his theories of murder, telling me about my editorial assignment, stalling, toying with me, refusing to come to Castle Doleful right now, even though I have told him nothing of how depressing and haunted it is.

"I will be happy to assess Mrs. Greeley's situation, time permitting, when we have at last scheduled the date for me to meet with Miss Fox, whenever that may be. I simply cannot come now."

"You don't understand. It is a desperate situation with Mrs. Greeley, and if your machine can help, why can't you come now and try?" I cannot fail Mr. Greeley, whatever my feelings are about Dr. Vincent's miracle healings.

"There are hundreds upon thousands of wives and mothers that are in need of my machine, the Vincent-ivizer."

"You call it the *Vincent-ivizer?*"

"Yes, not just after me, Miss Howe, but because the patient must have the *incentive* to be well."

"Ah." I do my best to appear impressed. I did not mean to insult his stupidly named machine.

"I have six more exhibitions this week. I see nowhere in this letter that he is prepared to make arrangements with Lovejoy's Hotel for my canceling demonstrations. Do you?" He's pretending he can actually read Mr. Greeley's handwriting and trying to bluff me into telling him what it says.

"I don't know the state of Mr. Greeley's finances, but I can safely assume that his position in this city ensures it. As it states clearly right here . . ." No one can read this handwriting, but two can play at the bluff game. I point to a word that appears to start with an *r-e*. It could be "remembering," "regardless," but I make a choice. "He is prepared to make any 'remuneration.' Did you not read that?"

"Hmm." He dabs at his mustache, removing a small blob of jelly.

"And has the lady decided yet on a course for supper?" The waiter has been asking this every ten minutes since we've arrived, always putting a strange emphasis on "lady" and never looking at me directly. I am out of place. Disturbing to the milieu.

Dr. Vincent, for his part, seems not at all perturbed by my inappropriate dress for such dining. Only once did he even seem to notice, and that was when we first sat down.

"Are those men's boots?" he asked.

I told him they were, in fact, the footwear of all proper ladies in Ohio. Whether he believed me or not, the answer seemed to agree with him, for he gave me a chummy sort of smile that I have not seen him give any other.

"I still don't have any appetite," I say to the waiter. "You don't need to ask again."

"Please only return when you are called," Dr. Vincent adds.

The strings of the violin whine three notes and a fourth that does not complete the phrase. It jars me, sets me on edge. I realize it is a lengthy journey back to Castle Doldrum, and it will be dark before we get there, even if we were to leave immediately.

"Mr. Greeley will pay whatever is necessary," I say, making my voice as pleasant and pleading as I can. "When I left, Mrs. Greeley was sleeping, at last, but she's had a miscarriage and hates the doctor who treats her. She calls him Dr. Bug."

"I will be frank with you, Miss Howe. I am not at all interested in the melancholic humors and female maladies that beset Mrs. Greeley. At the beginning of my career, I did make my practice helping women with similar complaints. I am far beyond that now. There are five hundred women with cases of melancholia for every one that I find a challenge. This is why I need my machine to be manufactured. I simply do not have the time. Mr. Greeley may be powerfully influential, but he does not have the capital to help me gain access to standardized assembly, and thus, I must exhibit in such places as these. Her melancholy isn't going anywhere. I can safely assume it will still be waiting for me when I arrive at a more convenient time."

His fork squeaks on the plate.

"It isn't only melancholia," I say. "She has fits of rage, like a caged animal. Behaves as if deranged. Biting people. Then after a session with Miss Fox, she seems fine, agreeable—sensible, even. Though she sees things that no one else sees, like weevils in wheat, and thinks her medicine is poison."

"I'm sure it *is* poison. Most of these tinctures are, the leading thought being that the poison in the medicine draws out the poison in the body. Or at the very least, subdues the patient into submission enough to tolerate the malady. On the other hand, someone may be poisoning her intentionally from within the household. Slipping arsenic into her food."

"Sir?" What a shocking accusation to make.

"From tales I've heard, she has long been a difficult person to like."

"She is very agreeable when in her right mind." A half-truth at best. I have never seen her in her right mind. "Who have you been talking to?"

"Miss Howe, you will learn it is always important to fully research any situation in which you are investing your time. I am a man who makes it his business to know things. I discover information in more ways than you can possibly realize. How I know things is not the point. I have agreed to visit Mr. Greeley and his household only because it will give me a unique opportunity to study Cathie Fox. My interest is in her and her alone. I am not even interested in attending a séance with this famous coloratura, Jenny Lind."

"That makes two of us."

"*You*, however, are interesting, Miss Howe." He chuckles. "So we will enjoy supper, and you can relay to Mr. Greeley my appreciation for his sending you here, but you will act as my proxy in assuring him that his wife can wait until we properly schedule a time for me to see Miss

Fox. Next month, perhaps. In the meantime, do please tell me more about yourself. And order something to eat."

"Really, I'm not hungry." My head turns toward a woman at the entrance who looks like she's wearing a full pheasant on the top of her head. How bizarre that feathers are a status symbol. The idea of eating anything with a face or feathers at this moment makes my stomach turn.

"You are suffering from a migraine?" he asks.

"No, I'm fine today." But how can anyone dine with the screechiness of that violin? "How do you know about my migraines? I never told you that."

"The way you move your feet in nervous apprehension. How you press the brows together on your forehead indicates that you have a most anxious temperament. You struggle to maintain focus, often distracted. Only where your will drives you due to a heightened sense of the dramatic—where there is great danger, or where you feel there is great injustice—do the other humors in your body rush to provide a sense of balance. Your migraines are due to your excitability and lack of mental discipline, paired with a desperate need to control others, as you cannot control yourself."

"That's not true, I . . ." I don't want to control anyone, and I am very disciplined when I am not stuck in a room of disgusting-looking food and women wearing dead animals as fashion statements, with corsets so tight they look like insects. A woman near the bar looks exactly like a shiny purple wasp—fine, I admit I am very distractible. "I don't see how any of those things would indicate that I get migraines, even if they were true."

"Oh, people are as easy to read as a book once you learn how to read their body. The woman you saw walk in the exhibition—please do not think I mended her feet or legs. It was always possible for her to move as she did. My machine helps the patient through balancing their will with their belief, their doubt with faith. For many, it is much easier to trust a machine than it is themselves. However, I could cure you of these headaches at this very moment. I don't need a machine."

He cuts the remainder of the meat in front of him into small pieces with methodical purpose. One, two, three small pieces.

"Have some supper."

He pushes a piece of possum onto his fork and holds it out toward me, like one would to a child.

The flesh glistens in the jelly. "Truly, sir, I have no appetite."

He pushes the fork into his mouth, chewing with exaggeration. "It is perfectly prepared. Quite delicious. It is a common meat here in the States, I understand. A delicacy to me, as we do not have possum where I am from."

"Where *are* you from?"

"I was born in a country that no longer exists, Miss Howe. I will not tax you to pretend you know of it. But I spent most of the formative years of my career in France, learning mesmerism in the tradition of the Marquis de Puységur—who trained with Franz Mesmer himself. Then I spent a decade in Austria before accepting a position at a university in England, where I developed this machine that marries all the disparate learnings about how to combat disease. I have been to all four corners of this Earth. One of the things one learns traveling is to eat the food of the culture. To eat of the land is to be of the land. I have consumed every manner of fish, fowl, and mammal—in one particular location, I partook of human flesh."

"I don't think that is something to brag about," I say, finding it hard to swallow.

"If you want to be healthy, it is important to not close the door to new experiences, especially ones that are as simple as opening one's mouth to a taste. If you will not let me serve you, serve yourself."

He tries to hand me his fork.

It repels me.

"You do eat meat."

"Yes, but I just—I can't eat *that*."

"Why?"

"It's the head, sir. The face. It seems like it could be sleeping . . . playing dead like possums do."

The fork goes into it with such force that I jump back. It sticks straight up in its snout. The handle is vibrating from the impact, like the poor thing's nose is twitching.

Dr. Vincent wears a benevolent expression on his face, as if he has just handed me a flower. He wants me to cry. He's daring me, somehow, to cry with that pretend look of care.

I won't give him the satisfaction. I meet his eyes with the blandest expression I can muster.

"There is some trauma in your life, Miss Howe, that you have buried deep inside you. If you do not uncover it, it will destroy you." He takes a long drink of his wine.

I am exercising extreme self-control, profound mental discipline. Finally, I get to a point where I can politely reply. "Has anyone ever told you that it's very rude to make assumptions about people?"

"Only Americans, who don't like to know anything, least of all about themselves."

I arrive here at a decisive feeling about Dr. Vincent. I hate him. I am no longer afraid of failing Mr. Greeley. I don't think I can bear to spend another moment in his presence.

I push back my chair.

He looks at me with surprise.

"Enjoy the rest of your evening, Dr. Vincent," I say, standing up. "Goodbye."

"Now, now," he says. "Come, come, don't be a little girl. You are stronger than that. You want something, don't give up. We are to work together, n'est-ce pas? Pardonnez-moi. Je n'aurais pas dû dire ça." He looks genuine in his apology. He even stands up, reaching a hand toward me.

People are staring at us. Pheasant Hat, Mr. Screechy Violin, and the waiter who wouldn't look at me who has changed his mind. All stare at me now, wondering what I have done to so upset Saint Vincent. If I leave, I might be tarred and feathered.

I sit back down, fuming, knowing I do need to get a grip on myself, I do need to calm down. The fork is no longer in the possum's face. I don't know when he removed it.

"Is everything quite all right?" The waiter has returned.

"Please take this dish away," Dr. Vincent orders.

I turn my head and don't watch as it is carried off.

"Quelle heure est-il?" Dr. Vincent takes out his pocket watch. With a little snap, he presses the bow to stare at the face. He sighs. I don't ask the time. How much I have wasted sitting here. He clicks it closed. The watch fob is golden, with a long braided chain. I wonder whether it is genuine gold.

The watch dangles, catching the candlelight; back and forth it moves. It is beautiful, really, how it shines as it sways. Back and forth, forth and back, back and forth. How fascinating, how a thing can move like that through the air. This must be how a cat feels watching a bird fly, watching a string move.

"Voulez-vous comprendre les mystères du monde? Je peux vous aider."

"The mystery of the world? I don't speak French."

"But you understand enough, and you relax when you hear it."

"I suppose."

"You are very relaxed now. Other sounds cease to concern you, other thoughts no longer trouble you. You just hear the sound of my voice."

The music of the violin has faded. The other patrons in the restaurant are only shadows. It's just me and him, here. Really, it's just me, watching this watch move back and forth, forth and back.

"Why does hearing someone speak in French relax you?"

"Oh, I don't know. It never did before."

"No?"

"Maybe yesterday. Maybe hearing it spoken by Jessica."

"Jessica?"

"Miss Elliot. Cathie's governess. She speaks it so beautifully."

"Toutes les femmes sont donc des sorcières?"

I am watching his watch, feeling sleepy, very sleepy . . . but I don't want to be sleepy.

Wake up, now, I tell myself. *Stay alert!*

My knee bounces up and hits the bottom of the table, clattering what's left of the dishes, spilling his wine.

"What are you doing with that watch?" I ask, feeling a bit woozy, like the morning after I had gotten into Aunt Clara's sherry.

"Nothing, I was just looking at the lateness of the hour." He looks alarmed, pulling his chain and watch back into his hand with the dexterity of a pickpocket. "You have a strong will, Miss Howe."

"Indeed, Dr. Vincent," I say. "I must be getting back. I will relay your thoughts to Mr. Greeley. That you will at some time be interested in meeting with the very famous Cathie Fox but are bored at how his wife suffers and have no *incentive* to help her, because although Mr. Greeley may have money and influence, he himself doesn't have enough to build a factory for your incredibly effective machine, the Vincent-ivizer. N'est-ce pas?"

"You purposely misunderstand me, Miss Howe." Dr. Vincent sighs, then erupts into a laugh. "Or else you'd realize that I have always intended to accompany you back to the estate tonight."

Chapter 20

Get back to the city to hear Frederick Douglass speak. Radicalize an eleven-year-old against the status quo. Get an abolitionist-supporting quote from Jenny Lind. Write an editorial that pretends to be about spirits but is sneakily about politics. Make sure Mr. Greeley knows just how arduous this task was that he gave me, so that he will listen to me. Eat more pie.

I take comfort in thinking of the things I need to do before I can successfully leave this state and get back to my Lady Jane. Yes, fine, I concede I am easily distractible, which can be a gift when I want to be distracted. Say, from finding myself stuck with Dr. Snake Oil, with a long ride ahead.

Black fringe and plush seats—this carriage is much nicer than the one I rode in on. I get the feeling that this is either Dr. Vincent's personal property, or he treats it as such. We sit across from each other, his hand on the trunk that contains his machine, which the driver knew to place on the seat next to him. He stares at me as if conducting a patient's examination.

"What do you believe in, Miss Howe? What is it that animates your limbs and motivates your movement?"

While I am glad that I am accomplishing the mission of bringing the doctor to the Greeley household, I am not interested in being further educated. I have had enough of Dr. Vincent to complete whatever piece he may have in the editorial I will write. Still, we have this whole ride ahead of us.

"I believe in equality, Dr. Vincent," I say. "The work for justice is what animates me. I believe that I am no more or less than anyone else, and my freedom to be whom I choose is my birthright. I hold these truths to be self-evident—as did the framers of our American Constitution."

"Ah." He chuckles. "I might have predicted you are one of those."

I will not elaborate to be further pried and poked. I try to see out the cab window into the grimy city.

"What have you experienced thus far from Cathie Fox, the spirit-telegraph?" he asks.

"Do you mean the knocking?"

"I have not heard it called that. Did you coin that turn of phrase?"

"I am not sure." It seems unlikely that I did.

"It is far catchier than 'the spirit-telegraph.' You have witnessed it?" He leans forward. His face appears strange in these shadows, his features obscured. I can clearly see the outline of his skull.

"I have witnessed it."

"Do share your thoughts with me, Miss Howe." Dusk is setting in, and perhaps it is too dark for him to read me like a book.

I ponder the length of the carriage ride and whether I prefer to listen to Dr. Vincent pontificate or to fill the time with my own discourse. I realize that whatever I say he will analyze, dissect, and hold for an appropriate time to use against me. This is the price we journalists pay to have our words in print. As I have not yet had this honor, I decide I will give practice to my editorial thoughts on the spirit-telegraph.

"There are certain things we take for granted, even if we do not like them. Death and taxes, according to Benjamin Franklin. I know this from his written word, which remains with us and contains something of the eternal spirit of the man. I do not need to find someone to try to drag his spirit from wherever it may be to rap out, in code, more aphorisms. We do have quite enough to easily extrapolate his beliefs or thoughts on any of our current situations. Many would disagree with me and would wish to consult him from the great beyond with regularity.

"A phenomenon, 'the knocking,' occurs regularly in the presence of Cathie Fox, a girl who is said to be a spirit-telegraph. This means that she can supposedly speak to those who are dead, whose spirits, apparently, are lounging about in Summerland, just waiting to share their new insights now that they have sloughed off their mortal coil.

"There is something troubling to me in all of this, I must admit. While many seem to find it the promised recompense of Saint Paul—'O grave where is thy victory, o death where is thy sting'—it seems to me a distraction from that which truly demands the attention of the living."

I am pleased with my monologue. Yes, there is the beginning of something there, once I can scratch each word into parchment and worry over its journalistic merit.

"Please give me an example of what you mean," Dr. Vincent asks.

"What I mean about what?" I said so many things. I can elaborate and exemplify, but I have already forgotten many of the trees in my bird's-eye flight over the forest.

"How speaking for the dead distracts those who are living."

"Oh, yes." That's an easy one. "Well, for example, Cathie knocks for Mrs. Greeley, who is very sick and disturbed. Mrs. Greeley now relies on this girl to not only relay messages through knocks from her dead son but also requests his spirit use Cathie's vocal cords, that she channel his voice. It is an alarming thing to witness."

"Indeed, I can imagine."

"I would say that Mrs. Greeley habitually uses Cathie Fox in the same way one may use a drug. Ultimately, this does not help her to let time heal her wounds of grief, and instead encourages her to continually renew the pain of the loss of her son."

"Ah. So knowing that his spirit is happy and content does nothing to create happiness and contentment for her. In your estimation."

"Certainly not. She would prefer to believe that she can in some way still control him, through Cathie Fox, than to allow that he is beyond where she can reach him."

"*Can* she reach him? Do you believe that it is genuine, this spirit-telegraph, or do you think it is theatrics?"

"I don't know." I truly don't at this moment. I can't seem to make up my mind one way or the other. "It seemed real when I witnessed it. Beyond what I can explain. Terrifying. I was very afraid of her, sir, the young girl. And I know she believes that she can speak to spirits. But I . . . To return to the question you asked me, I don't know what it is that animates her limbs. Uses her voice. I don't know what forces are moving through young Cathie Fox."

"Indeed." His voice is pleased. What I can see of his face reminds me of the bones beneath it. "I am most intrigued. As I stated, Mrs. Greeley's condition is far from rare. But to hear your account of Miss Fox quite excites me. Like a young Mozart with music, perhaps she has learned to play the realms of the emotional mind."

There is nothing in his words to make me suddenly feel trapped. Perhaps it is how he leans forward, that his mouth is open and his teeth shine. He smiles like a wolf. My self-congratulations at successfully fetching this charismatic quack for Mr. Greeley give way to feeling somehow duped and in danger.

"Maybe that's just another way of saying it's all just an act." I force a laugh. "People believe what they want to believe."

"That is correct," he says, as if it is the appropriate punctuation to end our dialogue.

The night grows darker, and each moment seems to lengthen in silence with it.

"Feel free to rest, Miss Howe. I know you have had quite a journey today," he says, his body relaxing into a curve against the back of the seat. "I will do the same."

But I do not dare close my eyes, and I do not believe, even as he snores softly, that he sleeps.

After what feels like days, the carriage finally makes its way up to the Greeley house. I am so excited to not be cramped in a carriage with Dr. Vincent that I forget he is chasing me into a haunted house.

It is an uproar of a welcome. The whole household—minus Mary Greeley—inhabits the front rooms. All at once, Mr. Greeley, Dr. Bing, and the Marthas encircle us, talking over each other to try to explain what has happened. Voices are hoarse, they snap at each other. This is the only thing that I can clearly determine:

Mary Greeley is in a coma.

Chapter 21

Castle Doldrum has imploded. It seems to hang lopsided in the lamp-light, as fingers point in blame and Mr. Greeley beseeches heaven and Dr. Vincent for intervention.

Martha, Dr. Bing, and I are the last to have seen Mary Greeley conscious. This afternoon, Martha entered her room to check on her, to find she'd soiled her sheets and could not be roused. Dr. Bing was quickly summoned to return, but he has not been able to awaken her.

"She went unconscious after a dose of medicine?" Dr. Vincent asks innocently enough.

"That has no bearing on her condition," Dr. Bing protests. After an initial welcoming of another of his profession to the fray, Dr. Bing gives up on problem-solving and slumps into a chair in the parlor, his head in his hands. "As I have stated, for now the thousandth time, it has nothing to do with the medicine I gave her. Nothing at all."

"But you gave her a double dose." It's the first thing I have said since we entered into this frenzy. A double dose, where I held her head for what may have been her last moments. *Et tu, Brute?* like Caesar, could be her last words. It may be a character flaw, but I spend little time entertaining the heavy twins of guilt and shame. So I am wholly unprepared for the sense of being crushed by both from inside.

"How dare you lie, Miss . . . whoever you are. I never gave her a double dose!" Dr. Bing's face twists with fury. "How dare you!"

"Excuse me, sir." I am highly offended. "I may be many things, but I am not a liar." Except when I told Dr. Vincent that all women in Ohio wear boots. And perhaps some small fibs here and there that I've forgotten about.

Dr. Bug (I will think of him only as such hereafter) retracts the accusation and then says, if not a lie, then it is my *mistake*. But furthermore: "No one is at fault but that of her body to handle this last miscarriage. These ignorant maids may also share some blame for failing to give her the daily drops of medicine, which would have calmed her body and slowed her bleeding and better enabled her to recover. And even if I did give her a double dose—which I did not—or even a triple dose, it would not have induced a coma."

Martha does not defend herself, nor confirm what I know we both heard.

"Perhaps in attending to Mrs. Greeley, you forgot some bread in the oven?" Dr. Vincent asks Martha, sniffing the air.

"Mrs. Greeley insisted we burn all the wheat," Martha says.

"And for what reason?" Dr. Vincent asks sweetly.

Martha hesitates.

"She thought she was being poisoned," I say. I wish I hadn't. Even though I had said as much to Dr. Vincent earlier, it stops the presses when I say it now. There is a momentary silence, in which I decide elaboration is necessary and will make it better. "She told me medieval demons were hallucinations caused by bad bread."

Accusations and recriminations spit from Dr. Bug's lips, landing on everyone, even Mr. Greeley. "If she cannot be taken care of in the home, she should be in an asylum!"

I am not sure which male voice points out that the only place Mary may be going now is the graveyard, but Jessica, appearing like an angel at Mr. Greeley's shoulder, assures him, "She will awaken. Have faith. She will be well."

Martha turns back to the business of cleaning things, moving things, bringing dishes, taking away dishes. Young Martha hugs the wall, sagging with the weight of Baby Charlotte, who we all know is not a baby and thus too heavy to be continually carried. Charlotte is still enamored with me, staring in my direction until I return the favor, and then she opens her mouth with delight, nearly to laugh, but no sound comes out. She has learned the rule for children: *to be seen and not heard.*

Dr. Vincent calmly stands in the center of the room. Everything in the house seems to have decided to bend to him, granting him some temporary lordship. Even the shadows seem to defer to his authority, swallowing the other shadows to illuminate where he looks. Now his eye is fixed on the most beautiful sight the scene has to offer: Miss Jessica Elliot. When I manage to break his gaze, he has the gall to wink at me, as if I were a conspirator in his brazen leering. He seems to have forgotten his original object of fascination, Cathie Fox, seated quietly in a chair in the corner, watching as if invisible. Our eyes meet. I can't read her expression.

"Please, Dr. Vincent, do something," Greeley begs. "Anything."

I notice a hairline crack in the wall behind Cathie, vertical. A possible break in the house's foundation. My eyes try to follow it, but I can't see where it stops or starts, and it turns a corner and disappears. I look back to see whether I can retrace it. Cathie's chair is empty.

"My treatments are only designed for conscious patients," Dr. Vincent says, with far more cheer in his voice than is appropriate.

Something grabs my arm.

I jump.

Cathie is right beside me, eyes glazed and red.

"I didn't see you there," I say.

She doesn't apologize for startling me. She has one hand clutched in a fist, the other tugs my sleeve. She should know better than to sneak up on me, even in a crowded and chaotic room.

Dr. Vincent continues to describe the nature of his invention to the desperate Mr. Greeley, and why it won't work to help his wife.

My arm is pulled again.

"What?" I snap at Cathie, not bothering to temper my annoyance.

"Your mother," Cathie whispers. "She has been making a ruckus all day at me. She wants me to tell you that she's here for you."

"Whoever you heard, it wasn't my mother." I wonder whether I could stomach seeing her again. I would bet she's kept drugged at the asylum so she's manageable. Perhaps I could catch her when she's awake enough that her eyes glitter, and get her to say more than three words, two of them being "buttons."

"She says she loves you and wants to help," Cathie insists.

"Stop it," I say, louder than I meant to be, but I don't appreciate the assumption of some helpful, loving mother that doesn't exist for me. Does Cathie always need to be the center of attention?

Dr. Vincent turns the whole of his figure to look down at me. No, not at me—at Cathie, by my side. He stalks toward her, mustache twitching, and crouches down slowly to meet her at eye level.

"Are you the famous Cathie Fox?" He offers her a hand, and she gives him the one that was tugging my sleeve. Her other hand stays closed. "You are far more mature and lovely than I was led to believe. You are a young lady, not a child."

"Thank you, sir."

"Would you be willing, in the name of experimentation, to use your powers as a spirit-telegraph to aid me in seeing if we can assist Mrs. Greeley?"

"Of course, sir. I am merely a vessel for the spirits."

He temples his fingers and bows his head like a swami. He stands upright with nimble bounce and turns to address the room. "If any-thing in heaven or on Earth can be done to help Mrs. Greeley, we shall do it!" he announces.

The hand that was tugging my sleeve now pinches me. Cathie unballs her fist to shove something in my hand. I know what it is without looking, stunned. However she managed the trick of appear-ing suddenly by my side, she takes the opposite approach to leave it, stomping away to join Dr. Vincent.

I have a moment where my belief gives way—Cathie is a magical child with special powers. But I pull myself back. My mother's spirit is still trapped in her broken mind. However Cathie guessed or divined the significance of this object, it's just a thing. I don't have to assign meaning to it.

My fingers open to see that it is black, with two holes like tiny eyes. A button.

Chapter 22

Mary Greeley lies motionless, covered in a starched white sheet, her body encircled by lit candles. Her room has taken on the quality of a small theater. Chairs have been dragged in from other rooms in the house so that Mr. Greeley, Jessica, Dr. Bug, Cathie, and I can all have proper seats. I am not sure why we need to be set up like a demonstration, but he insisted that we all understand the proper procedure. The Marthas, though they were the ones moving the furniture, are not included in the viewing space. They watch from the door, passing Baby Charlotte between them.

Dr. Vincent stands front and center, his machine on a table beneath a cloth.

"In 1774, Franz Mesmer discovered a force every bit as important as Newton's discovery of gravity, calling it *animal magnetism*. Initially using bits of iron and magnets, later he found he could cure his patients with the laying on of hands."

We are held in rapt attention. Even I suspend my doubt, clutching this black button in a side seam pocket like a secret talisman.

"To try and restore the imbalance of a humor without addressing the animal magnetism could be compared to trying to repair a roof by placing a bowl to catch where it leaks. To repair the roof, one must be prepared to climb a ladder."

A dramatic pause, and then the thesis:

"To heal the body, one must engage the mind." He lets us all settle in with that idea for a moment as he rolls up his sleeves. "The patient must have the *incentive* to heal. Now, the effectiveness of mesmerism has been proven beyond any doubt."

Dr. Vincent ignores Dr. Bug's snort.

"But it requires trained hands, and none of us can be a thousand places at one time. Thus, I have invented a machine that is small enough to be easily transported and simple enough to be put together by any doctor with the most rudimentary mechanical skill. Behold, the Vincent-ivizer—" He whisks away the red cloth with the flourish of a bullfighter, revealing the wood-and-copper box with a wheel atop that pivots and spins. "The fruit of my life's work, named after me, as I would my own son."

Are we to clap?

I have started to do so before I realize that no one else is joining me, and I quickly cease. It has been, however, already quite a performance. The tail end that I caught at the hotel was the boring bit. I do hate him—I have not forgotten the possum—but I cannot deny that Dr. Vincent is a highly skilled showman.

"Well, how does it work?" Dr. Bug leans forward as if to stand and gain closer inspection, but Vincent moves himself in front of his self-proclaimed progeny to deny him access.

"I will demonstrate the working of my Vincent-ivizer with this vital caveat: It was designed to work on conscious patients only. However, it is possible that even while unconscious, her mind may be reached with the most novel part of my machine."

He takes a readying breath, then opens the back of the box, pulling out a long coil attached to that hat made of wires that Vera Smith, back at his demonstration at the hotel, was wearing.

"Miss Elliot, would it be too much trouble to ask for your help with placing the Mind-Stimulator?" He holds out the headpiece toward her, coercing her into participation.

"I don't think I'm qualified." Her voice shakes uncharacteristically, as if she had thought she were, for once, invisible. "Maybe Dr. Bing would be better to help?"

"It is *your* assistance I am requesting," Dr. Vincent says.

She assents, slowly standing and moving next to him where he beckons. We are all invited to stare at her without reservation. What unexpected pleasure there is in unabashedly gazing at a gorgeous woman without fear of being seen in return. Of course it is *her* assistance he wants. Her appearance with him elevates his claims like an endorsement from John Keats: *Beauty is truth, truth beauty.*

"Place this upon her head, ensuring she has a wire here." He presses a finger to the center of Jessica's forehead in transfixing deliberation. "One follows here and then here," he adds, putting a hand on either side of her head. Through his touch, we who watch feel we can touch her, too. "The shaft of this coil rests against the back of her neck. Move her hair to get it to vibrate against the skin here." He moves his body behind her, his thumbs disappear behind the nape of her neck. We must imagine where they go.

I cannot see her blush, but I feel it. Each place he has touched her, I feel a mirroring prick on my skin, a dull sting. I don't like it, his fingers on her body.

"But do not be concerned with being overly 'correct.' The Mind-Stimulator will work, regardless." He hands her the helmet of wires, uncoiling a long cable attached to the back of it. "Much like sunlight, the flower will turn toward it."

Jessica must be careful, moving amid the candles in her wide yellow dress, the shimmer of it in this light taking on the color and quality of champagne. It glows and moves with her like a liquid. She effortlessly draws our collective gaze to her, needing no philosophies or soliloquies.

"Thank you, Miss Elliot," Mr. Greeley calls from his seat, as if he were the one to insist on her assistance. "I know how much Mother appreciates your kindness."

"You still haven't said what the machine will actually do," Dr. Bug grumbles.

"I will get into the technical aspects of the machine with you later, gentlemen. For now, and for the purposes of the ladies and the children, think of it working much like a clock. Or"—he gives Cathie an obsequious smile—"a windup toy."

As if Cathie plays with windup toys!

He twists a side crank, and the wheel atop the box spins while the Mind-Stimulator on Mary's head vibrates. The Vincent-ivizer is in action, but it has no apparent effect on the patient.

"Miss Fox," Dr. Vincent says, summoning Cathie, who has been sitting so still she could be forgotten. "Now I would like to ask you to call upon the spirits."

Cathie hesitates, then she moves her body forward until her feet touch the floor. She grips the arms of the chair, tipping herself like she's ready to spill from it. "If there is a spirit present, please rap once for yes, twice for no."

A small sound. One knock.

I can't tell where it's coming from.

"Is this the spirit of someone Mary Greeley knows? Once for yes—"

"He just knocked on the back of my chair!" Mr. Greeley says, his voice husky with emotion. "Oh, I feel my son's little hand on my shoulder."

The sounds of the machine and Mr. Greeley's sorrow make a strange type of rhythmic music. The spinning wheel of the Vincent-ivizer *whirs* and *tics*, the Mind-Stimulator vibrates, and Mr. Greeley repeats, "My son, my son, oh, my son!" It rises to a swell, undeniable in its tenor. Loss and grief, mixed with acceptance and hope, resonate in refrain.

My heart begins to pump, a sensation at the back of my nose like I might sneeze. I am surprised to find that tears are beginning to form. I remind myself that when I first witnessed this machine, I had to stifle a laugh that this was all just a show and creepy Dr. Vincent was like an actor playing some role and I didn't think any of this was real.

Except Mr. Greeley's grief *is* real. His loss is real.

His hope that it is the spirit of his son tapping the back of his chair, unbearably real.

I cannot deny the feeling of being swept up in these sounds. I allow myself to hear it with my heart and tell my mind to just listen. If this is like a play, then I will allow myself the catharsis. Mr. Greeley is openly weeping, and I weep with him.

Healing *is* possible, of course it is. Not just possible but the directive of all living things. It is the nature of our world to fill a void, for death to bring new life, that every end is another beginning.

Summerland! As I sit here, it seems obvious that it must be so. It is correct, it is true, that if we can all only *will* ourselves to heal, to be whole, everything in us responds to affirm that yes, we shall! Why, these tears of a father are like rain in a springtime. And after spring comes the summer of the soul. Summerland is not some distant heaven, it is right here with us, all the time. Summerland is real, Summerland is—

"Hogwash!" Dr. Bug blurts out. He stands up, nearly toppling his chair with his frame. "This is absolute humbuggery and balderdash, and I will not be part of it for another instant."

He lumbers out of the room, leaving a wake of empty space. I can hear him pushing past the Marthas, thumping his way down the steps.

Mr. Greeley blinks as if rudely awakened from a dream.

Cathie stands and walks over toward Mr. Greeley, her family's protector, then stops, as if seeing someone before him. She reaches out, like taking a child's invisible hand. She turns to face the unconscious figure in the bed, her back to us. A voice not her own speaks now.

"Don't worry, Papa," Pickie says. "I've been here all along, watching over her."

Chapter 23

It is the middle of the night, and I lie in bed, wondering about what is hovering over me. Something is moving up there, in the attic. It will be silent for a moment, and then, right above my head, a *bump bump bump bump*, like a child's fist pounding a door to be let in.

Or let out.

Is Pickie's spirit there in her room, watching over his mother? Or is he haunting from up there in the attic, where he was sent by her as a punishment when he was alive?

Mary Greeley is in a coma.

I think of Dr. Vincent's comment, before he put a fork into a sleeping possum's face: *"She is difficult to like . . . Someone may be slipping arsenic into her food."*

Was it a medical mistake of a double dose, or is someone purposely trying to kill Mary Greeley? I think about what I have seen and heard, and wonder who could possibly do such a thing and why.

I think of how Mary bit Young Martha's wrist, and her response: *"We do what we can to stay."*

"I hate her!" Cathie said. The pop of a wormy apple as she threw it into the fire. The intensity of Mary's threat to continue to control her: *"I will never let you take my son away from me."*

I won't let myself entertain that it could be something supernatural. Even if that's what Mary said herself. *"She says she felt its fingers on her neck last night."*

Or maybe there *was* poison in the wheat.

I turn onto my side, pressing my hands together beneath my head to raise up my neck a little, which has a bit of an ache. My history with arsenic poisoning is limited to the news.

I know that publications that recount the gory details of crime stories are trash, but maybe there's something educational, if not instructive, in diving into the mucky remains of a murder. Five years ago in Ohio, there was one that united the entire community in mutual horror and fascination. A woman had methodically poisoned her husband's supper night after night until he dropped dead of what everyone assumed to be some type of stomach disease. He was a domineering, abusive man who could well have been described as "difficult to like." No one would have known about this perfect crime if the woman hadn't allegedly bragged to her sister-in-law before the corpse was cold.

Knock knock from my ceiling. Undeniable.

Two knocks. Like one of those spirits telling Cathie no. Loud enough that I am sure there is someone up there. Someone lying on the attic floor, trying to get my attention.

I wait. It must be an animal. A rat or squirrel, moving something across the floor, a rabbit thumping his foot, a family of raccoons—I don't know. How many creatures can knock like that?

It is quiet again, whatever is up there.

A local chemist who was looking to popularize his understanding of the latest technology performed an autopsy to test the victim's organs. He proved the sister-in-law's suspicions. The abusive husband was indeed poisoned. Arsenic, to be specific.

First autopsy recorded, first proven arsenic poisoning in my little town . . . Believe me, suddenly every dead husband over the last decade was up for speculation. Murder Fever swept through the community. Everyone's jaw was moving on the topic for all season. Everyone was a detective, anyone could be a suspect. Never had arsenic been such a tonic. It was the most popular subject of extended family gatherings, fancy-lady neighborhood strolls, Christian moralizing. The story had something for the whole family. Husbands had reason to show more appreciation for the supper their wives had cooked, and suspicions enough to invite them to sit and partake rather than just serve. Wives hoarded a bitter vindication in a bad husband getting his just desserts. Spinster sisters could cluck louder about their in-laws. Oh, how thrilling to pass judgment and . . .

Thump.

I twist over in the bed; the weight of my head has made my hands numb.

Maybe I am determined to think Mary was intentionally poisoned to free myself of this awful feeling of shame for helping hold her down. Guilt for not punching Dr. Bug right in the face. She was calm, lucid, wanting to join the cause for women before his beaky face showed up and he sat on her chest like a vulture.

Bump bump bump bump. A scurrying, a scratching. A loud *thump.*

Something is definitely alive up there.

"Hello?" I call up.

I stand on my bed, cupping my palms around my mouth, trying to amplify my voice toward the attic. "Hello, can you hear me?"

More silence.

THUMP.

Enough. If it is something alive, I am not afraid of any animal.

If it is something dead, it cannot hurt me.

I will go up there. I will face it, whatever it is.

~

I wander outside my room into a house transfigured by night, lamp in my hand so I can see through the darkness. I look for the door to the attic, trying to recall whether I ever saw it. I don't think so. I cannot find it, so I look up, thinking it's perhaps one of those attic entrances built into the ceiling, a pull chain that releases a lever so the steps come down.

My lamp can detect nothing but the shadow that follows behind it.

All the warnings about not going up there, but I can't even see how I could. It is silent now, in any case, and has been silent since I began my search for it. Knocking no longer.

Another sound now compels me. Male voices, discussing something of grave importance, no doubt, by the rise and fall of strident tones.

I walk down the steps to the next floor and make my way across the hall. The voices come from Mr. Greeley's study, where the bright lamp-light and the open door show a sort of conference between Mr. Greeley, Dr. Vincent, and Dr. Bug. One is pacing, one philosophizing, and the other in his cups, respectively.

I turn the wick of my lamp all the way down, killing the light, so that I may neither be seen nor heard as I flatten myself behind the door. A narrow rectangle between the edge of the wall and the frame is enough window for me to see most of the room. I am instinctively driven to spy on them before I even evaluate the risk of getting caught.

"Look, I would pay good money just to watch Miss Elliot butter a piece of toast; I have no problem with that part of the demonstration. But when you add some hocus-pocus spirits, I can't swallow it." Dr. Bug is up pouring brandy for Dr. Vincent, who looks to be seated for a formal discussion, legs crossed.

"It is hardly a drinking occasion, Bing," Mr. Greeley says.

"You may be a teetotaler, but don't make the rest of us live in your misery. In our occupation, it is a necessity—eh, Vincent?" Dr. Bug pours himself what I can only assume is another slug in a series.

"Until I examine and work with the phenomenon, yes, it may seem fanciful." Dr. Vincent leans back in his chair, sipping. "But I do think there is promise that the spirit-telegraph could work in unison with the Vincent-ivizer."

"You're a smart man," Dr. Bug says. "Why mess with all this spirit stuff? We have treatments that we know are effective. Leeches have been used since the dawn of medicine. We all know the miraculous effects of laudanum." He slurs that last word.

"Yet if overadministered . . ." Dr. Vincent speaks calmly, steadily.

"I know my medicines," Dr. Bug swaggers. "I treat every man, woman, and child within the entirety of this town, and have for the last twenty years, so I will—"

"I mean no offense. I know you are greatly respected."

"That is correct." Dr. Bug sits, dribbling a bit of his brandy in the effort. "I never overadminister a medicine. It is not possible unless that patient has refused to build the aggregate tolerance."

"So is it the medicine or a lack of medicine, Dr. Bing?" Mr. Greeley asks, halting his pacing. "All witnesses say she was awake until you drugged her, and now she won't wake up." I cannot see where he has landed from my hidden position. "And please tell me, Dr. Vincent, what good is your machine balancing her humors and animal magnetism if she is a vegetable?"

There is enough silence for me to hear that someone wound the clock downstairs.

Tock tock.

"With all due respect, sir . . ." Dr. Vincent's vowels are in danger of swallowing his consonants with his accent. "I was petitioned to leave my busy exhibition schedule to attend to your sick wife. I am more than happy to depart at this very moment back to my room at the hotel."

"No, please, I apologize, I . . ." Mr. Greeley whimpers, having learned his lesson. "I deeply apologize. Your practice tonight is the first time I have had hope. I only wish you had been the one to attend to her last night."

Dr. Bug harrumphs, positioning his big bottom in the chair. "Well, that is a fine thank-you. I myself was dragged from bed last night to become the only man in this house! Your wife had a miscarriage—and where were you, Greeley? I saved her life. Saved it, I did! She'd have bled to death. She was out of her wits from withdrawal of her medicine, left in the care of some fresh-off-the-boat immigrants and that . . . that . . ."

Oh, he means me. He can't find a word to describe me.

"Young woman . . . I thought she was the maid, but . . . I still don't know who she is."

"She is a reporter," Mr. Greeley says.

"A reporter?" Dr. Bug howls. "A reporter? One of yours?"

"Yes, yes." Greeley either does not feel he has to clarify that he has never published me or has forgotten this fact. Either way, I puff out with far too much pride for a woman skulking in the shadow between a door and a wall.

"Well, I've heard it all now," Dr. Bug says, but I can see enough of his face to tell he is bluffing. He is second-guessing his tactic of calling me a liar, now knowing I could write a story about it. "I leave you and your wife to your Irish, your young wood thumper, and this Dr. Flimflam—" He motions to Dr. Vincent.

Dr. Vincent leaps up and forward like a pugilist.

"This *what*, sir?" His even voice belies his clutching of Dr. Bug's collar. "Do you insult me? If so, I advise you choose your words carefully."

Even if it is just a small split in the door, I have a perfect view for watching these two doctors duel it out. I hope they do.

"I—I—I . . . would not insult you," Dr. Bug sputters. "I don't insult you. I simply do not understand you."

"But I very much understand *you*." Dr. Vincent, while being half of Dr. Bug's girth, seems to have lifted him from the floor.

"No need for violence, no violence," Greeley pleads. "Please, gentlemen. Please, let's be civil, let's remember who we are. We are men of reason, men of education. Men in pursuit of wisdom."

Dr. Vincent releases Dr. Bug's collar. I am disappointed, for it would have been not only a major scoop but I'd also take quite vicarious pleasure in both of them sustaining a few blows to their smug faces.

Dr. Bug coughs, shaking his head, looking about the room as if trying to find where his status dropped on the floor.

"Well, that concludes my services for you, Mr. Greeley," Dr. Bug says, then begins finding his satchel and his brandy bottle in a swaying, slow-moving exodus. "Do not send for me again."

He stands, looking toward the darkened hallway, to the door I stand behind.

Does he see me? Will he see me?

If I am caught here, it could ruin everything I have built in gaining Mr. Greeley's trust, compromising my entire mission. Not only that . . . I am afraid of what the doctors would do to me. I have a vision of being pulled out and brought into the room and fully interrogated. Dr. Bug weighed down a woman and drugged her into a coma. He is drunk and ashamed, which is when men are most dangerous. Dr. Vincent shoved a fork in a possum's face. What might he do to mine?

Dr. Bug stares at the door.

I hold my breath.

He turns back to Mr. Greeley. "I cannot find my way out in the dark without a lamp."

"Apologies, Dr. Bing, yes, I will ring for . . ." Does Mr. Greeley not even know Martha's name? He pulls a bell. "For the maid."

I cannot take a breath of relief, for he will need to come out of the room, and it will not be difficult to detect my presence if he lingers at all near the door.

"Please do be cautious in how you speak of this night, Dr. Bing." Dr. Vincent is seated again, staring at the brandy in his glass. "Lest you come up against a suit of libel. Or malpractice."

I don't have time to move away, but Dr. Bug is in too much of a hurry to detect my presence, even as he has to push against the door.

He does not see me.

But she does.

Martha, holding a lamp far down the hall, locks eyes with me as she heads in my direction toward the study, her face set much as it was the first night of my arrival.

I press my finger to my lips.

Her eyes move from me without another glance back.

She keeps my secret, blocking the sight of me with her body as she helps the disgruntled and drunk Dr. Bug down the steps.

I keep my hiding spot.

"Where we cannot be helped by belief and will, we must surren-der to Providence." Dr. Vincent opens a window and dumps out his brandy. "Let us pray together, Mr. Greeley, that God may illuminate our path."

Chapter 24

Nothing illuminates the path back to my room. My night vision is better than most, developed by a fondness for staring up at treetops long after the sun has gone down. Trees, like everything else, change into more ethereal beings at night. But I am not currently outside, able to navigate with the pattern of stars and phases of the moon.

I am in a house that is most definitely haunted by the spirits of both the living and dead.

Step by step, one hand holding the unlit glass lamp, the other finding a wall, a banister.

Finally, my fingers find the frame of my open door, and I make my way to the desk to set the lamp down. I fall back into the bed with self-congratulations at my investigations.

Someone is in my bed!

I scream as a hand goes over my mouth.

"E. A., quiet, it's me."

It's Jessica. Relief and gladness, sudden and strong. I feel like she has been absent for weeks. How long has she been here?

"I've needed to talk to you. Alone. I would have come earlier, but Cathie was having trouble falling asleep. She's very upset about Mrs. Greeley. Where were you?"

"I was just . . ." I don't want to tell her I was spying on the men; it doesn't seem like the type of activity that would win her approval.

"Snooping around?" she says, knowing me too well already.

"I heard something in the attic," I say defensively.

"You didn't go up there, did you?"

"No."

"It's very haunted."

"Have you been up there?"

"Certainly not. I could tell you stories of things I've heard, about the evil spirit that lives there. But they frighten me, even to talk about." Her voice trembles.

"I thought you felt sorry for the spirits in this house."

"Not that one. It's cruel and feeds on fear. Truly, don't go up there. I will tell you that one of the maids who left last month went in there to dust, not knowing, and came out shaking and crying. She would never tell anyone what she saw and then quit on the spot."

She's scared, telling me this ghost story about the attic, but I can't feel any fear with her here. I feel like giggling, I am so excited by her company. It's too dark to see her with any clear definition, but my other senses take over. She's not above the covers, but under them, like someone who is planning to tuck in through the night. I maneuver my body so that I can join her there under the blanket.

Here we are, close as two peas in a pod. Oh, but I am trembling, too.

"I feel we've known each other forever," she whispers, finding my hand and lacing her fingers through mine.

Mary said the same thing to me last night. I pity Mary, but she repels me. I could not wait to get away from her from the first moment I laid eyes upon her. With Jessica, it's the opposite feeling. Every moment I am with her is too short, every distance between us too long.

"Where did you go last night?" I ask. "It would have been more bearable if you had been here."

"That is a very sweet thing to say, Miss E. A. I. O. U. I have a cousin in town, remember? I told you. She's a dear old thing who brought me over from England and recommended me for this post. I owe her everything. She was sick and needed me, so I couldn't refuse."

"Is she better now?"

"She was this morning when I left." Jessica's hands are so small, her skin so soft. In and out she laces our fingers. "And I wish you had been here when I returned. It was utter mayhem. I was the one who insisted they call back Dr. Bing; no one seemed to have the slightest idea what to do. When he got here, at first he claimed it was all normal and to be expected—a good thing, even. Until he realized that she couldn't be awakened. He said she was wild and raving when he had arrived, and that you—he thought you were her personal maid—would attest to that."

"I will not. She was lucid, making plans for the future, determined to survive. Then he arrived and she got very upset. He held her down and drugged her." I leave out that I aided and abetted his cause. "No matter the fact that he's denying it now, he most definitely said he gave her a double dose."

"Do not repeat that, E. A."

"Why not? It's the truth."

"You have no proof he said it."

"Martha heard it, too."

"Then she's denying it as well. She says she never heard him say that, so don't expect some salty cook to back you up. He's the authority here, not you. Your pointing fingers at him only brings attention to yourself, and you don't want that. Especially if she dies. Already he called you a liar, and if you try to accuse him, he will lose no pains to paint you as untrustworthy."

"He doesn't even know who I am."

"Well, none of us do, really."

It stings for a moment because it is true. I know I am an outsider here in this house, but in this bed, we are both inside. "I thought you said you felt like you've known me forever."

"Touché," she says, her hand leaving mine to touch my nose. "I feel I've known you for lifetimes."

"*Lifetimes?* Don't tell me you believe in souls returning? Reincarnation?"

"Why not believe in it? It makes perfect sense."

It makes no sense.

Although, it would be nice to think that I was a tough elephant in the time of Hannibal, crossing the Alps. Or a sleek black cat in ancient Egypt, companion to Cleopatra. Maybe in my previous life I was a great chestnut tree, with hundreds of branches reaching like arms to heaven.

Jessica's hands have left mine. She sits up, pulling away from me. "Why didn't you tell me that you are writing a story about Cathie?"

"Who told you that?"

"Horace, of course."

"*Horace?* You call him *Horace?*"

"Now, stop it. Don't try and make me laugh. I'm serious."

"Even his wife doesn't call him Horace, she calls him *Father.*"

"E. A., stop!" She is laughing so hard I can feel the bed starting to shake. I, of course, am laughing, too. It feels like victory.

I sit up as well, wanting our hands intertwined again.

"Mr. Greeley, then," she enunciates. "Your employer and mine. He's having a terrible time with all of this. I wouldn't put it past her doing it on purpose just to sabotage him."

"That's a terrible thing to say."

"It's true. It couldn't come at a worse time, with all the responsibilities of trying to run the paper amid all of these political uproars, and Miss Jenny Lind, the most famous woman in the world outside of Queen Victoria, is coming here for a séance to see what the spirit-telegraph is all about. I am doing the best I can to help out until . . . well, until the situation resolves itself, one way or another."

"The *situation?* Of his wife being in a coma?"

"Stop changing the subject. Why didn't you just tell me you were assigned to write about Cathie when I asked you?"

It is a genuine accusation, launched with hurt and aggression. I can understand it may seem that I have been hiding something. I must consider how to frame this. Truthfully, I wasn't assigned to write about Cathie when she first asked me. Of course, I wasn't assigned to anything. When I saw them in the orchard, it was tea and *Hamlet* and being told my mind was in the outhouse. Cathie crying, then begging me not to tell her governess about her "childish outburst" when all she wants to do is go home.

"Edith, answer me. Why didn't you tell me? Why didn't you tell *us*? Cathie is very sensitive about being investigated or written about in newspapers. Her family has been much abused by reporters. You're going to have to work very hard for her to trust you now."

I fall back onto my pillow, frustration gripping my throat. I want to yell, have a tantrum, punch the pillow. But that would be a very "childish outburst," and I can't see well enough to be sure I won't accidentally elbow Jessica in the face.

Earning an eleven-year-old's trust is not why I left the belly of the beast of Washington in the midst of a crippling defeat of human liberty. This is not why I rode for nine days on a hot, stinky, uncomfortable train with my back cramping, my bottom bruising as I tried to find someplace where I could write without spilling my inkpot. This is not why I poured everything in my head and heart into those useless pages that I tore to shreds. Kidnapping people and forcing them back to slave states where they may be beaten, tortured, raped, or murdered is the law of our land, and I am here in a warm bed in the Greeley home, being lectured about trust.

Most confusing of all, this undeniable proof that magnetism is real. Magnetism between bodies. Everything in me wants to press away every bit of space between me and her until I am stuck to her and she to me, so stuck that we can never be pulled apart.

Instead, I grab a pillow, stuff as much of it as I can into my mouth, and yell into it every profanity I know, concluding my tirade with "doughface."

"Oh, Edith. Even if Cathie may not trust you any longer, *I* do." She touches my back gently. "And Horace does, too. He wasn't sure you'd be able to get Dr. Vincent to come, and somehow you did it."

"I don't even know how I did it." Another frustration, but as her palms press softly into my shoulder blades, any negative feeling disappears.

There is no light coming in, anywhere. How fascinating the things I can still see—the glow of her cheek as she bends toward me, the shape of her head, her arms.

Whatever was pulling us apart now presses us together. Her hands around my arms, my hands around her head, my lips find hers. I pull back, appalled at myself. I do not know how I could let myself do something so brazenly offensive. Women share beds with women all the time; it is understood that none of us is so wicked and craven as to try to do what a man would. I start to stammer an apology, not knowing how I could possibly excuse what I have done, but am stopped by the depth of her kiss.

What does this all mean?

~

Frank Jackson proposed, in his way, when he learned I was leaving for Washington. He came to Aunt Clara's door in his Sunday clothes, even though it wasn't Sunday. He had shined his shoes and brought wildflowers. I was shocked, seeing him dressed up, holding a bouquet.

"Who are the flowers for?"

He fairly threw them at me.

"What's this for? What does this mean?"

"It means what you decide it means," he said. Then, with an intensity I found exceedingly difficult to bear, he looked right into my eyes. He would kiss me if I let him, and not stop there. He would burn through me like a prairie fire and wait for me to grow back enough green and gold to burn me up again.

He would bind me to him, and to this earth that he tilled and worked, and work and till me along with it until we were no different from any beast of burden working and breeding, harvest to harvest, until we were buried beneath the earth we had burned, tilled, seeded, tended, sowed, tended, harvested, and burned again.

No.

He knew my answer. He didn't even need to ask.

"You search your heart, as I have mine." He looked at me directly again with the prairie fire in his blue irises. "You know what it means."

He turned and walked away, leaving me to consider the bouquet.

Daisies, goldenrod, purple aster. Weeds, wildflowers, Ophelia's flowers.

Fell in the weeping brook . . . Till that her garments, heavy with their drink . . .

I didn't know what it meant.

~

Now I do. I could never burn for him, because I was meant to drown. That which I have been at the surface of my skin now dies in her hair, in her kisses, in the damp of the fabric between her breasts.

I drown myself in this woman in my bed.

Chapter 25

The foundation has shifted. I went to bed in one place and awoke in another. The house is still, a quiet that has allowed me to sleep through the morning.

I don't know what time Jessica rose from the bed, but the scent of her sweat and pressed powder comforts me like she remains in the room. I run my fingers over my lips—they feel chapped and stung. I have a momentary sense of vertigo, remembering. I linger in this cheerful room where I long to spend the day reading all these books Margaret Fuller wrote, soaking in the sweet secrets of . . .

Something is wrong up there.

It's like a whistle at a frequency I can't hear but feel, coming from the attic. It bends my ear to my neck with a warning. I pull my dress on quickly, neglecting to put on shoes in a rush to investigate the high and sharp soundless noise.

The notion was amusing to me last night, a room so haunted a maid quit her post after entering. It excited me that Jessica was scared, wanting to be close to me. Now I need to see what it is that made such a racket when I was alone and is now at a pitch that would drive away dogs.

Last night I couldn't find the entrance, but in the daylight it is perfectly obvious, this attic door. It is on the wall of the hallway, only a few feet from the doorframe that leads to my room. It is meant to be discreet, being the same color and texture as the wall. The small latch and knob are unassuming. The door is slightly warped, askew on its hinges, jutting out like a crooked tooth. The latch seems to be the only thing keeping it from falling open. I unhook it and twist the knob. It does not open, and after some brief tugs, I realize it won't budge without putting some shoulder into it.

My hands are suddenly shaking. I stare at them like they belong to someone else. This clenching in my stomach, the pinpricks on the back of my neck, and my trembling palms all indicate that the incessant warnings about the attic have succeeded in scaring me. Either that, or I am nearly faint with hunger. It has been a very long time since I have eaten. I rehook the latch and experience immediate relief. I don't need to explore the spooky attic. Not now, anyway. Right now, I just need breakfast.

I'm sure Martha will fix me something. A biscuit, a carrot, a cold mug of water, anything would be a healthy feast compared to a greasy piece of possum. Just thinking of Martha's worn face, her no-nonsense attitude, and her tireless care of all of us, I want to run and give her a big hug.

She's not in the kitchen, nor is her daughter. It is so quiet in this house. The beat of the grandfather clock is the only sound. No dishes clanking, no floors thumping, no wailing, no crying, just *tock tock*. Where are Jessica, Cathie, or the men? I laugh to myself, thinking perhaps I am Rip Van Winkle. Maybe I slept much longer than I thought.

I open the front door and venture outside.

What a gorgeous day it is! Barefoot, I can feel the cold, damp grass on my toes. The air is as crisp and sweet as the apples in the orchard. Fall is here in earnest. Some of the trees are boasting a costume change in color. Midas touched the leaves of the oaks out front—overnight they turned gold.

Birdsong begins to deafen every other sound. I raise my head to herald an immense flock of passenger pigeons. They cover the sky like a singing cloud, their wings beating a grand procession. I gaze up, gawking at their happy soaring city. I watch until they all pass beyond my sight line.

Where is Jessica? I am sorry I didn't get to watch the birds with her, but maybe we could go on a long walk into the forest, and I will say all the silly things that make her laugh. I walk around outside, not seeing anyone. At last, however, I see the Marthas in the distance. They stand in the back of the house with their washtubs and clotheslines. Baby Charlotte plays with her teacups and doll on a blanket near where they both scrub.

"Hullo! Marthas!" I call to them in a glad voice, waving my arms. "Hullo, Baby Charlotte!"

They don't return my greetings. Surely they must not see me yet.

I call again, but they remain unmoved. They talk to each other in quick hushed tones that stop when I get close. Baby Charlotte at least knows how to greet a friend, pulling herself up and running to grab my leg in a hug.

"I know you can talk," I say to her, crouching down. "Or at least make some sounds. Come on, now. Say hello. Now try it . . . hello." I elongate each of the sounds.

"Welo." She is eager to please me. "Well-oh."

"Very good. How clever you are!"

The Marthas still haven't acknowledged me. The water in the basin is pink, the sheets stained with rust-brown blood, though their hands move hard and fast across the washboard.

"It's beautiful weather today, isn't it?" I say to their backs. "The oaks out front are changing into the most beautiful shade of gold."

Young Martha's head twists as she gives her mother a sideways look and then turns back down. Maybe they just don't feel like talking.

"Where is everyone?" I ask.

Still nothing.

"What is going on here? Why are you not looking at me?" Being raised Quaker, I have no problem with the silent treatment, as long as I know why I'm getting it.

"Mr. Greeley is back in the city, doing his job," Martha replies, still focused on her work. "The others are somewhere about, I don't know. We're not their keepers. Do you need something? We are busy doing the laundry, which is hard backed up from yesterday. Plus a new guest, and prep for the ones we're to have this weekend. We've much to do this morning."

Martha scrub scrub scrubs.

"Well, has there been any change in Mrs. Greeley's condition?"

Martha's hands stop for a second. Her daughter looks at her and then quickly looks back to her own bucket.

"Wouldn't know about that, Miss Howe. We were hired to cook and do laundry, and we've enough with that. That's what we know, that's what we're here to do. That's it. No more attending to Mrs. Greeley. Temporarily, my daughter's to also be a nursemaid for Miss Charlotte, at least until Her Majesty brings someone else on with the proper training for that position."

"Her Majesty? You mean Mrs. Greeley?" I don't think I need to mention that she is in no condition to be bringing someone else on.

"Miss Elliot is taking charge of the household until Mrs. Greeley is better." Martha drops the sheet she scrubs and stands to face me, wiping her hands on her apron. "So Mr. Greeley has informed us. Miss Elliot may hire and fire 'at her discretion,' so he says. And so she herself has begun commanding us about what we are here to do and what we are not here to do, if we don't wish to be sacked."

"Hewwo! Hewwo!" Baby Charlotte tugs on my skirt.

"Hello, hello!" I coo back to her. "Listen to you! Very good!"

I suppose it makes sense. A household must be run. Jessica is the type to step in; she seems efficient at all matters of organization. Probably due to her being British.

"And she herself pulled up all high and mighty and said we aren't to be too familiar with any of Mr. Greeley's guests, including you."

"Hewwo, hewwo." Baby Charlotte pulls on my hand, all smiles, raising her arms for me to pick her up. I don't dare.

"I didn't ask Miss Elliot to do that, believe me." I suppose Jessica is taking it upon herself to make sure I am not conscripted into nurse-maiding again.

"HEWWO!" Baby Charlotte yells, and Young Martha abandons her laundry to scoop her up. She bounces her like an infant, shushing her as she carries her away from me as quickly as if she were beating an escape from a bear.

"I will talk to Miss Elliot because she doesn't understand that you all are my friends—"

"Don't you dare," Martha says, with so much venom I think I accidentally insulted her. "Don't you let our names into your mouth or out of it. You don't know how much trouble you've already gotten us into, waltzing in from the city, flapping your jaw, contradicting one doctor and talking about poison with the other, trying to blame us for the state Mrs. Greeley is in."

"No, my whole point was that it's the *doctor's* fault, not you—"

"You think if Mrs. Greeley dies, the doctor will take the blame? They'll blame us." Martha fixes me with a face like an iron shovel, hands on her hips. "Or you."

"Me?" I laugh before I can stop myself. It's just too ridiculous. Sure, I feel guilty about holding Mary's head, but that's to the credit of my character and certainly nothing to do with bearing any actual responsibility.

"Yes, you," she says to me with enough conviction to make a jury consider it. "I am not going to stick my neck out for you anymore. Prancing around in the night. Hiding behind doors, spying on people. I know the two of you are plotting something, doing devil knows what in the dark."

"The two of us?"

"Don't act innocent. I saw Miss Elliot coming from your room early this morning, smiling like a cat that ate the canary."

I feel my blood flush to my face, the back of my hand touches my chapped lips. I don't know what I am, but I know enough to know that whatever it is I am doing with Miss Elliot, I am not innocent.

"You may not be one of them," Martha says, returning to her washboard, plucking the cake of soap from the water and attacking the center of a large brown stain, "but you're not one of us."

Chapter 26

I am not sure how I got here. I don't recall walking back into the house, but I look down and see that my bare feet are on the pine plank floor of the kitchen. My mind feels separate from my body, disoriented and strange to myself. I want to start digging through crockery, conjure bread from the scent of scorched wheat—I am so hungry—but I don't dare mess through a kitchen where I am not welcome.

I stare at the dog bed where I slept the first night.

"Even the old dog ran away," Martha said.

(You should run away, too.)

I pull the button from my pocket.

(Button eyes)

I press it between my fingers, hold it in my palm, worry it like a stone. It has a pleasing smoothness on the edges, a texture in the center I find calming as I search for . . . yes. I need to eat something. With a vague sense of looking for an icebox, I open a door to see a small wooden staircase. I have to duck to avoid hitting my head as I go up. It turns one way and then the other, then ends midstep at a brick wall.

A wall . . .

No door, no window. Stairs leading literally nowhere.

Well, I suppose I shouldn't be surprised at anything in this place.

Maybe it is a false wall. Maybe it hides the missing body of the peddler. Ha.

Chiding myself for taking strange steps in the first place, I turn back down, thinking I should start leaving rocks or breadcrumbs or something behind me—buttons, if I had a pocketful.

But I just have this one.

Where am I?

I have opened the door I thought led back to the kitchen and find I am in a different room entirely and not sure what room it is . . . Oh, I am somehow on the other side of the house, in the dining room, with its large table I have never seen anyone eating at, its piano I have never heard anyone play, and curtains that are as thick and pink as tongues.

"This house is eating me alive!"

Where is everyone?

Martha said Mr. Greeley was back in the city, which of course he is, because he can't work in this house, he can't stand to be inside it, nicknaming his own house Castle Doldrum or Doleful, both meaning pretty much the same thing—sorrowful, depressing, mournful.

I should run back outside as Mr. Greeley always does and just eat apples, forage in the woods, never to return to this place.

But I can't forget my mission, my list of things to do, and above it all are these new feelings that make no sense to me . . . Where is Jessica?

The Marthas said this house whispered to them, made sad sounds of the children they've lost. Or maybe they were just talking about wind in the trees. I can't remember exactly what they said. I remember Cathie that first morning singing to Baby Charlotte, and I find I am humming that stupid song about a *bunch of blue ribbons* and standing in the nursery. I don't remember walking myself in here, and I certainly don't have a reason to be in this room, staring at the bright patterned wallpaper—bluebirds on green vines with yellow carnivorous flowers, waiting for the right moment to snap close their petals.

I look out the window to see the Marthas still scrubbing out back, Baby Charlotte is on her blanket again playing with her teacups, one of them I know is chipped . . .

A whimper.

Coming from behind me, I hear a starved little cry. I turn around from the window to see that there is an *infant* in the cradle. Oh, God. I have no food in my stomach, but bile hits the back of my throat.

Someone has left an infant in here and told no one.

How long has she been in here, neglected? Mary must not have miscarried, and in the crisis of her condition, everyone forgot this little one. I push back the yellow-brown lace that covers the cradle.

A baby, with eyes as black as mourning buttons.

I did not like her eyes.

I feel my chest heave with sorrow for her.

You couldn't take care of us both.

She hasn't been touched or held or fed; she can't even cry anymore, she's so hungry. My arms reach out to pick her up and hold her to me. She weighs nothing, nothing at all. I start to sing to her, trying to comfort her, a song I've never heard before but in a dream:

Poor little baby with her black button eyes, poor little button—

It plinks on the floor near my feet. I have dropped it.

Dazed . . . I am standing alone in the nursery before an empty cradle, holding my arms around myself, rocking back and forth on my bare feet. I hold nothing. There is nothing in the cradle. I bend down and pick up the button. I feel guilty and frightened in catching myself in the act of seeing things that are not there.

Hearing things, too. Voices I think I recognize.

I leave the nursery, following the sound.

But I walk slowly, wondering how much more my mind can take of Castle Dreadful.

~

The voices are coming from Mary's room. I put my ear to the door and can make out only some of the words.

"Many people . . . die if food is improperly . . . pneumonia, even . . . get water in the lungs . . ." It's Dr. Vincent. I can't hear another voice, but I have a fear and certainty that it is Jessica he's speaking to. Perhaps it is the cadence of what I can hear of his voice that reminds me of how he spoke to her during the demonstration.

There is a moment of silence. No one is speaking. In my mind's eye, I see the two of them together, hands intertwined, gazes locked—magnetized. I cannot bear the thought. I could knock, and decorum dictates I should, but instead I open the door without warning to discover what is behind it. Jessica and Dr. Vincent stand too close together, even as they move rapidly apart.

"Good news, Miss Howe," Jessica says with a perky formality that does nothing to ease my suspicions. She speaks to me as if she was not in my bed last night, as if I were familiar to her but not beloved. "The Vincent-ivizer has worked, and Mrs. Greeley is much better this morning." It is a mask of innocence, as if she had been standing across the room with the door wide open. Yet she knows she was in a room with a man, behind a closed door. Highly improper.

Mary Greeley doesn't look much better from where I am standing. She is still unconscious, lying prone on her bed with that wire hat—the Mind-Stimulator—attached to her head.

"Where's Cathie?" I ask, refraining from pointing out that Jessica is supposed to be giving instructions to her pupil, not fawning over whatever Dr. Vincent might be expostulating about with his nonspecific European accent and magnetic hands.

"She is taking an exam in our classroom. It's been a very busy morning."

This supposed classroom is a room I haven't seen before, but then again, it seems the rooms grow tumors of other rooms off them. I still don't know the full layout of this house, which even now is changing again beneath my feet. Where has Dr. Vincent been sleeping?

"As I was saying to Miss Elliot," he says, "my machine and I are needed in the city, but for now, it has exceeded my expectations, working on someone unconscious. This is why large-scale manufacture is needed." Dr. Vincent begins to remove the Mind-Stimulator. "Miss Elliot will be tending to the patient until I can return."

"You will help me, won't you, Edith?" she asks. "We need to sit Mary up and try and get some sugar water in her, and be careful to help her to drink it properly. Maybe if she keeps getting better, she could take some gruel. We'll have more help arriving soon, but for today, if you could help me manage."

Their hands touch as she helps him, lifting Mary Greeley's head so he can remove the part of the device that rests on the back of the neck, his hand large enough to cover hers, her hand beneath his like a concealed dove in a magic trick.

"Edith, are you all right?" she asks.

"Of course." My fingers are clutching the doorframe. Tightly.

"You slept half the day, and you look a little feverish. We can't have you getting sick, too." She moves away from him to put a hand to my forehead.

"I haven't eaten," I say.

"She refused food last night," Dr. Vincent says. "She wouldn't even have a taste of a most delicious dish that I offered her."

"Edith, why didn't you eat?"

"She suffers from migraines, an inversion of hysteria, which can kill the appetite."

"Yes, she was laid out the other day."

"I feel fine, I feel very well," I say. They are talking about me as if I am not here, as if they share something in their knowledge of me, which neither of them do—certainly not him. I hate the way they look at each other. "I just need to find a Graham biscuit or something somewhere to eat in this house." I try to pull her attention back to me.

"Of course you do. Let me go get that cook, always putting her nose in everything else and never actually doing any cooking when that's the one thing we actually need her to do . . . Edith, where are your shoes?"

"I am not wearing any."

"I can see that. Why not?"

"I did not put them on." I suppose this is not the answer she is looking for, flouncing past me in her skirts to yell at Martha and giving me a look I wish I knew how to read. I can't tell whether she's annoyed, amused, or concerned for me. She has left so quickly, leaving me alone with Dr. Vincent.

Strike that. Not alone.

Mary is here.

It is an unromantic business of disassembling the machine compared to the theatrics of its unveiling. Dr. Vincent remains silent as he unhooks the Mind-Stimulator, recoils the cord, detaches the circular spinning dial, and places it piece into piece, folding things I didn't realize could fold, until it is all neatly fitted together like a puzzle box.

"Mrs. Greeley is better?" I ask.

"A wonderful result that justified my missing this morning's exhibition. Though I must return now to the city. I will be back to work with Miss Fox. I have received an invitation to see her demonstrate her skills at Sunday's séance. Despite what I said last night, my curiosity is piqued to see what her spirits will perform for the coloratura, Jenny Lind." He is nervous, yammering. Very unlike the confident showman. Something was going on in here when I barged in.

I find myself standing over Mrs. Greeley, looking down at her face, her body. This is what "better" looks like? Her eyes do move behind her eyelids, her breath coming in a little faster. I see her swallow. It may be that the double dose Dr. Bug gave her is finally starting to wear off and it's nothing that the machine has done, but I don't need to keep Dr. Vincent here any longer with my skepticism. I am very pleased that he is leaving.

My foot touches something that makes me jump back, feeling like I've stepped on a worm. It's a leech, which must have gotten its fill of Mary's blood and fallen off some time ago. I move my foot quickly and bend over to examine it. Dark brown and ribbed, a truly frightening creature, a leech. It doesn't move, and seems rather, well, *crisp* for a healthy blood-sucking wee beast. I poke it with my forefinger.

There's nothing to fear, it's quite dead.

What is *that*, though? As I'm crouched down, I see that there's a vial carefully tucked in the corner against the wall beneath the bed.

I take it out to inspect it. *Tincture of rhubarb.* Less than half full. I remember Mary saying it helped her. "A superb tonic for the stomach," the label boasts.

Dr. Vincent has pulled it out of my hands before I can protest.

"I'll have this tested in the city."

"Tested? For what?"

"Just to see if what is inside is indeed as labeled. Druggists often have the lazy habit of putting different medicines in old vials. Or perhaps a careless maid, or crafty one, putting some of the prescribed medicine Mrs. Greeley refused to take in a more benign bottle." He is whispering to me, ducking his head close to mine. "A maid, a governess, even a child would have the means to do it."

"What are you suggesting?"

"No more than I said, but better to know more," he says musically, popping the vial into his pocket.

"Did you take all of the tinctures to be tested?" I now notice that *all* the vials and medicines that were in this room have disappeared.

"Means before motive," he says. "Poison is the preferred method used by women."

"And doctors," I add. How dare he. Sowing suspicions anywhere they might take root, just like Dr. Bug. All alike, these doctors.

"I do think Mrs. Greeley will recover," he says, picking up his machine to depart this room like an empty theater. "But wouldn't it be quite a coincidence for a young reporter to have such a front-row seat to a high-profile murder?"

It leads me to ponder what Mr. Greeley said when he sent me to collect Dr. Vincent.

There are no coincidences.

Chapter 27

No possum face here—just delicious apple pie. I didn't even realize just how hungry I was. I feel like my old self, now that I am getting some good food in my belly. A warm kitchen, with Jessica seated beside me, and I would swear this pie is even better than it was the first day I had it. I eat with such gusto that Jessica calls me a farmhand.

"I have worked as a farmhand," I say. A half-truth, as it was more a contest between me and Frank Jackson, who told me I was not as strong as I thought I was. I knew it was a trick to get me to help him bale hay.

"You need to have more than pie for breakfast. Do tell the cook what else you'd like."

"Yes, miss. What else d'you fancy?" Martha asks, speaking to me like we have never met.

"I'm not sure. This is great for now."

"Now or later, you just let me know. I'll be in here, baking up a storm, preparing for the guests this weekend." Despite how she treated me outside, her tone is pleasant and accommodating now.

"No need for that. We'll have other cooks for the weekend," Jessica says over her shoulder. "You have no experience cooking the sorts of food Miss Lind will be expecting. But the doctor has asked you to prepare a mixture of one part sugar to four parts water for Mrs. Greeley. And perhaps some gruel, depending on how she takes the water. Now, do offer Miss Howe something more to eat than a three-day-old pie."

"It's even better on the third day," I say, "and so delicious I'd be happy eating it every day for every meal."

"The lady doth protest too much," Jessica says.

"I can make whatever you like, Miss Howe," Martha says, sweet as sugar water. "How about some pancakes? We just got in good flour for that, and fresh buttermilk."

"What did Cathie eat this morning?" I ask her. I certainly don't want Martha to go to any extra trouble, but I could easily put eating a pancake on my list of goals.

"She wanted the pie, is all."

"She was very taciturn this morning," Jessica says to me. "You eat your fill and then some, Miss Howe. I am going to check on Cathie's progress with her exam."

Jessica exits, and I wait to hear a huff, a side comment, or a mutter under her breath from Martha. Some evidence of her frustration and anger at me and the situation of being ordered about by Jessica. *Whatever the two of us are plotting.* But she gives nary a snort, nor a clatter of a pan. She merely continues her work. She goes about the business of the kitchen as I make mine the finishing of this piece of pie.

"Would you like me to make you a nice hot pancake, Miss Howe?" she asks without malice, so there's no reason to fear her pouring a *nice hot* dose of arsenic in it.

"Yes, thank you, Martha," I say. I'm not one of them; the proof in the pudding is in simply sitting here and waiting to be served.

~

Jessica and I parade about Castle Doldrum arm in arm, like we own it. I have her all to myself for the moment. Mr. Greeley has returned to the Rookery, Dr. Vincent has ridden away in his carriage with his precious machine, Cathie is finishing her exam, and the Marthas are elsewhere, working.

Jessica is in charge of organizing the house for the séance, treating it as if she were planning a royal ball. Everything I noticed about the Greeley estate's sparse decor she sees as a personal affront to "Horace" himself.

"I am not suggesting it has to be Buckingham Palace," she says, "but this is the editor of the *New-York Daily Tribune*. Might he be allowed a landscape painting to draw the eye instead of a blank wall the color of last century?"

As an Ohio girl who has spent most of her life on farms, I definitely feel out of character when she consults my opinion on whether to feature Swedish food or typical American fare. Would it be a crime to serve both?

"You will try and dress the part," she tells me.

"I promise to wear shoes," I say, still barefoot at the present.

"Do you have something more . . ." She plucks the shoulder of my dress.

"Hmm, let me think . . ." I tease her, knowing I do have something she will prefer.

We race up the stairs, much like schoolchildren on a holiday. We don't even glance at the attic door, running past it into the special room where I sleep.

I close the door behind us as she throws herself onto the bed where I drowned in her presence last night.

I feel dizzy, remembering.

She laughs at me.

"What?"

"Edith, the way you look at me—"

"Yes?"

"Just be careful who sees you looking at me like that." Jessica sits up and pushes a hair back away from my face and smiles at me in such a way that I realize what I have been missing all my life up until now: her. I can't put my feelings into context. The only time I have heard of a woman being in love with another woman is in Shakespeare plays, and that's only when one is disguised as a man. The infatuation ends at the moment of discovery. Yet we both know what the other is, and here we are, in afternoon light with unspoken sonnets between us.

"I don't know how to hide how I look at you," I manage to say.

"Then you must learn," she says. "We must bind our feelings when we dress in the morning, as tight as we can take it, and then at night, in our beds, we may loosen as we like into each other. To display such feelings on your face is worse than a whore's rouge, to paint yourself in disgrace and dishonor. You do understand that, don't you?"

I know it from the tenacity with which everyone has always wished me to marry, and from silences and the unmentionables of women's affections for each other. The possibility of my loving a woman instead of a man is too shocking to even bear considering.

"Come on now, what do you have to show me?"

I open my trunk, letting her peek at the silk sleeve of the gown Lady Jane insisted I pack.

"Why have you been hiding this?" she gasps, pulling it out to reveal the blue-and-gray plaid with meticulous lace trim around the collar and pagoda sleeves. "It's beautiful!"

Lady Jane presented it to me like a graduation present. I had progressed from working in trousers and bare feet to the brown cotton professional dress I wear most days as I assist her. This gown, however, has signified I am now acceptable to accompany her to Washington parties and formal functions. I can't say I find it beautiful, though it astonishes me that my Lady Jane's hands sewed every stitch.

I admit that when I put it on, it does change the way I feel. The gown is a costume, a disguise in which I am better able to blend into a world where I need to do battle. In that way, it is like armor and probably about as comfortable. Along with the gown, I must wear a corset (of course), a crinoline, plus four petticoats. It also has a matching bonnet, which, in the latest style of our time, ensures I have no peripheral vision and thus must keep my eyes looking forward on the path ahead, much like a horse. As Jessica sighs over the stitching of the dress, I repack my trunk, and the sight of Frederick Douglass's autobiography snaps me back to reality with a sudden urgency.

"I have to get to the Broadway Tabernacle Church tomorrow," I tell her. "Frederick Douglass is speaking and I must see him. If I have to walk, I'll walk, but I will not miss the opportunity to hear him speak in person."

"You should wear this gown, Edith. And why don't you take Cathie? It will be an educational trip."

I cannot contain my enthusiasm for her brilliance. Two things from my agenda will be accomplished with the same trip. Nothing could radicalize Cathie the way that Frederick Douglass will. I kiss Jessica's cheek. Very European of me.

"And you most certainly will not walk," she says. "You will take a carriage, and as it is educational, it will be funded by the Greeley purse. I will be training new staff, and there will be furnishings coming in to get this place suitable to host someone with the stature of Jenny Lind, so it will be good to have you both out of my hair for the day." She puts her fingers into my hair when she says the word, and tugs a few strands, drawing my face close to hers.

Downstairs, a door slams itself shut.

Jessica moves away from me as if chastened.

"We'd better go and feed Mary."

Chapter 28

Mary's door is wide open. I didn't touch it, and Jessica says it was closed when she walked past it to get the sugar water from the kitchen. It wouldn't matter so much if Mary weren't twisted in the bed, head turned, hair falling across her face, arm dangling off the side. It's a disturbing sight. She looks ready to fall from the bed onto the floor.

"Oh, well, the door must have opened itself," Jessica says. "They do that in this house."

"They do?"

"Yes, and slam themselves shut, too. Haven't you noticed?"

I have noticed that many hang badly from their frames. The windows are drafty. So her door may have been shut, but not tightly, though I balk at giving my logical explanations. Whatever this house is, it is not logical.

Regardless of the open door, that Mary's body has changed position is some sort of sign. If she moved herself, it is progress. If someone else moved her . . .

No one else should have been in here.

The Marthas are outside. Cathie is in some classroom taking an exam. No one else is here.

No one living, anyway.

"Let's get her flat on her back," Jessica says, entering the room and placing the bowl on a small table. "You move her head, I'll move her legs."

Drool has spooled out of Mary's mouth and into her hair, her jaw slack. Her clammy skin, half-peeled lids, and saliva-soaked chin remind me of my mother at the asylum. Though I suppose my mother was more awake than this. Not much more.

We reposition her to the center of the bed.

Mary's eyes open for a moment, staring up at the ceiling.

Jessica grabs my arm.

"Mrs. Greeley?" I say.

Her pupils are wide and unseeing, and I wonder whether she's dead . . . But then I hear her breath come in, fast. She closes her eyes.

Even being in Jessica's presence, I hate helping with the task of feeding Mary, and I do a poor job of it. My eyes keep darting to the foot of the bed, as I wonder whether a little spirit stands there, watching.

~

The crack in the wall is substantial. It moves from the floor upward and branches out to either side of the parlor. In the lamplight and chaos of last night, I wasn't certain of the seriousness of its intentions. Today it is clear to me that this split is the sort that means life-threatening structural damage to the foundation, or at the very least, a house-hewing rift. It seems to me impossible at this moment, as Cathie and Jessica discuss the possibility of holding the séance in this room, that they do not note it. I want to point it out because it seems to be growing even as I look at it, but Cathie has already moved on. It is not the right room for the séance. And I keep my concern at the fissure to myself, for this house belongs to none of us.

Jessica awaits Cathie's directions. This twist of their roles is something I have not yet witnessed, and I find myself by turns amused and bewildered. We walk from room to room as they discuss which will be the most "inviting" for the spirits. Now that Cathie is here, Jessica keeps a measured distance from me, addressing me in a formal manner.

I try not to look at her *like that*, but it's difficult when I catch a furtive glance *like that* at me.

Cathie gives orders like a little princess familiar with dictating the terms of her comfort: The spirits prefer darkened rooms with drawn curtains. Those wishing to contact them should be able to sit comfortably around a table where their hands can be placed visibly on the surface, linked together in a circle. The spirits require that the chairs be arranged so that everyone can see everyone else, so that no one has reason to doubt that it is a genuine spirit making their presence known.

She makes the demands using words and phrases that indicate she is practiced in séances, particular in how she speaks. "Our silence is what allows the spirits to best be heard, the darkness is what best allows them to show their light."

The living room holds a table big enough to seat six comfortably and also a piano that seems to have never been dusted. I touch a key that makes a sour note. Never been dusted or tuned.

"Will this be a hospitable space for the spirits?" Jessica asks, with more deference than I have heard her offer anyone. She draws the curtains and creates a crepuscular atmosphere with no more than removing a sash and lowering her voice.

"The table is suitable," Cathie says. "And the spirits often appreciate a piano. Perhaps they will play."

"I hope they will tune it first." I sit on the bench and bang on a few keys together in disharmony.

Cathie moves to the center of the room, closes her eyes, drops her head forward, and . . .Well, I have no idea what she is doing. The quiet of the room reveals that there is no such thing as silence, for every small sound becomes amplified by the acoustics. The rustle of Jessica's skirt. The soft movement of my feet. Cathie's sharp breaths.

Enough time passes that my foot starts to go to sleep.

One knock—it seems to come from the table—becomes two, and the two become three.

"It's the other Greeley children from Summerland," Cathie whispers. "Pickie watches over his mother, but the others . . . They are here now. Miss Elliot, please greet them."

"Hello, children." Jessica's eyes are closed, her hands lift as if to welcome them. She is playing a part in this summoning.

The knocks pop about the room as if from every surface. I feel one coming from the bench where I sit, from the floor where my foot rests. My leg jumps as if I'd put it to a fire.

"This is your house," Cathie intones. "These rooms are your rooms. We would not invite in other spirits without your blessing. Each of you, please bless the proceedings with one knock—or your silence is your protest."

One, two, three clear and distinct knocks.

"Thank you," Cathie says. "Come, play."

Three little children run around the room, tapping all the surfaces. No, I don't actually see them. I don't see their little fists hitting the table, clattering the windowpanes. It is only imagination, my eyes trying to see in the shadows what makes the sounds.

And still the knocks persist, rhythms stopping and starting with loud beats, like children drumming on pots and pans. I can almost hear them laughing.

I want it to stop.

I wrap one of my hands in the other. I close my eyes and think about what I don't believe in.

I do not touch the piano, but behind me, the keys play.

I stand up to move and trip over myself, falling to the floor.

"Miss Howe?" Cathie claps her hands, releasing her pose and, I suppose, her spirit invocation. "Are you all right, Miss Howe?"

"Oh, yes, yes," I say, but those little children still seem to peek at me from the corners of the room. I am damp with sweat. "I was just trying to give the spirits better access to the piano."

Jessica hastens back to the window, opening the curtains, late-afternoon light revealing no children, of course. No little dead Greeley children are here.

I don't know what my expression is, but Cathie starts to laugh and Jessica joins her. My fear is apparently hilarious to them both, or maybe it is just the position in which I am sprawled on the floor. I get up and slip again on purpose, which makes them laugh even more.

Jessica gives me a hand and pulls me up, in which I take full advantage to turn into an embrace. Cathie comes and joins, and we all hug. I've made them laugh and forget for a moment about the ghosts of children, séances, and spirit-rappings. Jessica suggests that the rest of today's lessons happen with a picnic, and Cathie and I cheer.

Whatever is dead or dying inside this house, it is a beautiful day outside.

~

We are running, Cathie and I. It's a race! My bare feet glide across the grass. I could easily catch her, but I am allowing her to win. I gain on her, then I slow to let her fly ahead. It is flying, this unbridled running. Flying flying flying . . . I put out my arms like wings, and then she does, too. Two birds circling about, chirping calls to each other. Such a beautiful day to be wild and free.

Jessica lies on the blanket, staring up at the sky.

"I am going to catch you, Cathie!" I call out.

Shrieking, laughing, she's running faster, but I let myself enjoy the sensation of the earth beneath my feet. On a day like today, it's easy to believe in animal magnetism, to believe in Summerland, to believe that I've had many previous lives, and in all of them I have loved Jessica.

On a day like today, I believe spirits talk with a "Knock knock" and "Who's there?"

"It's you, Cathie, you're the turn of a knock-knock joke!" That makes Cathie laugh so hard she gives herself the hiccups. I tell her you can outrun the hiccups, but she doesn't believe me, so now I am proving it to her.

We are running through the orchards, and my feet are flying, but I will let her win, and everything is wonderful on this glorious day.

We run but then Cathie stops. We are somewhere I have not yet been. Four little graves, four *"beds out back,"* as Martha said that first morning. Cathie's hands run along each of the headstones.

"Touch the stones, Miss Howe," she says.

I will not, for I know if I do, the children will show me their faces the next time I dream.

"Mrs. Greeley said she will never let me go. You heard her. You were there." Cathie crouches down to trace Arthur's name.

"But, Cathie, she may die," I say, shocked that I offered it as some consolation without thinking. "Which would be a terrible thing, of course. But my point is, we don't know what will happen. You are not a prisoner, regardless. She cannot keep you here if you want to go."

"Perhaps Miss Lind will be so impressed with me, she will want to take me away with her."

It is possible. If she could make herself as indispensable to Miss Lind, somehow, as she's been to Mrs. Greeley. "But I thought you wanted to go home."

She turns away from me, gazes out at the open field before us.

"You will impress the Nightingale," I say to ease her mind. "Of this, I have no doubt. And also . . . Tag, you're it!" I poke her on the shoulder and run away from her.

She can't stay here in this little graveyard, contemplating how she'll survive, because she's "it" now and has to tag me. I run, and she follows, but I let her catch up to me.

"Tag! You're it!" she cheers, and I am chasing her now, running past the graves without stopping.

Yes, there are the dead, but I am not one of them! I am not there, in that grave, but out here to be fully alive in this . . .

This day!

Happy, because why ever be sad if Summerland is real? But today is even more perfect than Summerland, because it is the first real day of fall, and because it is the first real day of my life.

I don't know what it will be, the future—me and Jessica. Something has changed in me as fundamental as a new heart growing in my chest, and I run past graves, chasing a child who knocks for spirits, believing anything is possible, even if just for this moment. This is what it is, and only those who believe in it can know.

What it is to be in love.

Chapter 29

"Camptown races sing this song, doo-dah, doo-dah . . ."

As we ride this carriage into the city to hear Frederick Douglass speak, Cathie is acting silly and excitable, singing as if we were going to a hayride at harvest time. All my efforts to educate her about the importance of abolition and the current political situation are met with instantaneous agreement but no gravity. She says she knows Frederick Douglass, but when I try to convey how serious a person he is, and what an honor it is to be in his presence, she simply agrees. She has never read *Narrative of the Life of Frederick Douglass, An American Slave*, written by himself. Nor his newspaper, *The North Star*.

"Well, then, how can you say you know him?" I ask.

"He and I are friends," she says.

Of all the stupendous claims from Cathie Fox, from spirit-rapping to Summerland, this is the one I find the least credible. Cathie may be the biggest fibber outside Washington, DC.

The Broadway Tabernacle Church rises above all buildings that surround it and the city itself like the crown atop a queen.

"This looks more like a castle than a church!" she says, stepping out of the carriage.

It's the most beautiful building I've ever seen. A church for reform and equality, like the Quaker meetinghouse but with no appreciation of Friends' simplicity. This structure is of such glamour and Gothic beauty that each spire, each sparkle of colored glass, builds to another even taller tower, drawing the eye higher and higher unto heaven, like the very ideas of freedom and justice.

We make our way inside with throngs of other people, hushed and humbled by the architecture. Giant columns hold up an expansive domed ceiling, wide as heaven itself. It resembles more the illustrations I've seen of a Roman coliseum than a house of worship, especially with the pulpit set in the center. I can't even estimate how many hundreds of us there are, finding seats amid concentric circular levels that rise higher and higher.

"I have never seen such a place." Cathie gawks at our surroundings, and I grab her hand and tell her we need to keep moving, find a seat. "It's not just a castle but a whole kingdom!"

I find it more comparable to a forest, filled with birds before a storm, so many skirts rustling and people chirping. Women carry elaborate plumage of colorful feathers in their enormous hats. How many sad wings and tails were plucked to butter the bacon of a lady's head? Happily, there are also my dour, plain Quaker Friends in attendance, with dull attire that takes up significantly less property. Cathie is the smallest and youngest person here. When people notice her, they give her space, but with all the wide skirts and large feathered hats, it is hard to see her, and as people press in, I worry she'll be crushed.

Outside, the weather is brisk, but inside it's stuffy and already growing warm. Often in crowds like these, women are seated in the balcony, while the men are below, but here we are mixed together. As festive as we all appear, it is truly not the mood in the room. There's a rolling sort of feeling among us, each of us a drop in water being slowly heated, nearing a point where we all will boil.

We need inspiration. We need direction.

We feel powerless, helpless, and need our leaders to show us where to go. The scent of men challenged in their courage and the smell of women desperate in their purpose clog my nose, and I find myself sneezing four times without a handkerchief.

A trembling little man with kind, watery eyes offers me his. He has white whiskers on his hands. I accept his offer and blow a very unladylike amount of phlegm into it.

"Do keep it," he says when I try to hand it back.

"Can you see?" I ask Cathie as we push our way into a spot with a view to the center of the round. One would think the ladies would remove their hats, but it appears they are affixed to their heads for eternity.

"I can see better if I stand," she says. All the mirth Cathie and I had on the journey here has dissipated into a sweat of impatience.

The atmosphere of this room is acrid with disappointment—of complicity in the crimes of our country. Here, we are all the same choir awaiting our preacher, but we know we need a radical shift in song. We buzz with a shared sense of knowing. We had thought that progress, though slow and steady, had been happening. We had trusted that all our busywork was making a difference. We know better now.

Those whose famed escapes to freedom have been so hard fought and won—through miraculous feats of physical endurance, such as Henry Box Brown, who managed to fold, conceal, and have himself shipped to safety. Or ingenuity, such as Ellen and William Craft, Ellen pretending to be a white man traveling with her "slave," actually her husband. They are now, at this exact moment, on the run again. Everyone knows someone who is at risk or who has already disappeared.

We, too, may be shackled and imprisoned, should we help others hide or escape. Yet here we are, men and women holding fast to our sense of moral necessity, our fear and frustration rolling off each other as William Lloyd Garrison takes to the pulpit. The sermon begins.

"We may be personally defeated, but our principles—never!"

We respond with a hero's welcome.

"There must be no compromise with slavery. None whatsoever!" It is my first time seeing Garrison in person, and it thrills me as he begins his oratory. What he lacks in stature, he makes up for in vocabulary, using twelve words for every necessary two about how we must not relent, must use moral persuasion as our tactics, and never give an inch.

I find myself wondering, what does it mean to not give an inch, when you have been kidnapped and dragged thousands of miles?

I begin to lose focus as he continues speaking. My mind turns back and forward upon itself. Everything has changed for me. I cannot even look back a week but to feel I was a different person then as now. Who I am, what my future will be, everything now needs to include Jessica. No thought begins or ends without the memory of her hand touching mine, her crooked tooth visible only when she laughs with abandon and forgets to cover her mouth . . . What is it to be free if I am not free to be with her?

Garrison is still talking, words that become sentences that become phrases, inviting applause at the end of them.

"My singularity is that when I say that freedom is of God and slavery is of the devil, I mean just what I say. My fanaticism is that I insist on the American people abolishing slavery or ceasing to prate on the rights of man."

He continues to give space for cheers, but the responses are now half-hearted.

Has it been five minutes or ten that he has been talking? Isn't he here to introduce the main event, Mr. Douglass? He just keeps going on as if he will conjure Douglass through the power of churning each word. It is ten minutes, then twenty, then forever. There is no doubt of Garrison's commitment, but we are not the same people we were when he began this tour, before the passing of the Compromise. We are beyond words at this point. What is it that we must *do*?

"Douglass!" some man has the temerity to shout in one of the pauses meant for Garrison's applause.

Garrison ignores it, continuing on.

"Douglass!" the voice rings out again, this time when Garrison is midsentence. Then another voice joins the first. Then another. Until it becomes a chant.

"Douglass! Douglass! Douglass!" His very name rouses us from our seats. With our standing ovation to Douglass, who is not yet here, Garrison finally concedes an early exit. We cheer and chant and wait for our demands to be met.

At last, he appears. An imperious figure of a man who towers over everyone in the room, both physically and spiritually. We are wild at his manifestation. The presence of Frederick Douglass fills the hall with the power of a prophet, and I tremble, humbled to my very core.

He lifts his hands, and we all hush.

"I want to thank my friend Mr. Garrison for his ideals, dedication, and work toward this cause. But he cannot speak as I can, from experience. He cannot refer you to a back covered with scars, as I can. He has never felt the blood that has sprung out as the lash embedded in my flesh."

We are silenced. Like Christ's passion, his body has borne the sins of this nation.

He is here, resurrected, to show us our damnation. Will he also show us the path to our redemption?

"The blood of the slave is on the skirts of the Northern people."

The pride with which I dressed the part of a lady this morning returns to me in shame. The blood is not just a metaphor for our continuing to do our daily business as usual, or in our dough-faced representatives who wheedle and concede. The actual skirts and petticoats we wear are made of cotton, the blood crop of the South. The sound of rustling, a constant wherever women are present, is as still as I have ever heard. We have been turned to stone.

"If I speak harshly, my excuse is that I speak in fetters of your own forging. Remember that oppression has the power to make even a wise man mad. Our fault here today will not be that we pleaded the case of the slave too vehemently, but with unnatural calmness and composure."

I remember how I wrote my editorial, fingers pressed upon my quill, weighing each word on the subject as if morality were a mathematical proof. But there is no morality where violence is used to balance the equation. Composure is the luxury of the complicit. It is our duty to be angry. *"It is a sin to be polite in times like these."*

"This Compromise reveals with great clearness the extent to which slavery has shot its leprous distillment through the lifeblood of the nation. What mean ye that ye bruise and bind my people? Will justice sleep forever?"

At this, a woman's voice behind me cries out in pain, "Awake!"

"Repent of this wickedness!"

"I repent!" a man's voice. Then a woman's. Then everyone.

I am speaking in tongues, but only two words. Hot tears baptize my face.

"I repent! I repent!" We all cry for mercy.

"Repentance is not submission, it is action. Just this past week in Boston, Southern bounty hunters arrived, expecting the full support of the law, and were met with a surprise. Crowds of people surrounded them with shouts, taunts, and threats, and hunted them. People of all walks of life in that freedom-loving city, the birthplace of the American Revolution, shouting, 'We the people! We will not give up our friends, our neighbors, to tyranny! We the people are created equal!'" Douglass gives us something to root for, to cheer for.

And so we cheer loudly.

"This is what has happened in Boston. What will happen here in New York? Will you be patient with tyranny?"

"No!" I thump the floor with my feet.

"Will you be diplomatic?"

"No!" I am a spirit, demanding to be heard, in a temple full of avenging angels thundering together. "No, no!"

"We the people!" he calls.

"We the people!" we respond.

"We the people are created equal!" he finishes.

"We the people are created equal!" we echo back in one voice.

"We the people! We the people! We the people are created equal!" We chant as a chorus, again and again, until he raises his hands, pressing us down into silence so that he may finish his sermon.

"Slavery must be attacked in its stronghold, or the sun of this guilty nation must go down in blood."

A cry of assent bursts forth from the congregation, but a voice in my head overpowers even the voice of the prophet with a quiet certainty:

It will be so, it will be so.

A vision grips me. Blood rising like a wave, covering fields upon fields. Fires burning, everything consumed in angry conflagration. It is coming, it will be so, it cannot be otherwise, for blood will have blood, fire will have fire, and I cannot stop it, I cannot . . . breathe.

I can't get my breath, my corset is too tight, I bow my head and grip the pew ahead to keep from fainting.

Don't think of blood, don't think of fire—

Think of her.

Soft and powerful as an angel, the love I share with Jessica shields me, breathes for me.

I will not faint. With her love as my guiding star, I raise my head again. I shall face that which must come.

But it is coming . . . waves of blood enough to drown us all.

Douglass thanks all of us for coming before stepping off the stage.

People begin to move out of their seats.

"We are all in this together!" says the little man who gave me his handkerchief, shaking my hand.

"We are!" I agree, though some of us are more in it than others. Everyone is now trying to exit. I reach out to grab Cathie's hand, but she is gone. I look to my left, to my right. No sign of her.

I don't know when she disappeared.

"Have you seen a little girl?" I ask people all around me. "She was just here."

They stare at me with no help to offer.

"Cathie Fox!" I call out. "Cathie Fox, where are you?!"

Chapter 30

"If it's a fight they want, they'll get it!" a man says next to me.

"Yes, they will!" I reply. "We're ready!" As if this sixty-year-old man and I, a twenty-year-old woman who just nearly passed out because my corset is too tight, are ready to pick up the bayonets and run through the bounty hunters.

"Cathie!" I call out again, now feeling very desperate.

A basket for donations is shoved into my chest by a blue-feathered bonnet riding a pink, wrinkled face. "Support the cause!"

It's hard to hear anything amid the constant cries for organizing, advocacy, new bills to be proposed, or outright revolt. Feathers, skirts, trousers, hats, people pressing in on people as I cry out, "Has anyone seen a young girl? I am missing a young girl."

"Is that your missing child?" a woman asks, her voice hoarse from chanting and eyes red from crying. She points to the front of a processional line where devotees stack in hopes of handshakes and blessings from Mr. Douglass. Now, an astonishing sight. There is Cathie being held in a hug by the man himself. He lifts her up like she weighs nothing and puts her on his shoulders.

"Behold, the spirit-telegraph!" he booms, loud enough that I can hear from my position all the way at the back of the line. "And my dear friend, the famous Cathie Fox!"

I try to press my way forward through the gauntlet of bodies.

He is being led away, still harboring Cathie, but I'm able to use her as a beacon until they disappear behind a wall of stout men. I push and slide, maneuvering myself between hips and backs to make my way to the gatekeepers.

"I am here with Cathie Fox, I am her chaperone," I insist to one of the men, who ignores me. I try the same tactic with another man who blocks the people's access, but he is unmoved. "The young girl with Mr. Douglass, she is my charge. I am her chaperone, so I must find her, it's most urgent," I try with a third burly, bearded man, using all the I-am-so-helpless-please-help-me feminine wiles I ever saw another woman use. I even bat my eyes at him.

His jaw softens.

Good Lord, it's working. He pulls me past him and through a door into a small hallway. I am led outside an antechamber, left alone to wait.

"There's someone insisting that she belongs with the young girl," the man says, popping his head inside the room. "She says she is Miss Fox's chaperone."

"Oh, that's Miss Howe," I hear Cathie say. "She must be so worried. Let her in!"

I am granted admittance into a large echoing room with a mural of heaven on the ceiling. I hang toward the edge of the wall as Cathie twirls around, watching her skirts flare. They are talking about people I don't know. Amy and Isaac Post are the names I gather.

"Well, Amy just had her fiftieth-birthday party, but she wrote to me that it was not complete because I was absent," Cathie brags. "I wish I could have been there. I love visiting their house."

"Their home is one of the most comfortable places I know on Earth," Douglass says.

I am far too cowed to contribute anything, especially in a conversation where a spirit-telegraph and an abolitionist prophet are updating each other on mutual friends about whom I know nothing. I attempt to get a grip on my nerves. I find it helps to stare up toward the mural that begs the question: If a million angels fit on a pinhead, how many can fit on this twenty-foot ceiling?

Mr. Douglass tells Cathie about Isaac Post's recent experiments with something called "spirit-writing," where apparently Mr. Post has spoken to George Washington, Benjamin Franklin, and had a wonderful chat with Nat Turner.

Somehow, between the lines of their continued conversation, I start to piece together the puzzle of how Mr. Douglass and Cathie Fox know each other. They were introduced through this couple, the Posts, who are both instrumental "friends of the spirits." They have encouraged the Fox family communication with the great beyond from the outset, and are also a major hub of the Underground Railroad.

I am humbled. Cathie is part of a vital network of people who are on the front lines of the abolitionist movement, far more connected than I am. I have been thinking to influence Cathie in a direction where she has already landed and set up camp.

"Let us agree we can each have more than one best friend, but who is this friend you brought with you?" Douglass asks, pointing at me, and I realize I haven't even introduced myself.

"I am E. A. Howe, sir. I am a newspaper woman. You are my hero, sir. I do not have sufficient words to tell you how much I admire you." What a stupid way for me to introduce myself. At least I said it so quickly there's a good chance he couldn't make out the words.

"She came here to write about the Compromise, but now she's writing about me," Cathie informs him. "Apparently, Mr. Greeley thought her position against it was too radical to print."

"Is that so?" he asks, his leonine gaze so intense I have to look away.

"Yes, well, also he said it seemed that I was moralizing like a schoolgirl, which I know is an insult, but as an unknown journalist, I probably should have sent it to him with just my initials. Then he wouldn't have known I was a woman. Anyway, my first purpose at the estate is to convince him to have the *Tribune* come out strongly against the Compromise." Fifty words when I only needed one, which was *yes*.

Then I add insult to injury by somehow talking more.

"But he says he doesn't take advice from anyone except maybe Benjamin Franklin, who is, of course, dead. But then he said I could write about Cathie because she's a spirit-telegraph, and I've accepted that assignment. I guess I'm hoping that maybe something will happen so that the spirits influence him where I cannot."

Whew. I take a deep breath. I have a newfound compassion for William Lloyd Garrison using so many words when people want fewer.

"Perhaps the spirits can convince where morality, decency, and reason fail," Mr. Douglass says. "For too long, religion has served the hierarchy and oppression of the master. None are more cruel than those who feel emboldened by their God to rule. A new day is dawning. The spirit realm is here for each of us, to know the immortality and progression of our soul that refuses to be ruled by any master. The spirit realm is here, equally, for all. Is that not so, Miss Fox?" He smiles at his friend.

"Anyone can do it, who is willing to learn," she says.

Ben Franklin might as well have just handed me his kite and key, as a bolt of inspiration strikes me.

It's not that the idea of the spirit-telegraph delivering a message for equality hasn't occurred to me before—I thought to sneakily influence Cathie from the moment I accepted the task to write about her. It just didn't occur to me that the Fox family telegraph has been spelling out this message from the first moment, bringing in the help from a heaven we've all been praying for. Summerland, an afterlife of neither heaven nor hell, but a place where the spirit continues to learn and grow, is a radical concept. Anyone can access the spirit realm if they are willing to open their ears to hear the knocking. The message from heaven is clear, and it's the same one we've been chanting: We the people are created equal.

The sense of absolute joy I feel makes me want to soar up to the ceiling and pinch that fat Cupid's cheek.

Of course the Posts encouraged the young Fox sisters to spread their knowledge. The tale of how they taught a spirit to communicate with the living moved faster than the wind. It was everywhere, almost immediately. Hearing the story was in and of itself a type of invitation to try it. Talking to spirits, as it turns out, is incredibly contagious. This world of people accustomed to countless wars fought for millennia over what happens after this life can hereby prove it for themselves. The messages one receives are not from some preacher, some church authority, or politician. They are what you believe they are, they mean what you make of them, and in that way, the messages of the spirits are the most genuine messages one can receive. Anyone can ask for it.

Knock and it shall be answered.

"About your editorial on the Compromise, Miss Howe," Mr. Douglass says to me. "I am certain *I* would not find it too radical. If you send it to me, I will consider it for my paper, which you may have heard of. It's called *The North Star.*"

"I am a subscriber." Also, I have probably actually died and gone to heaven. The only thing better than being published by the *Tribune* would be to be published by *The North Star.* Honestly, I never even considered it possible.

"If I publish it, I would like to use your full name so that people may know a woman wrote it."

"Right is of no sex, truth is of no color," I say, echoing the motto of his paper. I do not mention I have torn the editorial to shreds, which means I will need to rewrite it from scratch.

Garrison enters the antechamber, a compress around his neck. After complaining that his throat is sore, he tells Douglass it's time for them to travel back to the "safe house."

I feel so terrible, having joined the fray of people chanting Garrison offstage. He seems sad and sick. I want to tell him something about how much I appreciate all he does, but I am afraid of how lengthy my speech has become, and that I fear too much of a good thing in his reply. He should rest his voice.

I give him my best encouraging smile.

"I look forward to reading your editorial, Miss Howe," Douglass says. "And, Miss Fox, commend me to the spirits, for all the comfort and wisdom they give."

Any doubt I've ever had about the truth of the spirits has been erased. Suddenly, I can even understand Greeley's directive that I should pursue the spirit-telegraph with the same passion as I had for abolition, for I see now that they are, in fact, intertwined. A headline fit for the editorial I will write about Cathie prints itself on my mind:

THE SPIRIT-TELEGRAPH IS THE GREAT EQUALIZER

Chapter 31

Cathie may be famous, important, and a great equalizer, but she's also just a kid.

A kid who is being very annoying.

This carriage is taking us back to the Greeley estate, but she doesn't want to return there just yet. She protests that Miss Elliot said we should get dinner and stay in a hotel overnight, but I am saying no. I want to get back to my Jessica tonight, tell her all the things I have seen and felt and now understand. I cannot wait to tell her of my epiphany about the radical equality of the spirit-telegraph. I know she will love it.

But the spirit-telegraph herself, at this moment, is testy, tired, and complaining that she's hungry. "Only the spirits are free in this life," she says, rapping her knuckles against the carriage window. "Yes, no, yes, no, yes, no . . ." She sings a repetitive little song.

"What are you chattering on about?"

"What are *you* chattering about. It's your leg having the fits."

Yes, my leg is going up and down, up and down. So what? I give her a withering look. I suppose she's not the only one who is testy.

"You're not Splitfoot, you're Stompfoot," she adds.

I have no idea what she means by that and don't really care. Children and the things they say . . . I am missing Jessica, who would never tolerate this amount of whining and would know how to get it to stop.

"There's a rock in my shoe," she says, bending over to grab her foot. How lucky she is to be able to do that—the joy of wearing no corset.

She puts her stinky foot on my lap.

"Do you keep onions in your shoes?" I wave my hand in front of my nose.

"No onions," she says with a light kick. "Just garlic."

She takes off her stocking and puts her bare toes back on my lap. I grab her foot and tickle it so she'll remove it. She squeals and moves it away, then puts it back, and I tickle it again, causing her to get a case of the uncontrollable giggles.

"Don't tickle Mr. Splitfoot!" she shrieks. "He'll get you!" She nearly shoves her big toe right up my nostril.

"Enough," I say. "Let's calm ourselves."

"Get her, Mr. Splitfoot!" She presses her big toe against her second toe with a most impressive SNAP.

"Cathie, calm down now." Snapping fingers is hard enough; I've never known anyone who can snap their toes, and with an alarmingly loud sound.

"Mr. Splitfoot, will you calm down?" Cathie pulls her leg back to her, flexible enough to cradle her knee in her arm like a baby as she talks to her foot. "Yes or no?"

She stretches her leg across me and pushes her toes against the wooden wall of the carriage.

She snaps her toes twice.

KNOCK KNOCK.

The knocks reverberate like they are emanating from the carriage wall right behind my head.

"Mr. Splitfoot says NO!" she screeches with laughter. "He will not calm down!"

She laughs and laughs.

Clomp clomp clomp go the horses' hooves.

Rattle rattle rattle go the carriage wheels.

There are noises of the city outside, but inside my mind, a tornado is brewing.

Cathie's laughter starts to fade, then dies completely.

"Miss Elliot is going to be very mad at you for not feeding me supper." She pouts, putting her foot back into her shoe. She realizes she has said something to me without intending to say it. Or rather, her foot has. She ceases speaking to me entirely and closes her eyes, signaling she no longer wants to interact. I can sense her discomfort and tension. She got away from herself. She didn't mean to do that.

I feel triumphant but conflicted, as if I just solved a murder mystery and found out that the culprit was someone I love.

I know who he is—Mr. Splitfoot.

He is the *split* in her *foot*, the space between her big and second toes. Behold, the phenomenon of the knocking.

The spirit-telegraph is housed in a shoe.

$Chapter\ 32$

**THE DEVIL AND CATHIE FOX:
THE UNAUTHORIZED RADICAL
REINTERPRETATION OF THE STORY SHARED
BY CATHIE FOX EARLIER THIS WEEK**
—as imagined by E. A. Howe

Hell hath no cruelty like young girls, bored.

Maggie and Cathie Fox, on the cusp of adolescence, walked the woods of rural Hydesville, trying to out-scare the other. It was the end of March 1848, and the long, suffocating, cramped winter was at last giving way to spring. While two years apart, they were as close as twins, especially now that they had been separated from the bustle of Rochester and all their friends to this nowhere hamlet to live in a creepy, dark, haunted little cottage.

The house, like any old timber-built, scrimped-nails structure, moaned with every breath of wind and continually complained about the pains in its boards as it settled into the cold of the night. It thumped, bumped, knocked. The Fox sisters told each other tales of the slit throat and blood gurgles of whatever ghost it was that was making noises in the darkness.

At night, they impressed each other by helping the house haunt— using strings to pull objects slowly up the stairs as their mother sat upright in bed, crying out:

Did you hear that? Is there someone on the stairs?

Light a match, light a match, I say! There is no one there!
No one there!

This made them laugh themselves into hysterics as they walked and mocked, in the pleasured age-old pastime of preadolescence, reducing the sincere emotions of adults to sources of humor. Even and especially those they love.

It had been an abrupt move from the bustling city of Rochester, a port city, to the relatively small town of Hydesville, to provide a more rural, woodsy simple life for their daughters—and the absence of temptation of drink for their father.

One pities the mother of Maggie and Cathie Fox, a woman with two generations of children broken by the ten years of estrangement and then reunion with her alcoholic husband. Her older children had known a drunk father with a temper who abandoned them. The younger ones knew a quiet, repentant, and sober man, but also a bitter one. Their mother doted on her second-chance children, and she was certain they'd inherited from her line the family gift of second sight. She was psychic, her own mother was psychic, and they came from a long line of psychics.

The young Fox sisters had a great finale planned for April Fools' Day. Cathie had taught herself how to snap her toes in the same way she could snap her fingers. Cathie had then taught her sister Maggie how to do it, and the two had been practicing their snapping. First fingers, then toes, then toes, then fingers. Back and forth they would snap, loving how when they snapped with their feet, it would make such a lovely thump in the wood of a floor or a bedpost.

And thus they did plan to further persecute their poor mother, who, alas, had persecuted them with the boredom of living in Hydesville.

It was a joke that went too far.

After a suitable amount of raps that appeared to knock on doors, tables, floors, and prevented any semblance of sleep in the house, lamps were then lit, investigations were made, and still nothing could be detected making the noises. Even Maggie and Cathie traded so seamlessly between each other that they couldn't quite be sure which of them was keeping it going. Their eyes would meet with the agreement that it was enough now, and then there would be another *KNOCK*.

Their mother was crying with exhaustion and fear, and Cathie felt it was time to come clean. She jumped out of bed with the intention to demonstrate how the trick was done and hopefully receive relief and begrudging applause from their overwrought mother. Cathie snapped her fingers and said, "Mr. Splitfoot, do as I do . . ."

And thus began a game of twenty questions with Cathie's fingers doing the snaps and the "ghosts" (Maggie, still in the bed) doing the knocks, giving Mrs. Fox details only those in their family knew to be true. Questions that could be answered with varying numbers of raps, such as all their ages and the number of children Mrs. Fox had borne (including the one who died). They expected that Mrs. Fox would see, if the ghost knew these things and other family secrets, that she would suspect who was actually haunting her house.

This knowledge did not prove to Mrs. Fox that the "spirit" was actually one of her live daughters playing a trick, however. Instead, it only proved her belief that this spirit knew all the things that only the "other side" of life could show.

Cathie even said, "I think perhaps it is a joke for April Fools' Day, Mother."

Mr. Fox's face was as inscrutable as stone in the low light. He had not ever punished his second-chance children as he had his older ones, but they had heard of his sparing-no-rod techniques, and this served to frighten them.

As Mrs. Fox became more and more astounded, they became further entrenched in the trick. The sisters agreed: They must admit nothing.

Convinced of the genuine evidence of a poltergeist, Mrs. Fox was the April Fool, sending her husband off to fetch the neighbors to hear the tales of Mr. Splitfoot.

Neighbors knew that the Fox house was haunted. The original owners of the home had moved shortly after the rumors reached their peak, leaving behind a house that began to acquire a reputation. The next two renters complained of nightly noises.

The girls were in for it now. There was no way out but to tunnel farther down.

Thus, the girls were called upon to speak to the spirits in the house with a growing audience of neighbors and townsfolk.

The girls learned to speak letters of the alphabet for the spirit to choose, and thus knocked out the story of a crime in a drumbeat rhythm on the resonant wood of the Hydesville house. Oh, hear the tale of the death of the peddler, of tragic ends and injustice delivered. What a sad and bitter end, to have had his throat slit, his blood drained into a bowl, his body shoved into a false wall in the basement and covered with bricks . . . and all for what? Beautiful thimbles, thread, and the gold in his peddler's trunk.

But the radical story here, the public agreed, was not the one of the tragic peddler.

It was the idea of talking to spirits and hearing them talk back. It was a parable, no physical evidence needed for it to be believed.

The parable, a metaphorical story perfected in the Gospels, is not true because it is factual. It is true because it makes our lives better when we believe it.

~

I compose this editorial in my head as I sit here, attempting to convince myself that this last line is what I believe.

I want to protect this trick like I want to protect this child.

I cannot expose Cathie Fox, eleven years old, her sleeping head on my shoulder as we clop along in this carriage.

I must never reveal the secret about the knocking.

Chapter 33

No songs or excitement from Cathie as the carriage arrives back at Castle Doldrum. I have to wake her, and she groans and whines. It's already dark outside, even though it is not late. Fall just began, but it's already threatening winter.

I don't use the brass Federal Eagle to knock, or knock at all, because I know this house now. I don't need to wait on ceremony. I merely enter, operating under the assumption that it is the same place I left this morning.

This, however, is not correct. We left this morning and it was one house, and now, walking in this evening, it's clearly another. New lamps shine in the parlor on end tables I've never seen before. I am stepping on a rug that wasn't here earlier.

"Who are you?" A new maid intercepts me and Cathie, thinking that we might be intruders.

"I'm E. A. Howe. Who are *you?*"

"What are you doing back here?" Jessica's voice demands, seemingly disembodied, and then orders the maid to another post. She descends the steps quickly.

"I told her, Miss Elliot, that you wanted us to stay up there tonight," Cathie says, "but she wouldn't listen." She tattles like she was born doing it. "She said we needed to get back straightaway, and I haven't even had supper."

"You haven't had supper?" Jessica is angry at me in a way I cannot account for, until I see him behind her on the stairs.

Dr. Vincent.

He towers over the whole of the room from his place on the stairs, surveying me like lord and master. As he descends, he nonsensically seems to lengthen, grow taller.

Jessica huffs past me, taking Cathie into the kitchen.

"What are you doing back here?" I say to him. "I had thought your schedule was filled with exhibitions."

"Oh, the invitation to witness the séance was too much to pass up," he says with that accent from nowhere, coming closer and closer to me, looming over me.

"The séance is not until tomorrow," I remind him, refusing to allow myself to shrink before him.

"Yes, well, I wished to check on Mrs. Greeley, see how well Miss Elliot had taken my instructions for care." He bores into my brain with his chameleon eyes. Anything he wants, he takes. They may have spent the whole day together, eating little sandwiches and tea cakes, having a picnic. He may have tried to make her sleepy with his gold watch, touched her with his magnetized hands. "Have you been troubled by any more headaches, Miss Howe?"

The longcase clock *tock tocks.*

He wants to call a migraine into my head, put white holes in my vision at his will. No, no, I need to get hold of myself. I won't let him read my mind or put things in there.

"You can learn many things from that which afflicts you, even seeing your own blind spots," he says, now close enough for me to smell his mustache oil.

Another new maid brushes past me with linens, and another lights a new lamp, illuminating the doorway into the dining room before disappearing inside. The maids appear to be multiplying.

I rush away from him to follow the new maid and the new light, wondering where Jessica has gone.

Castle Doldrum is a broken puzzle box house. These pieces do not fold in on each other or fit together like Dr. Vincent's machine. The house, of course, is a metaphor for my own mental and emotional state at this moment. Metaphor being a much used—even overused—rhetorical device by editorial writers. As comforting as metaphor may be, however, there is also this *actual* house, where I find it very difficult to orient myself one day to the next, or even one morning to the same evening.

New people work in the kitchen, but I have a desperate need for the Marthas, even if they ignore me and accuse me of plotting against them. Where are they? I can't even find my voice to ask these new cooks. Cathie seems unperturbed with the changes in personnel, eating heartily the food in front of her.

"I told you she wanted us to stay in the city, Miss Howe," she says with her mouth full. "But now that we're back, I'll admit I'm glad. I want to get a good night's rest before the séance tomorrow. Who knows where it could take me? It's the most important demonstration of my career."

Career! That's the first time I've heard such a word from her. It is especially incongruous from an eleven-year-old chewing with her mouth open. I sit down next to her, hoping Jessica will appear. Cathie seems to have forgotten that she almost shoved Mr. Splitfoot up my nose.

"Would you like something to eat?" a woman asks me.

My corset feels too tight to allow my stomach to expand. "Maybe later," I tell her.

I wander away from the kitchen, my feet attempting to find steady footing in this newly altered environment. A new mirror hangs in the hall, and I don't recognize myself in it. It's the silk gown, I suppose. I very much want to change out of it. I take a lamp from a table, both of which I've never seen before, and walk upstairs. I can see light coming from Mary Greeley's bedroom, but I don't walk by there on the way back to my room.

Jessica helped me with my corset and crinoline this morning, when everything was different. Now I have to get out of it myself. It is a frustrating effort of lifting delicate, fitted fabric without tearing it, of twisting my arms behind my back to unlace the ties that bind me. Eventually, I get myself free, put on my nightdress, and wander back downstairs.

The clock *tock tocks*. This aspect of the house has remained steady, that rhythm. An hour has passed since I last looked at it. Where is Jessica?

I prowl around the ground floor until finally I see her, standing next to Dr. Vincent in the dining room. He holds her hand in his.

"What are you doing?" I ask, my voice sounding rude.

"I am showing Miss Elliot how there are different centers in the hand that connect to the body's humors." He grins. "Much more effective than palm-reading."

"Miss Howe, you are not appropriately dressed to be seen." She pulls her hand from his, blushing. She is flustered at being discovered. Upset, even.

The house has tumors. There are rooms that have no way into them but other rooms. Just when I think I finally managed to understand the layout, I see a maid coming through a door that I thought was a closet, a wall where I thought there was a window. This must be Jessica's vision of the house, fed full of lamplight, furnishings, and new people, appearing welcoming, even while the wood rots and walls crack and Dr. Vincent coils around her tighter and I want to grab her and run but I cannot because I . . .

I have not bound up my feelings tight as a corset. I am not appropriately dressed to be seen.

"Miss Elliot?" Mr. Greeley appears from what I believed to be a shadow in the corner of the parlor but I suppose is some sort of portal. He is home from the Rookery, then. He must have come down from wherever he sleeps. Jessica cannot say anything more to me about my nightdress, because he is in his nightshirt, with the wrong buttons buttoned together. His eyes are blinking like he was awoken unwillingly.

"Who are all of these people?" he asks Jessica as yet another maid walks by.

"They are here to help us prepare for Miss Lind and the séance tomorrow," Jessica says, "changing the bedding and preparing the menus. I apologize if any are disturbing your rest, but there is so much to do. They will all be heading to the servants' quarters shortly for the evening."

I had no idea there were servants' quarters.

"I have the most painful piles," he says. "I am finding it hard to sleep."

"Would you like some hot milk?" she asks.

Dr. Vincent has retreated into a red velvet chair I don't remember seeing before, his hands steepled, watching.

Greeley seems confused about where he is, muttering about how tomorrow's headlines need to be sorted and a broken typesetting machine. "And I have played the middle too long on this Compromise," I distinctly hear him say, though to no one but himself. "The *Tribune* is going to need to make a stand, one way or another."

"Consult the spirits, sir," I say, snapping into action, and he jumps in alarm. Even though I have been standing here this whole time, he did not see me. "Maybe the spirits will convince where reason, decency, and morality fail. That's what Frederick Douglass said to Cathie earlier today when we met with him."

"You were speaking with Douglass today?" He looks at me as if I have twelve heads, all of them with radical notions.

I am surprised that Jessica didn't tell him about the educational trip he paid for. Or she could have told him and he forgot, as he does so many things. She doesn't remind him now.

"Yes, sir, I was there today along with at least two thousand others at the Broadway Tabernacle Church, cheering for Frederick Douglass, booing the Compromise."

A woman in a starched apron appears in the room then, with a tray, offering him a cup of hot milk.

"Miss Elliot, who are all of these people?"

"Horace, remember? They are here for Miss Lind's visit tomorrow."

"But Miss Lind will not need all of this fuss and to-do. She is the most modest, simple sort of person. That is her charm."

He takes the milk, however, and dutifully drinks the entire cup like a hungry calf. He doesn't seem to notice the new rugs, lamps, and landscape paintings, or if he does, he makes no comment. I wonder whether he actually sees what is around him or he is so much in his mind that even physical things are a distraction from the stories he is shaping in his head.

The hot milk reminds him of something.

"Where is Charlotte?" he asks, with such urgency that I pity him. I live so much in my mind, too, that I sometimes forget my surroundings. It is an awful feeling, that sudden shock you have when you realize that there is something very big and very important you have forgotten about.

I can see it plainly. He just remembered that he still has a living daughter.

"Baby Charlotte is happy," Jessica says. "I assure you, Horace. She is tucked asleep in bed."

"No, please, I need to see her at once," he says, pulling strands of his neckbeard.

"I can have her awakened, if you like," she says with plain disapproval.

"Yes, I like!" he says, as if he fears Charlotte, too, has gone to Summerland like his other children.

Jessica continues to ignore me, heading out of the room, leaving me to hang around like forgotten wallpaper with Mr. Greeley and Dr. Vincent, who appears to be resting his eyes. I don't believe it for a second.

Oh, but here is Young Martha. What a relief. It is so good to see her, and she is not nearly as skilled at ignoring me as either her mother or Jessica. She gives me a kind of ashamed glance of her eyes and a little smile. She is dressed in a different outfit than I've seen her in before, a clean blue cotton dress and a bright-white starched apron she is still tying on when she enters the room. Jessica whispers something to her, and she performs her best curtsy and disappears, only to reappear a minute later with Baby Charlotte in her arms, her back curving with the weight of holding her. Charlotte clasps her hands around Young Martha's neck, and when Mr. Greeley tries to take her, she screams and bursts into tears.

Mr. Greeley relents and gives up this wild notion to have any relationship with his daughter, quickly handing her back to Young Martha. In doing so, he stumbles over Dr. Vincent's feet. He sees him for the first time since he wandered into this room from wherever he was before.

"You! I've been looking for you!" he says, though it is clear to all of us that he hasn't. "Why isn't your machine hooked up to Mother? I went to check on her, and your machine was gone!"

"It already did its work; it doesn't need to be reapplied," Dr. Vincent says, profoundly bored.

"But she has still not awakened. She is still in the same situation. Put it back on her."

"It has already done what good it can do," Dr. Vincent says.

Greeley starts to yell, then beg, offering whatever Dr. Vincent wants—testimonials, articles, access to all his important friends. It is a humiliating thing to watch, Greeley only stops short of getting on his knees. Dr. Vincent finally relents, saying that he will guarantee nothing, but he will go ahead and place the machine back on Mrs. Greeley if Miss Elliot will help him reaffix it.

"No, I can't," Jessica says, her lip shaking. "I tried to hire a nurse, but I couldn't find one on this short notice. I can't do it anymore, Horace." She looks at him, taking his hand as if she holds it every night and twice before breakfast. "I can't do it. It's terrible to see her like this. I can't even go into that room anymore."

Wrong-buttoned and milk-mustached, Mr. Greeley turns to me, another mission to impart.

"Miss Howe, will you help Dr. Vincent? Just until we can get another nurse in here or the situation resolves itself."

Using the exact same words that Jessica did with me the other night.

"The situation." Quite a euphemism for a coma.

Chapter 34

It's not a good idea to keep one's eyes closed when walking with an oil lamp, but I do it all the same. Let Dr. Vincent be the first to see little Pickie, if he is there to be seen. I am carrying the lamp because Dr. Vincent only trusts himself to carry this precious machine, but that means I am entering the room first. Needless to say, as much as I dislike walking behind Dr. Vincent, I find the presence of him following me far worse, especially when the first thing I fear I will see in Mary's room is the figure of her child at the edge of her bed.

When I open my eyes, I see that all the lamps in the room are already lit.

"You were in here earlier?" I ask.

"I told you I came early to check on my patient, Miss Howe. Did you purposefully not hear, or were you too busy concocting other fantasies?" Dr. Vincent is surly that it is me assisting him rather than Jessica. When he doesn't get his way, his magnetism starts to lose its pull. "She is in worse condition today than she was when I left yesterday."

I am not making my own assessment of Mrs. Greeley just yet because I'm entranced again at the real-haired portraits of the Greeley children, finding a familiarity in their painted faces and touching their hair halos.

"I believe you are here to assist me," Dr. Vincent says, trying his best to maneuver his machine onto a table as a solo effort.

I put down the lamp and pull over a table.

"Help me to lift her head," he instructs, taking out the Mind-Stimulator.

Dr. Vincent and I support Mary's head, just like I did with Dr. Bug. Different night, different doctor, all humbug. At least tonight I don't have to sit through his whole production again.

"How is she worse?" I ask, because she seems to me much the same.

"Her heart rate is slower, her eyes are less responsive to light, her breath is more irregular."

"Oh," I say.

"The sheets were changed. Who changed them?" he asks.

"I don't know. I wasn't here today. But there have been maids running around with linens since I returned."

"How about yesterday?"

"I don't know."

"Were the regular maids in here that you know of?"

"You mean the Marthas?"

"Yes, I suppose, if those are their names. The Irish mother and daughter."

I know they were out back, attacking the stains, scrubbing. I don't want to tell him that, though. He seems as liable to blame them for nothing as Dr. Bug. Martha said to keep her name out of my mouth, and here I've just gone again and used it.

"I don't know who has been in here," I say, which is the truth.

"And Miss Elliot tells me you assisted her in all things yesterday. You helped to give her sugar water, correct?"

"Yes," I say without hesitating, even though it is hard for me to properly recall anything but where I was in proximity to Jessica's glance, touch, and the transcendence of time with her.

"Who prepared the sugar water?"

"I don't know." It's not a lie, because even though I heard Jessica tell Martha to do it, I didn't actually witness its preparation. Jessica went to get it, and I met her in Mary's room

"What do you know, Miss Howe, about that dropper you found, the tincture of rhubarb?"

"Nothing, but I think I already told you she said it helped her stomach. That was the one medicine she would take."

The questions make me uncomfortable, even more so than I am just by virtue of being here in this dark room with Dr. Vincent and a sleeping Mary. He is cornering the women who have been here caretaking. I don't even know if I believe that Mary's condition has worsened. But I do believe that Dr. Vincent plays some sort of game with the inhabitants of Castle Doleful, a complicated one that I am poor at anticipating, like chess.

He cranks his machine, making the wheel spin with a *whir-tic tic*, and the Mind-Stimulator's coils vibrate. When I first saw him demonstrate this machine, there was something almost pleasant to me about the *whir-tic* sounds. Now I find them grating and unsettling.

He crouches down and speaks into her ear. "Hello, Mary Cheney Greeley. This is Dr. Jules Vincent. You are now being healed of any disease." He reminds me of Dr. Frankenstein, trying to bring life back into a corpse. "Your body is releasing any poisons you have ingested, and you will awake tomorrow your good old self and know the miracle of the Vincent-ivizer!"

I almost expect a bolt of lightning. But there is only the continued *whir-tic* of the machine that works like a windup toy.

"Well, as you said, it only works on the conscious mind." Why am I trying to make him feel better about the fact that she didn't suddenly burst to life?

"Yes," Dr. Vincent says. "Though I believe there is a part of her more conscious than she appears."

Even as he says it, I feel like I can sense her, beneath that clammy skin, pushing herself upward from the depths of where she sleeps, even if it is just in a dream.

"I would have preferred to have Miss Elliot, you understand," he says. *Oh, I understand.* "But you are a competent assistant, and I believe

I am very close to knowing all there is to know about Mrs. Greeley's current *situation*."

So he has noted the euphemism as well. Probably wishes he'd come up with it.

"Well, it's a backhanded compliment at best, Dr. Vincent, but you're welcome." I am more than happy to keep him as far from Jessica as I possibly can.

"Tomorrow," Dr. Vincent says to me. "You will assist me again."

I bow with a performance of deference. If he is Dr. Frankenstein, I suppose that makes me . . . whatever Dr. Frankenstein's assistant was named. Fritz?

He turns down the wicks of the lamps and ushers us out of the room, closing the door behind us. He hands me the lamp and pulls something from his pocket. I see, as he crouches down to mark the doorknob, that it is a stick of grease paint. He seems to be painting a very intricate symbol.

"What are you doing?" I ask.

"It's for protection."

"Protection against what?" I am wondering whether it is a secret symbol to guard against evil spirits. I didn't realize that, as a supposed man of science, he would go in for something like this sort of witchcraft.

"I will know if anyone enters this room between now and the morning. Even if someone tried, they would not be able to copy the symbol. And if someone touches the handle, the grease will stick to their hand. It is difficult to get off the skin, and if I wonder who is entering, I need only to ask someone to read their palm. Or balance their humors, as I did with Miss Elliot's hand earlier."

There is something he is insinuating to me with that last little statement. Asking me to recall how he touched her, what he was looking for. He is trying to plant something in my mind. I don't appreciate how he puts things into my head without invitation.

"They could just use a cloth to turn the handle," I point out.

"They won't see it unless someone alerts them to it." He pushes his index finger out toward me, as if an accusation.

"You think someone's coming in here, and doing what to her?"

He doesn't answer that.

"The door does open and close itself, you know," I say.

"Does it?" His mustache twitches.

"The house is . . ."

"Haunted?" he says with an insufferable smile.

I don't nod.

"Miss Howe . . ." He rises up, straightening his back with a long articulation to demonstrate his height over me. He presses his shoulder against the door to show it does not yield and that he has fully secured the catch. "Tonight, I assure you that this door will not open nor close without a human hand."

"I never said it was haunted," I say. "I may not be a man of science, but I am a woman who understands basic physics."

"Yes, Miss Howe. You are quite the skeptic," he says, making it sound like the point of a joke. "Meet me here at seven o'clock tomorrow morning to help me rewind the machine." He doubles his grin so that, with his mustache, it seems to take over the whole of his face. "*Outside* the door. Now, I'm off to bed."

Where that bed is, I cannot fathom, and after he walks a few steps into the hallway, he disappears into the darkness.

Chapter 35

I never said this house was haunted, but I thought it plenty. Whatever this house is—

THUMP. I need to get out of here.

It's driving me mad (*like my mother*).

THUMP THUMP THUMP.

I pull the pillow over my ears.

This house is eating me alive!

The house has surely changed, but it is still the same house of thuds and bumps and bad dreams and so much NOISE.

Whirrrrr-tic.

Add now the sound of the Vincent-ivizer and all the new staff scurrying around like mice.

THUMP.

Something is in the attic. I am sure of it. Maybe someone is trapped in there, trying to get out, but no one will go in, because they are too scared of ghosts, and so the person up there will die of starvation and then actually *become* a ghost.

That is an example of irony.

Irony, like metaphor, is a commonly used rhetorical device in news stories. Irony is employed particularly in headlines or open paragraphs to hook the reader—

THUMP.

No, regardless of the potentially ironic results, I am not going to investigate. Especially as I am waiting for her. However, after this amount of agonizing, it may be time for me to admit it. I do not think she will be coming to my bed.

I am beginning to doubt this love. Not what I feel for her, but I doubt that I can assess what she feels for me. If she doesn't love me the way that I love her, then . . . what can I possibly do about it? There is nothing I can do. Nothing but . . .

I don't want to stay in this house anymore. I don't like these feelings and these thoughts I am having. Even when I think that being in love is the most wonderful thing, it still makes me quite sick to my stomach. Feverish, dizzy, and like I am being tossed about on these emotions I can't control. It's like being seasick. Not that I have ever been on the sea.

Tap tap.

That's a knock, that's—

She is here. She enters my room. Relief rocks me like a broken fever. She blows out the candle and climbs into bed.

"What took you so long?" I ask.

"Listen, Edith, you've no conception of how many plates I am trying to spin here. Can you please be quiet and hold me a minute?"

Her body curls into my mine like a semicolon.

I cannot hear any more sounds from the attic. I seem to only hear them when I am alone in here, the thumping perhaps acting as echoes for the thoughts in my brain. Now I hear nothing but my love's breath, and feel nothing but the sweetness of the spoon of her body.

"Why did you ignore me when I came in tonight?" I can't keep quiet for very long.

"I hardly ignored you. I was furious with you."

"Why were you furious with me?"

"Because you say one thing and do another, and show up when I have ten thousand things to do, and add feeding Cathie and getting her to bed to the top of my list when that is why I told you to stay in the city."

"Why aren't you furious with me now?"

"Because I'm too tired and I need you too much. Now, shut up and hold me."

The same measure of jealousy, pain, stomach-knotting agony has turned to solace, comfort, a floating sense of ecstasy in holding her. I never want to let her go.

But I can't let it go. "What did you do with Dr. Vincent all day?"

"Oh, cheese and crust, Edith. Are you really that jealous?"

"'Cheese and crust'? Is that how you curse?"

"Answer my question. Are you really that jealous?"

"Yes." I am far more jealous than she even realizes. I resent every moment of their proximity.

"Don't be. What do you think, that I like Dr. Vincent just because he is an extremely handsome, charismatic, famous, and eligible widower?" She says this, but her voice is teasing, and she kisses me as she does.

"I didn't know he was a widower."

"He married a middle-aged baroness, twice his age when they wed. She died and now he has all of her money. But not enough to manufacture his machine."

"How do you know this about him if you didn't spend the day together?"

She stops kissing me. She puts her hands into my hair and gives it a pull.

"That hurts." It doesn't. Actually feels sort of nice.

"Good," she says. "I don't like him. I find him unsettling. There's something cruel about him, haven't you noticed?"

"Most certainly." A fork impaled in a dead creature's face still quivers in my mind.

"Listen, I need to talk to you. It's important. It's about our future together."

I could cry with happiness that she just said those three words, "our future together."

"You do want us to have a future together, don't you?" she asks.

"Yes," I say far too loudly. "Yes, yes."

"I have been thinking about how we can do it. And then I had a premonition. One of those visions I have, that I always trust."

"What was it?"

"Mary Greeley is going to die, Edith. I saw it. And I saw . . . other things."

Tic-whirr, says the Vincent-ivizer from downstairs. *Tock,* says the pendulum clock in the wrong rhythm.

"I will be the next Mrs. Greeley," she says.

I stiffen, go cold. I take my hands away from her. "You can't be serious."

"Why wouldn't I be? I'll make a wonderful match for him. He is already an incredibly important man, but she has been a weight around his neck, dragging him down. With me, he could be so much more. With me as his wife, he could be president."

"Jessica, you can't marry him. You don't love him."

"I am sure I could learn to. He is a kind man. Thoughtful. Idealistic. There's much about him one could learn to love."

"You have nothing in common," I say, my mind reeling. She talks like this while she is in bed with me, saying it is about our future together while it is actually about *Horace.*

"By all accounts, he and Mary had much in common," she says, "and what a nightmare she turned out to be."

"She has been stuck at home, sick and pregnant, while he gets to live the life of the mind and to be important. She gave him the money for his first paper from her inheritance, and while he was out getting to state all of his important opinions, she was at home, alone, trying to obsessively live up to the ideal of a clean house. She cares about ideas and learning and wants to go to speeches, have a life outside the house. Women need to be able to pursue their interests, same as men."

"Women are different. We are not the same as men."

"And men aren't the same as men, either. All of this classifying people into who they are because they are a man or a woman, all of these pretenses of their superiority because of race or sex. No, we are none of us are the *same*, but we are all equal. We all equally need and deserve to survive and to have the opportunity to have meaning, which must be self-determined . . ."

She presses a hand over my mouth to stop me from continuing.

"You will wake the whole house," she whispers.

I would wake the whole house, too, and I want to, but for her hand.

I pull it off me and get out of the bed.

"Edith, come on. Don't be a child."

I walk over to the desk. Why, Margaret Fuller worked at this desk. Now there was an inspirational woman who understood equality, even in marriage. I do my best to light a candle. Why do women think they have to marry? What if we all just refused? I suppose I haven't had many women in my life besides Aunt Clara and Lady Jane, both of whom have rather unconventional views on marriage and family. Lady Jane left her husband and children to start this assignment in Washington, and Aunt Clara, despite her wish that I marry, seems resigned that I will sooner turn into a dryad.

I can't get the match to light. I sit in the dark.

"E. A.," Jessica calls out softly. "Come now, come back."

"You don't want to marry him," I say.

"But I do, see, for then I can also be with you," she says.

I crawl back into bed but keep my distance. At least I know she is thinking about a future with me instead of one without.

"How do you figure that?" I say finally.

"Well, you could stay on as Cathie's tutor."

"Why does everyone want to give me a different job than the one I have? I am a—"

"Newspaper woman," she says in unison with me. "Well, then there's that. Didn't the first newspaper woman in America stay here, in this very room? Why couldn't you stay on here?"

I suppose I could. Stay here for more crisp-apple, blue-sky days of fall. Cold, snowy days cuddled by a fire in the winter. Spring days when everything comes alive. Summer days.

Summerland.

"Tell me the premonition," I say.

"I was walking outside in the orchard. Clear as day, I saw her grave, right next to all her children. And his, too. It was years and years from now. You were with me. We were older, much older. We were holding hands. No gloves, and the back of our hands, Edith, they had started to wrinkle. I couldn't see the dates on the grave. The numbers weren't clear, but her grave was covered with moss. She'd been dead for some time. But he . . . he had just died. Decades from now. But we were together, all that time."

Years spent together. Together for so much time that the backs of our hands wrinkle.

That is a future, a premonition, I want to believe in.

She begins to touch me in ways she hasn't before.

She knows things about me that I don't even know. Parts of me I didn't even know existed are willed into life by her fingers, her lips, her tongue, the press of her palms.

What is she doing to me?

She is killing me.

I am laughing, crying, shoving a pillow in my mouth to keep from screaming. Feathers in my mouth, biting on the pillow, flying somewhere inside my body.

She is resurrecting me.

I am flesh made spirit possessed—it rocks through my body from the inside of my skull to the curl of my toes, and my heart bursts with a new life below my belly, wet and raw, shivering.

A warm, gentle wave of sleep reaches out to pull me back to a forgotten beginning, before I was even born.

"We will stay together," she says.

"Yes." How sweet that we now have a boat where we two can rest atop this wave.

And maybe now can last forever.

PART III

SWEDISH NIGHTINGALE ATTENDS
SÉANCE AT GREELEY ESTATE, EVENT
SHROUDED IN MYSTERY

Chapter 36

She sings, and blessed are those who hear, for their ears ring with the eternal realm of the angels. Newspaper men have written that, much like the experience of touching heaven, there is no possible way to describe the voice of Jenny Lind. That doesn't stop them from getting paid to try. P.T. Barnum, the tour manager, has reporters in every city on his dole to write fanfare creating need and desire. The papers explode with Lind-mania, signaling to the public its duty to greet her at every port as if for a religious festival. She has come to America to bless us en masse with high-class culture. The woman herself, the papers claim, is likewise angelic in her humility and commitment to giving money to charity, thus the perfect vessel for her sublime voice.

The papers lack only one story about Jenny Lind, and that's the one I am developing. I have a unique angle. Nothing looks better on a celebrity angel than a good cause with a dash of controversy. I wake this morning looking forward to this evening's séance with a renewed thirst for justice and sense of commitment, for I have been in the presence of Frederick Douglass. And while I believe I have figured out the very humble origins of the knocking, I now see communication with spirits as a powerful force for equality.

Miss Jenny Lind is the most powerful mouthpiece in America. Tonight, I have the opportunity to convince her to speak out for what is right, and I know the spirits will aid in this endeavor. She will come out to me, debutante-style, as an abolitionist—and I will shove it in the face of every doughy Northerner and slaving Southerner. She will sing for freedom Happily Ever After.

There is a fly in my ointment. What a groaning duty it is to have to wait for Dr. Vincent. I stand outside Mary's door, my resentment bubbling. The clock has already done its seven chimes; I was here by the seventh and he was not. I do this for Mr. Greeley, I remind myself, because Jessica does not wish to assist Dr. Vincent any longer. Better it be me than her, anyway, alone with him.

I examine the doorknob he so carefully marked. It does not seem to have been smudged, smeared, or in any way disturbed.

Surprising, considering all the new staff bustling past me.

"Move it, miss." An older maid with thick arms and a strong accent tries to enter the room. "I need to change the sheets."

"Just wait," I say, and because she isn't waiting, I have to slap her hand away from the doorknob, lest she become a suspect in whatever concoction Dr. Vincent is working up. "I am very sorry, but there is paint all over the handle, and I didn't want your hands to get dirty."

"You think I'd rather be hit than dirtied?" If she didn't have sheets in her arms, she'd likely have struck me in return. Let's be clear that I barely touched her.

"Look, this preposterous doctor is going to think whoever gets this paint on their hands is an attempted murderer, and I don't know you, but I don't think that is something you signed on for."

Dr. Vincent finally shows his mug. He is late and moves without urgency.

"I was on time, and here's your suspicious sheet-changer in the flesh," I say, motioning to the maid, "who was about to open the door and implicate herself."

"Hello," he says to her, crouching at the door to inspect the knob. "Pardon Miss Howe, she has a rather dramatic way of doing things."

"Nobody's touched the door," I say, with no attempt to hide my I-told-you-so tone.

"Can I do my job?" the maid asks. "Or do I need to take it up with Miss Elliot?"

"Oh, I am sure the woman of the house, Mrs. Mary Greeley, would much appreciate the changed sheets." Dr. Vincent takes out his kerchief and wipes off the doorknob. "If she still lives and breathes."

It didn't occur to me that Mrs. Greeley might have died during the night, but the idea that we may walk in and discover this makes me hang back and let them enter first.

"She lives," Dr. Vincent declares from inside the room, beckoning to me.

He puts his hands beneath the wire coils of the Mind-Stimulator to gently remove it from her head. He and I both lift Mary's body as the maid pulls out the sheet and puts a new one beneath her. Mary seems more alive than she was last night. There seems to be more tension to her muscles, more speed to her breath. It's enough for me to be a little more open-minded about the effectiveness of his stupid machine.

Dr. Vincent is conveniently fiddling with his boxy progeny on the other side of the room when the real work of removing soiled clothing is needed. I help the maid remove the makeshift nappy from Mary's body.

"Just like changing a big baby," the maid says, with enough camaraderie that I feel forgiven for slapping her hand from the door.

I find myself thinking about my mother in the asylum. I wonder whether she needs to be *changed like a big baby* or whether she's able to control her bodily functions. I think back with a new perspective to what I saw of her during my visit, recalling that she was holding herself upright in the chair. Her eyes were open and she said a word. She was more awake than Mary Greeley is now. I wonder now if she was deeply drugged, and what she might be able to say if sober.

"Uh," Mary utters, startling me. "Ah, uh . . ."

"Better and better!" Dr. Vincent shouts, running over to her. "Mary Cheney Greeley, can you hear me?" The excitement in his voice suggests she is about to open her eyes and answer. She doesn't respond to the question, but that doesn't mean she doesn't hear.

Having changed the sheets and the diaper, the maid looks at Dr. Vincent for permission to leave, even though I am far more a member of this household than he is.

"Please bring some gruel for me here," he orders her. "It is for me, not the patient, should anyone ask. I will be eating it."

The maid puts one foot behind the other and performs a mini-curtsy, an absurd gesture of deference, especially as Dr. Vincent looks at least a decade younger than she.

He motions for me to help him rehook and reposition the Mind-Stimulator back onto Mary's head.

"I truly did not think this machine would be so effective." I am woman enough to admit that I am very impressed with her improvement. "Honestly, I had thought a lot of it was just . . . bells and whistles."

"It is, Miss Howe," he says, returning to the box and twisting the crank that sets the coils vibrating. "Mostly bells and whistles. But perhaps you'd be amazed at how much we humans need things that look a certain way in order to *feel* a certain way."

The Vincent-ivizer is humming, the wheel slowly spinning. It reminds me of the back-and-forth of his gold watch. He must intentionally do this to people, put them in a dream state and get them to say things to him that they would otherwise not say. He is a thought thief, and yet here is Mary Greeley as a testament to his work. He spoke something into her ear about getting better, and here she is, better.

"Belief and will," I say, echoing back the words he uses. "People get better because they think they will—but when unconscious, is there still a place where a person's belief and will can be reached?"

"In this case, Miss Howe, entirely different forces are at play." He grins at me like we are old chums. "Perhaps you would be willing to discuss those with me. I am very interested in your perspective."

"Perhaps some other time," I say, disdaining his chummy smile. I am not about to share my thoughts with someone who would otherwise steal them. "We are all so very busy this morning. Do you require any further assistance?" I attempt to copy the maid's curtsy.

"How are your migraines, Miss Howe?" He has crossed the room and now stands far too close to me.

"Oh, they are all gone, Dr. Vincent," I say with emphatic cheer. I am not taken in by this creepy quack, whatever his feigned concern. "I'm fit as a fiddle."

"The next time you see those bright diamond-shaped lights that are the harbingers of the crippling pain, I advise you to do this." He takes my right hand with such quick mechanical precision that I do not back away. He presses between my index finger and thumb. "Miss Howe," he says, speaking low and fast, "I know that you have an aversion to me, as you do some of the memories you've buried deep in your mind. Please know I have no judgment about your amorous feelings for Miss Elliot."

Why do I not rip my hand from his, fling denials in his face? Perhaps it is his calm manner and that there is something not altogether unpleasant about his hand showing me a space where migraines are born and can therefore be stopped from seeding.

"Those feelings, you must realize, are not in her best interest, nor yours."

"You don't know me and you don't know her." It had felt like it was a soft touch, but now I realize it is a vise grip he has on me. I truly don't care how he looks at Jessica. I do care how she looks back at him. Despite her protestations, he has her ensorcelled.

"No, but I can read people, Miss Howe, as easily as reading a book. Miss Elliot is as predictable as a penny dreadful. It may be today, tomorrow, or next week. But pending my, or your, intervention, she will administer the fatal dose of laudanum to Mrs. Greeley."

He releases my hand.

"That is a wallop of an accusation, Dr. Vincent," I say as calmly as I can. He aims to shock me. He thinks I will plead *Oh, no,* or *Oh, how,* or *She would never.* I understand his tactics. He stabs right into the place where one is most tender. "A truly pernicious suspicion to pin on the one person who has been helping to keep her alive. Miss Elliot has been feeding her, changing her these past few days, while you are out strutting your feathers and waving your hands." I mimic his mesmerized stares and gestures.

He chuckles at my imitation, then guffaws outright as if I did it for his entertainment. It was not my intention to amuse, and I feel myself wilting.

"Oh, Miss Howe." His laughter subsides. "Whatever your opinion is of me, please do know I am rooting for you. Do as you will. I will not make any trouble for either of you. I do not have pretenses, such as yours, that I work for justice."

"Right, of course not. You have no pretenses at all," I spew at him. His accusation turns over in my stomach, sickening me. It is disgusting. He conjectured before even coming here that Mary was being poisoned, and since arriving he has done everything he can to find a suspect to fit his theory. He's trying to turn my mind against Jessica. Telling me what is in my best interest or hers—as if he cared about either. "You don't work for justice, and you're not a real healer, so why do you do all of this?"

"Science, of course." He is serious. "The science of the mind."

I do my best to throw a mocking laugh at him, but it sounds forced and weak. I shake with anger, impotent to respond.

"Hot gruel, for the doctor," the maid says, standing in the doorway with a steaming bowl. Her voice breaks the spell Dr. Vincent was attempting to put on me. "And Mr. Greeley requests your presence in the study, miss."

"The doctor may need you to assist him," I whisper to the maid on my rapid flight to the door, never happier in my life to be summoned anywhere.

"Assist him in eating gruel?" she asks.

"Miss Howe . . ." Dr. Vincent says, unwilling to release me or even acknowledge that I am now free.

I will not turn back. In case he is reading my mind, I fasten there an image of his face with a fork stabbed into it.

"Believe it or not, Miss Howe, you are very lucky I am here to help you," he calls after me.

Chapter 37

Mr. Greeley stands behind his desk, humming to himself, looking out at the canopy of leaves from his window. When I enter his study, he doesn't notice. The books have multiplied since the last time I was in this room. There are new stacks on the floor, forming precariously balanced columns. I wish to plop myself in front of one and spend a day discovering each title. But not *this* day. I start to grow concerned that he may never turn around.

"You asked to see me, sir?" I say, notifying him of my continuing presence.

"Ah, Miss Howe," he chirps. "I believe I have some news that will please you."

Mr. Greeley looks better today, in even greater measure than his wife. His face is clean-shaven, oiled, pink as a baby's. His neckbeard looks carefully coiffed, his frock coat clean and pressed. He struts behind his desk with mirth enough I surmise Jessica spent the morning preening him and serving his breakfast.

"I have decided that I—and therefore, the *Tribune*—will be announcing my position against this Compromise, in particular, this execrable Fugitive Slave Act."

I shout in jubilation. I yell to the rooftops praises to all divine forces for their miraculous intercession. Then I grab him in a bear hug that likely embarrasses him, though he laughs heartily. We both do, for a moment. I do realize, however, that calling evil what it is does not typically eradicate it.

"I know you will write with conviction and eloquence," I say. "And it will educate many Americans who were before confused about what this Compromise really means. May I ask what finally convinced you?"

"Your presence here was not in vain. It did cause me to think more deeply about certain things I have taken for granted. But ultimately, it was speaking with my son that convinced me."

"Oh, did Cathie have a message for you?" I could just kiss those stinky feet of hers.

"No, it wasn't through the spirit-telegraph. I can't tell you how I heard his voice. It wasn't like hearing in the typical way. Yet I heard him, clear as a bell. Last night, I came here into my study, rereading letters from my friends, thinking of all those that I have known who have come and gone. Thinking of the child I have, still alive. I asked for my son's forgiveness. I believe he is here, watching over Mother, and will be here until it is time for him to take her with him to Summerland."

"Mrs. Greeley is better today . . ." I start.

"I do not think she will recover." He takes a breath. "Mother has always been sickly. She doted on Pickie so, until he rebelled against her, and then . . . their relationship became more tumultuous. I'll never forget his face, once when she had him by the arm, as he yelled, 'O, you ugly creature!' as if it would stay her hand. I never intervened, all those times she corrected his behavior. She often beat him. Locked him in the attic. The sounds he would make up there I could not abide, and so I would leave. The household was her domain, and I would not go against her. I knew he'd eventually understand why she could not spare the rod. That we each have our spheres, men and women. I do not allow her interference in mine, and I would stay out of hers. I did not think my role as a father called for it. I thought one day he would understand when he grew up."

He turns to look out his window, into the light of this day.

"*Does* he understand?" I ask. Between Mr. Splitfoot, the Vincent-ivizer, and Jessica's premonition about our future together, the only thing I am sure I believe anymore is that each of us *choose* what we will believe. If Mr. Greeley believes that he spoke with Pickie, then it is as true for him as that he is speaking here with me.

"We need forgiveness not just for what we do but for what we don't do," he answers. "I hope I will not err again, in keeping silent and turning my back on my duty. I will do what I can, with the tools that I have, for this country that I love."

I am glad for Mr. Greeley and his choices this morning, neck-beard and all.

"Now," he says, clapping his arms around mine, "how are you doing with your article on the spirit-telegraph?"

"It is going extremely well." Actually, I haven't started it.

"I am certain that tonight's experience will be the perfect lead-in—everyone will want to read about Jenny Lind's reaction."

"Most certainly." I am not breaking out into a cold sweat, as I am confident Jenny Lind's impending statement of support of abolition in this editorial I haven't begun writing—ostensibly about the spirit-telegraph, but really about equality—will pull the whole thing together.

"Your argument for the presence of spirits should not be solely based on the account of this evening, however. You must be reasoned. Measured." He says this as if he is worried, as if he doubts my reasoning and measurements. "I trust that by this point you have had plenty of experiences with the knocking that is heard around Miss Fox."

"Indeed, sir." More than plenty, and more than I will reveal.

"I know Dr. Vincent is already planning different ways to use and patent the spirit technology."

"Mm-hmm." I would bet those ways will involve bells, whistles, and a spinning circle.

"We both know how powerful the spirits are in their ability to provide comfort and faith. But there are those who refuse, for whatever reason, to believe. I have it on good authority that there is a medical panel at the Academy in Rochester that is working on an article discrediting the girls. We will provide a different approach."

"Yes, sir."

"Can you have something for me to read by tomorrow?"

"Oh, yes." My goodness. I must go lock myself in the room and figure out how to write favorably about Cathie Fox—the spirit-telegraph—without lying through my teeth.

"Wonderful! I've been meaning to write Mrs. Swisshelm to tell her what a help you have been to this household . . . Oh, that reminds me. She sent this for you, care of me at my office. I am sorry, it arrived earlier this week, and then I forgot it." He hunts about his desk, opening drawers, closing them, picking up books and setting them down. At last he finds it and hands it to me. An intriguingly thick envelope addressed in my Lady Jane's exquisite handwriting holds the promise of . . .

My stomach drops when my hands touch the sealed letter.

I can't explain how I know it, but something is wrong.

<h1 style="text-align:center">Chapter 38</h1>

Lady Jane's hands have the skill to sew something as delicate as lace. She loses herself so completely when she paints portraits that she decided she must quit, lest her family never have supper. In the swoop of her lettering, I can read her concern, and I am frightened for what the message inside may be. I sit at the desk—where Margaret Fuller herself penned letters—and break the wax seal.

> Dear E. A.,
> This letter arrived from your Aunt Clara the day after you left. I've never known your Aunt Clara to be a letter writer, so it did worry me. Unlike you, I know that it is unacceptable to open letters addressed to others. (I have forgiven, but I have not forgotten).
> Please do write to me and let me know after you have read her letter that all is well, both with her and with your work there.
> Persist in your purpose.
> The bread and circuses of Washington is as you left it, minus your one righteous soul. May you soon return to assist me in this fight, having succeeded in your mission there.
> You are much missed.

Be of good cheer. All is for the good for those
who love God.
But do not be polite.
Yours Truly,
Jane

The letter tucked within is addressed by the shaky hand of my
dear Aunt Clara. Baby bird without feathers, her hand—wrinkled, blue
veined, papery soft. How I wish I could be held close right now by her.
As a child, I would squirm, always wanting to break free. Unless I was
sick or hurt or scared. Then I would run to hold her when I saw shadows move or heard the screams of something being caught in the woods.
How I loved her skin, the comfort of her smell of muscle ointment and
peppermint soap.

I press the letter to my cheek, like it is her own face.

I am afraid to open it. Eventually, I do.

Dear Edith,

I hope the wickedness of Washington has made you
think again and you will return home. Come and keep
an old woman company.

I know you want nothing to do with her, but it
is my duty to inform you that I got word from the
Friends Asylum that your mother died last week in her
sleep. She was buried the following day in their plot
with a small stone bearing her name and the dates best
they knew for when she was born to the day she died.

I told you growing up that you were an orphan,
which was true in spirit if not in fact. Now that the
fact is the same as the truth, I hope it brings you peace.

Do come home.

I remain,

Your Aunt Clara

There is no breath in my lungs, no beat in my heart. I am dead, too, for a moment. I feel like I am somewhere outside my body, looking down at myself. The idea I hold of myself as E. A. Howe is suspended at the moment in a brutal question.

Where is my mother?

Given that she died more than a week ago, it is possible that her spirit was there in the nursery, that first day, knocking over the teacup. That she was there in the wind, when Cathie claimed to have seen her. Somehow gave her a button, free of her body and able to know things she didn't or couldn't have when alive. She could be here, right now.

Or more likely, she is gone, along with every chance I ever had to know her, to be with her, to understand what happened that broke her mind into pieces.

I breathe in huge gulps of the grief-stricken air of this house, adding to it my own sorrow. My mother's ghost joins that of the children who haunt this place—but of course she will only stay as long as I do. It is *me* who she haunts.

It's easy to say it was all a coincidence, that Cathie made those sounds and said she saw my mother, who I had thought was still alive but who actually had just died. It doesn't prove anything. But proof is a cold thing, and I need nothing as cold as proof right now.

It would be easy enough to prove that none of the things I value most in the world actually exist. Not truth, not liberty, not equality. Even love, which to me seems to be as much a giver of life as the sun, could be a figment of imagination. Tears run quickly down my face, my breath coming in sharp jags to my abdomen in a way that feels as if I have never cried before in my life. Not as a child, not as an adult, I have never really cried until now. My body sways with it, possessed.

Now I am truly an orphan.

My mother is dead. I never thought it would hurt for that to be true, not after I saw how she was alive. Yet every part of me aches, reaching for some sort of solace. If I could only know what it is that I hope for.

If I could choose what I knew to be true, would it be a reality where the spirits of the dead could speak to the living?

My mother spent most of my life in an asylum, drugged and non-sensical. What could she possibly have to say to me that are not just my own words blowing back in the wind, lost from their context, making no sense?

A fight for her very soul.

If I want to continue to stake a claim on coincidences, I could say that there is no connection between Mary Greeley's condition and my mother's. But at this exact moment, it feels better to allow that these threads are part of a divine tapestry, as Horace Greeley said. That—

Knock knock.

Jessica is here.

Chapter 39

She is inside before I properly tell her to enter—copper eyes darting, breathing hard, like she was moving swiftly. I am not composed in the manner she expected. My eyes and nose are running to the river. Seeing her makes me whimper for her to hold and console me.

"Oh, heavens, E. A." There is no manner of a hankie or a hug available in Jessica Elliot. "What is going on?"

"My mother is dead."

"Yes, I know, so is mine. Why are you crying about it right now?"

"You don't understand. You see, I said I was an orphan . . ." I suppose I never really understood the Quaker obsession with truth until this moment. Even a lie that seems small and makes your life easier, in moments like these creates great difficulty.

"I don't have time to talk about your childhood, E. A. I need you to collect your faculties and compose yourself. Now, come on, take this." She hands me a book.

It is a beautiful blue clothbound version of "The Nightingale" by Hans Christian Andersen. I am momentarily entranced by the illustration on the cover. Two birds sit side by side. A brown, simple bird and one fashioned as an elaborate bejeweled work of art. "It's like us," I say. "One plain and one so beautiful."

"Oh, cheeses, Edith." She grabs my chin and looks me in the eye. "I need you to be clearheaded and no-nonsense, do you understand?"

I nod.

"Listen carefully so I don't have to repeat it." Her voice is low, her face close enough to kiss. I can read her lips so she doesn't need to pronounce the full words. "After Jenny Lind arrives, everyone will be downstairs to greet her. I will ask you to go and fetch this book for me, for her to sign for Cathie. Before you do that, you do this."

She reaches into her upper sleeve and pulls something out. Something small, which she places into my palm. A vial.

She tugs gently on my bottom lip and touches a place at the base of my gums.

"A full dropper. Wait until it absorbs, don't let any dribble out."

She doesn't even say who it's for—of course not. We both know.

"Then you will come back in here, grab the book, hide the vial in this room, and hide it well. I will tell you what to do with it later."

She pulls away from me so that I am the one left holding the book and the vial.

"Then you bring the book to me downstairs. Do you understand?"

I'm frozen at the moment. I can't move to nod, but of course I understand what she is asking me to do.

"Don't look at me like that, E. A. I didn't put her in this state. You and I both know it was Dr. Bing who did this to her."

I do know that. It was a double dose from Dr. Bug, no matter how he denies it. Except . . . maybe there was laudanum in her tincture of rhubarb, maybe Jessica hid it in there to try to get her to take her medicine because she was easier to manage that way. But if Mary finished that tincture and then received the double dose, that would account for an overdose.

"As it is now, she will never wake up," Jessica says. "And she'll stay like this, needing full-time care. It could be years. It could be forever."

Yes, like my mother. All those years, like a breathing corpse in a chair.

"I'd do it myself," she says, "but Dr. Vincent is watching me, always. He never takes his eyes off me. He's playing some game with my mind.

He has me in a snare, Edith. He knows about *us*, I don't know how he does, but he's blackmailing me. He wants me, he wants me very badly."

Of course he does. Everyone does.

"I was prepared to do it and never say a word about it to you," she says. I know it's true. It's what she has meant to do all along. "I wanted to keep you innocent of it, keep you up here, my love, with your beautiful thoughts about justice and goodness . . ."

"Miss Elliot?" There are sounds on the steps. One of the new staff, calling up.

She would have done it and never said a word to me, except for that I brought back this doctor, who is blackmailing her with his suspicions, so it has to be me who does this for her.

"I had that premonition about us, Edith. But the thing is, you believe it, and so you will make it come true. Do you understand?"

I do. It's a strategic plan. It's laid out like a clear mathematical equation, a step-by-step solution. Simple. Everyone will be so busy thinking about the séance no one will think about Mary Greeley in her coma. When she finally passes, no one will be surprised. Even *Horace* expects his wife to die, and when she does, he will ask Jessica to marry him in a matter of blinks.

I can live right here in this room, waiting for her to visit me every night.

"Miss Elliot?" the voice calls again. "Are you up there?"

She stands up, sets her face, and opens the door. "Yes?"

"Mr. Greeley is asking for you."

"I will be there momentarily. I am trying to get our newspaper woman to wear something presentable for tonight."

She closes the door, pressing her back against it, and stares at me, her chest heaving with fear, a prairie fire in her eyes.

She is the reason painters paint, poets rhyme, and men go to war.

Chapter 40

I hold a murder weapon in one hand and a children's fairy tale in the other.

Other words of my torn editorial fly through my mind—*complicit, good and evil, a deal with the devil where we all burn.* How many days I've wandered about, believing I was in love with someone I didn't know at all. Believing love was simply an ecstatic shudder of my body, the desire to cover every inch of hers with my kisses. How little I know Jessica is nothing compared to how little she knows me.

People do kill for love—fools. Now I start to doubt the depth of Mary's so-called coma, for perhaps Jessica has been continuing to dose her, hoping to send her under for good. I don't know how long she has been poisoning her—weeks, days, or just since Dr. Bug's double dose? It could have begun as innocently as a trick to get her to take her medicine, making her easier to manage. Or maybe she hasn't poisoned her yet at all, and it is just this one dropper, a coup de grâce, that she is asking me to deliver.

I can't help but see my own mother in Mary. She must have been heavily drugged when I saw her at the asylum all those years ago. If I had been less afraid of her, more willing to face who she is—who she *was.*

My mother is dead now.

I can never see her face again, nor take her hands in mine. See what could remain of her mind, what me there was left in her, and what of her in me. I regret that I have let my fear, my denial of her, prevent me from returning to figure out the mystery of what happened to her, what snapped and made her kill my brother and attempt to push me under.

"They would have hung her . . ." A memory of what Aunt Clara said about my mother warns me. There is more danger here in this house than I realized.

Fear grabs my shoulders and starts to shake them.

This could be a setup.

Mary still may die. I don't trust Dr. Vincent, I certainly can't trust Jessica, and even the Marthas were fine with throwing wild accusations in my direction. My fear is grounded in the reality that I did, in fact—whether I was aware of it or not—help Jessica feed Mary Greeley. And I absolutely did hold her head still so that a doctor could poison her enough to almost kill her.

I don't know what is in the vial. Dr. Vincent suggested it would be laudanum, but it could be anything. If I dump it on the floor, I fear it could burn like acid. If I take it outside and bury it, I could be seen doing so. I must hide it.

I take down the collections of Margaret Fuller, guilty as a thief, seeing which of her books of essays or letters this vial, this instrument of death, can hide behind.

I choose *The Great Lawsuit: Man versus Men, Woman versus Women.*

On second thought, I might as well put Dr. Vincent's greasepaint on the spine, it seems so utterly obvious. Of course I would put it there, should someone come in here looking for it. Jessica, who would kill a defenseless woman, would not balk in pointing her pink-mooned finger in my direction if she thought it would help her, just like in a penny dreadful.

No, I cannot hide behind Margaret Fuller. I cannot hide it in a desk, under the frame of the bedpost, like that rhubarb tincture Dr. Vincent grabbed from my hands. There is no suitable place anywhere in this room to hide it—too much exposure here, every cranny or disguise easily revealed.

Of course, there is an obvious solution. The best place to put it is in the room everyone is too scared to enter.

~

The attic door waits for me. It has been waiting for me since I arrived here. I make sure no one is coming up the stairs to see me lift the latch, twist the knob. This old door sags on its hinges, making it crooked, wedging it into the frame. I must put some shoulder into it to get it to comply.

Small wooden stairs lead up to the unknown. I hesitate a moment, thinking of the *thuds* and *thumps* and every sincere warning to *not go up there*. The vial burns into my clutched hand like a guilty conscience, urging me to take the steps quickly.

Finally arrived at this foreboding space, I take a long look around. It is dark in here, but I'm able to see. Deep shadows corner the dust motes that swim in the light from an east-facing window, a century of dirt on the glass. A broken piece of the ceiling lets in a pinprick of sun from above me. The sweet smell of something rotting makes me gag.

Something is definitely dead in here. Last night, that must have been what I heard, something alive that failed to escape. But would it so quickly rot?

There it is.

I see the dead body. A bird—a starling—lies in the center of the floor.

Poor thing, what noise it made struggling to get out. All in vain. I should have come up earlier, helped her get out of here. Instead, I was thinking about irony while she beat her wings and broke her beak in desperation.

Then again, maybe it was something else. It's strange how the bird's body is situated, as if the attic placed it for me here, like a cat leaves a gift for its caretakers. The attic itself has a presence, offering this to me, inviting me to come in and sit down. The bird is just one small thing. There are so many dead things to imagine, now that I am up here.

Pickie was locked in here, terrified. His screams still hang in the air. I can see with his eyes, the eyes of a terrified child. How the shadows play with the pinprick of light in the corners. Faces of phantoms in the cobwebs trapped like insects, cocooned in grief, sucked of all vitality, husks of life. In the creaks of the boards, I hear the cries of the dead, warped in the wood. The floor moves as I walk, like a mouth opening. The smell of decay, a bait for the creatures who feed on that which is rotten.

It is a fitting place to hide this murder weapon. I am drawn to the farthest corner, where a broken slat opens into a dark hole in the wall. I drop the vial into it. Strange, I don't hear it plop or plink, as if it was caught by a goblin's waiting hand.

I turn to leave. The boards remind me of a hangman's galley. I avoid looking at the bird's corpse. My urgency to escape this attic is growing even as I note that the door is now shut.

There are scratches on it, hundreds of them dug into it where he wanted to be let out when she locked him in. A great pity for little Pickie overcomes me.

People remember bad things that happen to them. Places remember, too. Held between these attic walls, the breath he screamed from his lungs. On the door where he clawed until his fingers bled, the buckle in the wood where he kicked.

Let me out!

I try the door. It rattles but doesn't yield. I apply pressure.

I am not a weak or small person. I chop wood, throw bales of hay. I can get this door open.

I slam my weight against it. It's a small latch, it should break, but it doesn't budge. My shoulder screams in pain where I hit the door. I bang against it, but the sound somehow muffles, or maybe I just can't hear it with the ringing in my ears.

The pinprick of light in the broken ceiling becomes as distant as a star. The attic grows wide and fat, expanding in all directions, and I shrink inside it, the smell of death in my nose, my ears ringing with panic. The spirit of Pickie is inside me, and I have been locked in here for being too wild, because there is a bad spirit in here who will take me to hell if I don't learn to mind my mother. I see through the eyes of a little boy that there is no escape, even as I am crawling back to the center of the floor that is the ceiling of the room where E. A. sleeps, thinking perhaps I am in a nightmare and I will be able to wake her up.

THUMP

My fist beats the attic floor, and it is a child's fist. Two knocks mean NO. I do not want this nightmare.

THUMP THUMP

How terrible to only be able to speak in knocks, to otherwise be silent and ignored by the living. How horrible it is to be dead.

Yes, yes, and all must die—the attic speaks in a whine too high to normally hear, but I can hear it now, louder than that of the ringing in my ears. *Yes*—it feeds on fear and eats the cries of children like a sweet treat—*and you cannot escape your own mind.* My thoughts start spinning into each other.

Then the whine in my ears becomes Mary's voice; she is my mother now, and I am a child locked in here as she tells me of the horrors of hell as I scream.

No! No! No! My fists beat the floor, and on the other side of it, I know I am in a different timeline, lying in the bed, trying to ignore my own fist knocking.

Let me out! Let me out!

I pull out the button from deep in my pocket, and it takes me back into my own body as E. A. I know what the button means.

Memories spill out all at once like a gutted animal. A face, close to mine, singing, speaking, whispering the word. It's what she called me.

A figure takes shape. It is neither the woman I see in my dreams nor the one I saw at the asylum, but I know she is the spirit of both.

She is an outline made of a bluish light, she has no facial features, and I can see through her.

"Yes, it was my nickname for you," she says in a voice I hear somewhere other than my ears but vibrates in my bones. "You were as small as a button, and your eyes were little button eyes."

I toss the button away from me; it rolls across the attic floor, into a cobweb, where it is clutched, stuck in a gray, sticky mess like my mother's mind for all these years.

"You tried to drown me, and you killed my brother!" I yell at this coinage of my brain.

"I couldn't take care of you then. I couldn't take care of myself. But I can help you now."

Your mother never loved you. Jessica never loved you. No one ever loved you because there is no love—the attic whines. *There is no justice. No mercy. Only violence, only cruelty, only death.*

"The air is bad here, you need to get out. I can only help you if you ask me," the apparition of my mother says.

My shoulder and fist are sore, and I am lying on my back next to a dead starling, stuck in this space where the only light is . . .

The window.

Can you fly? This rotting bird couldn't see the glass. Her brain swelled until she died here on the floor. Are you smarter than a bird? The attic floor shakes beneath me like it is laughing.

Outside the window, I can see laundry, hanging, floating like clothes with no people in them, sheets like the skins of beds in which I drowned but was never loved.

Break the glass, jump out; whether you fly or fall, at least it's over—

"Edith Ann Howe," my mother orders me. "March yourself away from this window, back to that door, and kick it from its hinges."

"But there is no love," I cry at her.

"My button, you are surrounded by love. Even now, love holds you and is here to float you away from those who would harm you to those who will help you."

I feel it and I know it is true. Yes. And I *am* loved—by my Aunt Clara, quiet, creaky, and determined. I am loved by my Lady Jane, who inspires me and mentors me. And I allow it, to sense that, in her own way, she loved me, too—my mother. All the good mothers and terrible mothers, who cradle us and bury us, love us in their own way.

I don't march myself, but I do manage to make my way back to the attic door, where a child's hands scratched into the wood. An indentation where a little foot kicked but couldn't break through.

I kick the door. It doesn't budge.

I try again, putting into my foot all my strength, self-righteousness, and fury.

It quivers but does not break. I make sure to aim where the wood is already starting to buckle, where a little boy did his best to escape.

"Mother," I say aloud, with the quiet resolution of all children who know how to forgive. "Please help me out of this place."

My foot breaks a hole into the door, big enough for my leg to push through.

Ripping my stockings, I pull my leg back out. I slam the door again with my shoulder, and it comes off its hinges entirely, breaking open.

I am free.

Chapter 41

"Miss Howe?"

I have lost track of the time, as I do when my pen is scratching parchment and I am whispering to it the words I wish to appear. Thoughts become tangible things, ideas wriggle to fix themselves into solid sentences for thorough interrogation of their purpose on the page.

A young wisp of a maid stands at the door, her arms full of pretty things, her face flummoxed by what she sees. Oh, the room looks like a shipwreck. Margaret Fuller's works scattered hither and yon. I must look a fright, too, with my splintery skirts and hair going who knows where.

"Miss Elliot has sent me to help you dress in your gown, and to do your hair," she says. "She also has sent up this shawl and brooch for you to wear, if you would like. She says they are her particular favorites, and she thinks that the gems in the brooch will suit your eyes."

"Oh, they will, will they?" I almost reach for it without wiping the ink off my fingers, then decide it's better not to touch it at all.

"Very lovely," I say, though it is quite a lot of brooch for a little pin.

"She thinks your hair would look fetching in a Grecian plait, which I am skilled in doing."

"What is your name?"

"Agnes, miss."

"That is a good name." I would prefer Agnes to Edith, certainly. "Agnes, have you ever seen or read *Hamlet*?"

"No, miss. Shall I clear a place for you to sit so I can style your hair?"

"No, no. But do sit yourself and talk to me for a moment." I must have been writing for hours at this point. My fingers have started to cramp. "I am working on an editorial on the goings-on around this place. The knocking, specifically, and there is a part in *Hamlet* where he says, 'There are more things in heaven and earth, Horatio, than are dreamt of in your philosophy.' I am wondering what role imagination plays in belief. Are you religious?"

"Yes, miss. Please let me fix your hair. Miss Elliot said you wouldn't like it, but to tell you that she insists. Also to tell you that we must begin immediately, as Miss Jenny Lind is due to arrive shortly and you must be ready."

I feel very optimistic about my editorial thus far, like a pattern is starting to become clear to me. An idea. There is no belief or knowledge, even, without the imagination. It precedes both belief and will. It must be imagined before it can be believed.

I find myself submitting to the Grecian plait, as it will allow me to fully interrogate Agnes all the while on her belief systems and how she came to them. She is doing the best she can with the knots in my hair I have neglected to brush out. Her hands shake from time to time. I can tell she is very nervous. Scared, perhaps, of me, of the mess of this room, of the broken door to the stinking attic.

I refuse the shawl and the brooch. They are quite lovely—for another person. I will not in any way be badgered into wearing my gown, either. I will be attending tonight's séance as a journalist, and I will be dressed as one.

~

"Quite a to-do," Greeley says, walking from room to room, inspecting the new mirror, the new rug, the new lamps. The new staff, which seems to double in number every time I look away.

Miss Lind will be arriving soon, so I have made my way downstairs to join in the last-minute preparations, which continue on with haste.

"Are all of these things here to stay?" he asks Jessica.

"Only if you like them. Otherwise, they are temporary. Just so Miss Lind feels at home."

"I have told you, she needs none of this. She is the most humble, unassuming person. All this to-do is quite unnecessary. Mother would not . . ." He looks up at the ceiling as if she were hovering there. He does not finish the sentence. There would be nothing new, nothing shiny, were Mary Greeley the one entertaining. She might have thought it better to refuse entertaining in the house at all and instead host Miss Lind in the barn.

As it is, Castle Doleful is putting on the airs of Castle Delightful, tapers burning in reflective, colorful, bright little sconces, curtains pulled and sashed like a fancy-wasped corset, the chandelier in the living room lowered with each and every candle lit.

"These ornaments are, according to my understanding," Jessica says, "typical of the expectations of European guests far less luminary than Miss Lind." She looks like a queen in a gray satin dress with beads and brocades so intricate they must have cost a dressmaker her eyes to stitch them. "We must offer her a proper supper, as our esteemed guest."

The Greeleys are strict vegetarians, teetotalers, and adherents to the Graham diet, but for this event all nutritional abominations will be tolerated. Cakes, puddings, lingonberries, meatballs in the Swedish style, and champagne to wash it all down.

"I am so excited to try the lingonberry torte," Cathie says. She is meticulously crafted in a blue pinafore, her hair pulled into two tight braids. Jessica looks dressed for a ball, and Cathie looks like a young lamb ready to prance out into the fields. This, I assume, is so she appears most humble and innocent for the special guest.

I have put on the same functional brown dress I wore when I first arrived here in the rain.

"I am sorry that you were not pleased with the brooch," Jessica says. "The gems are genuine bohemian garnets." She doesn't mention that I refused to wear my gown or her shawl, as I complied at least with the hairstyle. Every part of my skull feels pulled and pinched into submission.

Jessica has always kept distance between us whenever anyone else is around. Now it no longer troubles or disturbs my mind. It allows me to see her with objectivity. I tell myself that what I loved truly was a figment of my imagination, my own invention of Jessica Elliot, a woman whose character matched her beauty. I am not the first woman in the world to misjudge someone's motivations. My mind consoles me with dry logic and cool reason. Meanwhile, there's a humid howling beneath my belly that insists it has zero interest in her character and needs only her embrace. I must admit, when I find myself circling her orbit, I start to question how much my mind is in charge if my body decides to mutiny.

Cathie and I press our faces against the window, looking out to witness carriages arriving, horses trotting up the long drive where a lifetime ago I pulled my trunk up behind me in a storm. We watch Miss Jenny Lind's entourage emerge from the coaches. Greeley was not expecting so many. He thought she would be accompanied by one, or perhaps two additional guests, not twenty.

People spill inside the front parlor and hall. The sudden bursts of chatter with free-flowing superlatives in the introductions are made and continued. Her composer, her violinist, her pianist, her personal secretary, and her lady's maid—all were brought here as part of the tour, as she never goes anywhere without them. Much hand-kissing, pressing, shaking. Curtsies and bows. Not worthy of introduction are the valets that each of her retinue employ, nor the maid of her maid. I cannot yet see Miss Lind, who stands in the center of the crowd, obscured by the rings of her entourage.

Ah, there she is, winding toward Mr. Greeley. I admit, I feel a sense of honor and trepidation as I am offered to Miss Lind for her consideration as he beckons me into the fold.

"And this is Miss Howe, a reporter of mine," Mr. Greeley says.

I wonder whether or not I need to curtsy. I decide to do my best.

She returns the favor, and I am smitten. What a charming little person she is, with a peach of a face, a graceful little figure, and such an open expression of curiosity.

Her secretary, a tall, thin man, translates for her in Swedish something that Mr. Greeley said. She seems confused about the word *reporter*.

"I write for newspapers," I clarify.

"Oh, newspapers." She has a darling Swedish accent.

"She is writing about Cathie Fox—the spirit-telegraph," Mr. Greeley says.

"How do you feel about the abolition movement, Miss Lind?" I ask, with full confidence that she will wax rhapsodic on its virtues now that she has been directly asked. "A statement of support from your powerful voice will greatly help this unquestionably good cause. Especially in the South, where you are soon to tour."

There may be some confusion with the language. I am not sure what *abolition* translates to in Swedish, so perhaps I need to explain the tenets to her. Her open expression has now closed, and her personal secretary is rapidly turning from his chat with Greeley, as if I were hiding a dagger up my sleeve. I center myself and try again.

"I know you are to tour in the Southern states, and your strong statement about their abhorrent practice of institutional kidnapping and enslavement—"

"No, I did not say," she says with a horrified expression. "I say nothing."

"But if you did, if you would, if you—"

"Miss Lind makes no such statement." Her personal secretary cuts me off, blocking her from my view, and his hands stretch out as if to throttle me. "Miss Lind in no way speaks any words that would offend her hosts in the South."

"Miss Lind, even a very simple statement," I call to her back, which is moving away from me and through a wall of maids and valets.

"In no way does she endorse any viewpoint that would offend any of her hosts in the South," the secretary says again, with such emphasis that I realize it has been rehearsed exactly for questions such as mine.

"No politics, Miss Howe," Mr. Greeley says, putting his hand on my shoulder. "This night is not about that."

"It's not politics, it's—"

"Let our honored guest experience the beauty of the spirit world, Miss Howe," Mr. Greeley says, like a warning.

I brace my disappointment by reminding myself that the night has not yet even begun. I shall bide my time.

"So where is the little girl who sings for the spirits?" Miss Lind's broken English rings out. We all pull back like curtains to reveal the smallest and humblest of us all, Cathie Fox, waiting patiently on a settee to be called forth.

Cathie walks to Miss Lind with an assurance none of us adults have mastered.

"You, then, are the mouthpiece to heaven?" Miss Lind says with a self-conscious Swedish lilt, grasping Cathie's hands.

"I am most humbly in your service and honored." Cathie curtsies, as graceful as I've seen her.

Without warning, Miss Lind pulls her into an embrace. A joyous laughter erupts at this unexpected intimacy and circles out to engulf the room. "What a sweet little girl! How old are you?"

"Eleven."

Miss Lind opens her mouth wide, and the most sublime sound in the world pours out:

> "Ah! May the red rose live alway,
> To smile upon earth and sky!"

Pure and sweet like cool running streams and wildflower-covered hills. My mind becomes clear, my heart becomes glad. Her voice is the sound of goodness, faith, rippling like a happy bird foretelling nothing but springtime. Though I have never been to an opera, I have heard this type of singing before. But I have never heard a voice like this. Yes, a nightingale is an apt description. It is a pure, free sound that lifts the heart.

> "Why should the beautiful ever weep?
> Why should the beautiful die?"

She stops singing and we all reflexively respond in applause. We just heard the reason she is more famous than Queen Victoria, and far better loved.

"And now, you must make the spirits sing for me," Miss Lind says to Cathie. "You show me that the beautiful do not die."

The pianist—the "most skilled in all of Europe," according to Miss Lind's introduction—sits down at the piano with a long glissando, decrying how terribly it is out of tune. He plays "Nelly Bly," singing with clear articulation of the "de" and "hab."

> "Nelly Bly! Nelly Bly! Bring de broom along,
> We'll sweep the kitchen clean my dear and hab a little song!"

There is some confusion around supper, for the entourage had thought that no supper would be served and there are plans for that later at the hotel. Jessica tries to wrangle the best course of action with the secretary, amid the carousing tale of Nellie Bly.

Miss Lind is not hungry, not even for meatballs or lingonberry, though she's amused at the offer. She and her composer dialogue back and forth in their own language, the content related with merriment to the secretary. Apparently, the composer will accept small plates being delivered to him to sample. He will not turn down the opportunity to try the American attempt at Swedish dishes, and judge accordingly, no doubt.

The violinist joins in the next round of "Nelly Bly."

"It is best for the séance to commence after sunset," Jessica informs the secretary, straining to be heard over the rousing next verse.

"Therefore, supper should be served soon, and Miss Lind can just partake of fruit, if that might please her."

"Miss Lind does not understand why it needs to be after sunset, and she wants to ensure a good night's rest at the hotel. She had understood from Mr. Greeley that this was a demonstration only, not a supper." The secretary does not need to further consult with Miss Lind to relay this all back to Jessica. He apparently shares a mind with her.

"It's too much of a to-do, Miss Elliot, as I said before," Mr. Greeley blusters, embarrassed. "I never said we should have supper, and now there will be all this food going to waste."

Jessica does not react to being scolded, neither capitulating nor apologizing. Instead, she merely consults the composer, who seems quite happy with the lingonberries and meatballs.

His satisfaction charms Miss Lind, who would not deny such pleasure to her retinue. Small plates, then, rather than a full supper, shall be brought and delivered to each person who would like to sample what America has to offer of the Swedish dish.

If Jessica is despondent at the alteration in plans, she does not show it, pivoting to insert herself next to Miss Lind. She inquires with enunciation and volume so that the meatball-eating composer, the personal secretary, Mr. Greeley, Dr. Vincent, and the blushing maid he is chatting with can no doubt attest to hear:

"Miss Lind, I would like to make a present of your friend Hans Christian Andersen's book 'The Nightingale' to Cathie. Would you do me the honor of signing it for her?"

"Oh, Miss Elliot, thank you," Cathie responds as if on cue. "I love all of his stories, and that one most of all. It would mean so much to me, Miss Lind, for you to sign it."

"Of course I will sign it, child," the Swedish Nightingale humbly demurs.

"My sister Maggie will be wild with envy!"

"Oh, Miss Howe, will you fetch it for me?" Jessica asks. "I left it upstairs in your room."

Dr. Vincent was correct about my distractibility. I had somehow thought if I disposed of the vial of poison, that would be the end of it. Clearly, Jessica thinks all will go according to plan, that I am ready to slay a sick woman so she can usurp her position. That my mind will bow to her bidding merely because my body is magnetized to her touch. I am taking too long to respond.

"Would you like me to go?" Little Agnes, the maid, suddenly appears to offer. "I know where it is."

"I will go," I say, snapping to attention. I can get the book, despite that I am not playing her chess game, being pulled like a pawn to be sacrificed.

I make my way upstairs, yet my feet feel heavy as I move forward, like attempting to walk in water. Everyone is down in the hall except for me and Mary. Jessica will not see what I do or do not do. I don't need to see Mary or go near her. And I don't want to.

Why, then, are my legs walking me there? The *whir* and the *tic* of the Vincent-ivizer are nearly unendurable, making a grating whine, yet they seem to warn me that I am overlooking something very important. Is it something to do with Dr. Vincent? I have a distinct impression of him saying "check" and gloating over a chessboard. By going to her room, I'm putting myself straight into checkmate. A particularly upsetting comparison to think of, especially since I am a terrible chess player.

I find myself at Mary's door, no greasepaint on the knob, no mark to show someone entering or exiting. Not that it would matter—the door is wide open.

Why am I going into this room at all?

She lies there, unconscious. This mother, not my mother. But like my mother. The Mind-Stimulator whirs on her head, light from the window and shadows from the trees pass over the dead portraits of the Greeley children, their dead hair like golden halos.

I stand over her body, noting that her eyes move beneath her lids, that her breath comes in more quickly, that she is better, that it is possible she can awaken, and I suddenly realize why I am here. I speak aloud.

I ask for her forgiveness for anything I have done that may have caused her harm, intentionally or in my ignorance. In particular, for holding her head as a doctor forced her to take something she knew was poison. I weep for the death of my own abusive mother. I cry for the woman I will never know, and I allow that it is possible that her spirit cares for me after her death in a way she never could in life.

I ask that Mary wake up. I do this all with solemnity and sincerity, there in the watching presence of Pickie, if I can believe in that sort of thing—which, for the moment, I can. Then I do something I don't remember ever doing before.

I kneel by her side and pray for her. I may not have faith in this gesture, but enough people do that I figure it can't hurt.

Chapter 42

No one asks where I have been. I'm not sure how long I was gone, except that it was enough time for plates to be filled and emptied, for people to drape themselves on furniture and be waited on, and for the sun to set, making it dark enough that one can fully appreciate the work it took to light each candle in the chandelier.

"Here is the book," I say, holding it up. The look of loving appreciation on Jessica's face, the way her hand lingers on mine, causes a momentary insurrection in my body. Luckily, she turns from me quickly to present the fairy tale for signing. Much pomp, little circumstance. The delivery of the autograph from Jenny Lind has concluded. I have a temporary stay in the execution of Jessica's full disappointment in me.

"It is time now, everyone, for us to gather for this special event." Jessica draws us into the living room for the séance, but people need to be corralled. There is none of the showmanship that Dr. Vincent displays in his own exhibitions, and he offers none of his usual intense gazes or magnetic hand-waving. He is still enjoying his food and his champagne, lingering near the door, chatting with the violinist. I hear him say something about his own years of study on the instrument.

Mr. Greeley tries to take charge of the situation. He gives instructions for everyone to find a seat at the round table at the living room's center, but Jessica wants everyone placed in certain positions. There are only six chairs for the table, so other seats need to be brought in if Miss Lind insists—as her secretary huffily confirms—that all her musicians and he himself, of course, be included. After four more chairs are brought in and placed, Miss Lind's personal maid is banished with the other valets and maids to the kitchen.

There are now ten of us remaining.

"Now, it's all very simple in how it works," Greeley explains. "We make a hand-holding chain. This is how the séance is conducted."

"There must be confusion with your French," says the secretary. "*Séance* means 'sitting,' not holding hands." He says something in Swedish, which makes all the Swedes laugh. I would wager that there is much fun being made of Mr. Greeley, but I cannot confirm it because I don't know Swedish.

"Our hands make a circuit for the spirits," Cathie's voice rings out. "But more than our hands, they need our reverence." She cuts through the chatter, her sincerity hushing the Swedes. "Our reverence makes them welcome."

The atmosphere of the room begins to thicken, soften. Those of us selected to stay find the gravity in our bodies. Questions course through our veins. What are we here for? Why have we been chosen? What is to happen to us?

"We must be quiet, that they may be heard," Cathie intones in a chant-like cadence. "It is in silence where spirits speak the loudest. Our humility is their exaltation."

The clear confidence of her instruction enables the Lind party members to be directed where they will be seated, though the arrangement must be altered, as Miss Lind insists that she be seated between her composer and her secretary. She is clearly uncomfortable with touching anyone's hands she doesn't know. Mr. Greeley will sit directly across from Miss Lind—I suppose it is a place of honor—and I somehow wind up with the violinist to my left and Dr. Vincent to my right. I do not protest. I am here for whatever it is we are about to witness, and if I need to hold Dr. Vincent's hand, I will suffer it.

"Before we begin," Cathie says, "I will honor you all with a special request for the spirits."

The adults all turn their eyes to her in expectation. Something thrilling is about to occur, we all know it. Even I—who've heard more than enough from Cathie Fox's spirit-rapping—can't help but feel I am at the mouth of some opening mystery.

"There was a time," she says, "when spirits played the piano for me and my sister. I ask that we leave the cover open. Might we also have the violin placed on the piano, in case the spirits wish to play?"

"Oh, no, I am the only one who touches my violin." The violinist begins what will clearly be a losing battle, as Miss Lind makes a forceful Swedish remark. "I do not know who this spirit is or if they can play, or if they will break a string."

Miss Lind says something that changes his mind, and he relents, placing his violin as requested with the air of someone saying good-bye forever.

"We now may be seated," Cathie says.

We sit, negotiating the positions of our bustles and britches with the backs of the mismatched chairs.

"Shall I lower the lights?" Jessica asks.

Cathie nods, the weight of her head dropping down. Slowly, she lifts her head with her eyes set straight ahead without a blink.

Jessica walks over to each light and dims it, a shadow lengthening from every corner.

"Take the hands of the ones next to you," Cathie says, "and hold them so we can all see them here on the table. They will function as a circuit for the spirits to pass through."

Jenny Lind says something in Swedish, and the violinist says something back, even as he slides his hand into mine.

"Miss Lind is nervous," the violinist whispers to me. "She had not expected it would make her feel this way. Is it always like this?"

"It's my first séance, too. I don't know." It is a phenomenon in and of itself, holding hands with a stranger. I am aware, of course, that my hands are already hot, sweaty, and mannish, especially holding the delicate fingers of the violinist. I hope I don't harm his livelihood. I don't want to take Dr. Vincent's magnetic-fork-plunging fingers, but once I do, I'm pleasantly surprised that they are not made of snakeskin or plaster. It's just a hand, like any other. I can feel that he has calluses on his finger pads from where he carries his machine back and forth.

So here I am, seated at a low-lit table with Jenny Lind and Horace Greeley, holding hands with a mesmerist and a violinist, in a chain of fools awaiting a performance from an eleven-year-old's foot. And this is my first real assignment as a journalist.

I have to remind myself that I believe I know how she produces the knocking sounds, because I feel in danger of forgetting. Something is happening in all of us, linking like this—pulsing with breath and blood, expectation, hope, fear.

"There is a presence in this room, do you feel it?" Cathie asks.

I am not saying it isn't just my imagination, "just" being that limiting adverb that puts imagination in a box with toys, but I *do* sense something else is here, within the space of our circle. Some *thing* that had not been here before, now descends upon us.

A presence of . . . I don't know what. But there is a tangible feeling of unease.

"Någon rörde mig på axeln," someone says, I think the composer. "Someone just touched me on the shoulder."

A murmur passes around the chain, the violinist twisting his head. "Who tapped me?" he asks.

"It's a spirit," Cathie says. "A gentle spirit who is making her presence known."

Soft fingers touch the back of my neck. My eyes are open, I can see no person in my periphery. Who is touching me?

A bass note is struck on the piano.

I jump straight up in my seat.

The light is low in the room, but we can all plainly see our collection of hands gripping each other's. There is no person at the piano. Dr. Vincent's hand squeezes on mine in a quick pulse; when I look at him, he grins.

Whispers between the guests are quelled by Cathie's voice saying, "Shhhhh . . . What spirit is here?"

The notes sound again, and a series of knocks shudder the table.

Jenny Lind squeals something in Swedish and then English. "Who did that?"

"We have joined together to ask the spirits if they have a message for Miss Jenny Lind," Cathie says. "Knock once for yes."

I hear the knock softly, but it must be louder where she sits, for Jenny exclaims, "Mr. Greeley, that must have been you!"

"You see my hand," Greeley says to her. "I could not knock."

"You did it. It banged right here in front of me, and you are the only one close enough to do it!"

Strings pluck once, twice, then make a screeching yowl on the violin.

The violinist's delicate hand belies his strength. He grips my hand with such force I feel he'll crush my knuckles.

A heat comes through my body—the need to break the chain, the desire to run. I tell myself I must stay where I am, to stay in control of myself and my fear.

"Perhaps we should see what message the spirit has, Miss Lind," Greeley says. "This is the purpose for which you've come here."

"Ja, yes," she says.

"Spirit, please knock once for yes, twice for no," Cathie says. "Do you understand?"

Knock.

"We are here tonight, spirit, to prove to Jenny Lind the truth of the spirit world. Do you have a message for her?"

Knock.

"Ask the spirit, Jenny Lind," Cathie says. "If the spirit is here for you, ask what the spirit has to say."

"Ja, yes," she says. "I don't know, in English, how to ask this."

"Then ask in your language."

Jenny Lind utters some words in Swedish.

Two knocks.

Her face contorts in surprise.

She asks another question.

One knock.

Miss Lind gasps. Whatever answer she is getting, it is shocking to her. She asks one thing more, and a flurry of knocks shake the table.

"Mr. Greeley, you are doing this!" Miss Lind yells at him. "You are the one knocking!"

"I most certainly am not." Greeley breaks the chain to put his hands on top of his head. "I am not! Here are my hands, see!"

"Someone is doing this!"

"Everyone, put your hands on your head," Greeley says, chuckling. "Cathie, you, too!"

We all put our hands on our heads. A relief, I must say, for my hands are quite sweaty.

The knocks have stopped for the moment.

We all start laughing, looking one to another. It is too funny! The sight of all of us, hands on tops of heads, left to right, across and around, seeing each other's faces in full expression of fright, is so comical we have to laugh. What a hilarious situation, and how ridiculous we all look. Even creepy Dr. Vincent's face is transfixed with joy. What fun! What fun to be scared about nothing!

Dum duh . . . two low notes, *BANG!*—the lid of the piano slams down.

None of us are laughing anymore.

Thud-bump.

"The spirit," Cathie says, hands on head, "needs to say something. I will say the alphabet, and wait for a knock on the letter of the name of the spirit. A . . . B . . . C . . . D—"

A knock.

"Her name begins with a *D*," Cathie says.

"But how is this happening?" Jenny says, looking from person to person. "Who is doing this?"

Mr. Greeley is still full of mirth. "This is far more activity than I have seen before," he exults. "The spirits have turned out wonderfully for you, Miss Lind."

"I do not like it," she says.

"It is a marvelous instrument. You are getting a message from the other side!"

Jenny asks another question, in Swedish.

Knock. Knock.

Jenny looks around, all of us still wearing our hands as hats. "But who knows this about me?" she asks in English.

There is a sudden *whoosh*. Half of the candles in the chandelier go out, as if snuffed, leaving our faces cloaked in shadow, shrinking the visible room.

Hands start to come down from heads. The violinist's are shaking.

"Who is the spirit?" I ask him in a whisper.

"It is a rival who died at the Royal Academy," he says.

"A, B, C, D, E, F, G, H, I, J, K, L, M—"

Knock.

". . . N, O—"

Knock.

". . . P, Q, R—"

Knock.

"A, B, C, D—"

Knock.

"A—"

Knock.

"Morda. Morda?" Cathie asks.

THUD.

Jenny Lind begins making high-pitched, keening noises.

"But tell us," Cathie says, "what you know *now*, spirit? From the other side?"

The center of the table erupts in a series of shuddering knocks.

Then stops.

"Be at peace, Jenny Lind," Cathie's voice says. "She sees now, in Summerland, what she did not see on Earth."

The dam bursts on Jenny Lind's tears, and the circle is broken as her entourage move from their chairs. She is patted, embraced. People rush to give her their handkerchiefs, possibly hoping she will bless them with her sacred tears. They treat her like a saint.

Is it done, then, speaking with this rival? Or will she materialize further to tap shoulders, knock tables, and pluck strings?

"Oh, what a wonderful science," Dr. Vincent exclaims, breathless. "This far exceeds my expectations for what a child can—"

A scream shatters above us.

Our eyes tilt upward.

"Enough, I don't wish to play anymore," Jenny says, but we have all clasped hands again, as if for protection.

A door slams!

A howling wind slams another door shut, closer to us!

The whole ceiling shudders!

Poundings like giant fists onto the stairs, and it is coming down for us, coming, coming.

"THIS HOUSE WILL COME DOWN!"

Do we move? Do we breathe? We do not. We just clasp hands in the half-light of the room, as some sort of fury moves closer.

"TAKE! THIS HOUSE! DOWN!"

It is coming.

Reasonless, faceless, furious, a moving wall of sound. We pray for it to pass, to have mercy, to depart. We have tampered with something from beyond, awakened something that slept, that rages from above and is descending upon us.

It is closer now.

We did not know—but we are not innocent—how these forces we have drawn forth will burst our dams of logic, break our brains of categorical solutions. We understand nothing, we know nothing, we are nothing to this thing descending closer and closer to obliterate the world we know.

It is coming . . . for us.

We do not know what it is. We do not want to know. But it is here.

The door of the living room flies open.

"TAKE THIS HOUSE DOWN!"

An apparition in white, hands outstretched, screaming.

We topple over each other, getting up from the table, trying to run, but where to hide? Just get as far away as possible. Except brave Mr. Greeley.

Mr. Greeley runs *to* the apparition and catches it with both arms.

It folds over and into his body, limp.

"It's a miracle," he cries, loud enough to reach the heavens. "A miracle!"

Chapter 43

There is a small white light in the center of my vision, like a fairy gas lamp stuck to my eyeball. I press that place between my thumb and index finger. Dr. Vincent be damned, it does seem to help alleviate the pain, at least the one in my head.

Jenny Lind and her entourage are leaving in a rush. Mr. Greeley attempts a blubbering explanation of why the appearance of Mary Greeley is a wonderful—rather than a horrifying—event, but this seems difficult to translate into Swedish.

Cathie, knees pulled into her chest, looks very much like a child awaiting a punishment.

"It is a strange gift that disturbs," Jenny Lind says to her by way of parting. "You are an instrument for the spirits, but beware of those who play you without care." She stifles a sob as a maid appears with a coat befitting an emperor's nightingale and wraps her in it. "Beware, little spirit-singer!" she calls out as her entourage encircles her and floats her away.

The secretary herds the remainder of the Lind party as I attempt to stall him in my journalistic duty.

"Who was the spirit?" I ask him. "Why was she so upset? I couldn't understand what she was saying."

He hesitates. Then, with a practiced patter, he states, "As Miss Lind has remarked in many interviews thus far, while she was young and in music school, she destroyed her voice from abusive training and misuse.

She could not sing or even speak for about two years. The voice you hear from Miss Lind is the one that she had to piece back together herself, note by note."

"Why did the spirit so upset her?" My throat burns. All the yelling I did in the attic is coming back to haunt me. "The violinist said it was a rival."

"When Miss Lind had to leave school, another young coloratura became the top singer and went on to great success before dying young. The spirit claimed she was murdered by someone Miss Lind knew and loved. There is no more to say in the matter, and no proving or disproving it, as that person is dead. I must go now. We are due at the hotel. You will need to clear any statements you wish to make with Miss Lind's press manager, and should you try and fabricate any statement at all that would offend our hosts in the South, we will not hesitate to take legal action."

"Legal action?" I have never heard of anything so ridiculous. I don't even know what that is. People print whatever they want here. That's the freedom of the press.

Oh no. The light in the center of my vision is getting bigger.

"It was an astounding success," I hear Dr. Vincent's voice. "It is much better, child, to terrify than to merely entertain." He is speaking to Cathie, who appears ready to burst into tears. I feel awful for her, knowing how badly she wanted to impress Miss Lind. Perhaps she performed *too* well.

I can't account for how she did it. How could Cathie accomplish all those things? The violin, the piano, the touching on the shoulder. Even just the knocks alone from one girl's foot seem beyond comprehension. I have no way to explain it, and at this moment I couldn't even begin to try. Perhaps Jessica is helping, the two of them working together . . .

The pain has started to take over my head, the light blotting out more of my vision.

Jessica . . . I can't see her, I can't feel her. She's as distant as someone else's dream.

Chapter 44

I am sick enough to die.

Blinding light giving way to a fever. I am retching into a chamber pot, my throat on fire, my stomach throwing everything back up.

A migraine knocked me down, and a flu means to finish me. Head, stomach, throat, but the most painful is my broken heart. Jessica does not come to my bed. She does not visit me. I do not hear her voice, or any voice. My sheets are soaked with sweat, but no one changes them. They are leaving me alone to die.

Instead of dying, I dream. I can't remember what.

⁓

Black tea, broth. Someone changed the chamber pot.

A hand on my head.

"Don't touch her, we don't know if it's contagious." It's Martha's voice, and the hand belongs to her daughter.

"Then how will we know when the fever has passed?"

The Marthas are taking care of me, whether I am one of them or not. I don't know how I deserve the grace and care they give to me, that they give to everyone in this household.

Later, voices outside the door.

Men talking, strident and cocksure. Like doctors, but not for me, for Castle Doldrum. Assessing. I hear them outside the room, taking out the pieces of the attic door, talking through the walls. They whistle cheerfully as they diagnose fatal flaws. Wood rot, especially in the attic. Poor construction, cracked beams, the very foundation sinking. The house is coming down around me. I will be another ghost in this house, but maybe I will be the last.

No. I refuse to be a ghost.

I am dreaming, but I remember this as it's happening. I feel arms around me. I am part of a happy family I never knew—a father, a mother, a brother—I am a child in a cradle, and they sit around a warm room and look at me with love in their eyes. But now I am no longer a child; I am me, now in this bed, and they are watching over me.

My mother's face I see in this dream as I never saw her life—intelligent, striking, full of fierce love. My father's face is like seeing my own in a mirror, except there is a thumbprint dimple in his chin and a jaw that could break raw acorns. And my brother—I know it's my brother even though I can't make out his features. I know by the way he's teasing me: "Oh, you're gonna live like you always do. Stop crying, you're through the worst of it."

But it isn't just the spirits of my family watching over me. The hot broth the Marthas have brought me is medicine. The water, from a deep well, wishes to restore me. The boiled-down stalks of root vegetables that grew fat in the dirt—I can taste onion, carrot, garlic, and the healing of sage, the savor of salt—call me back to this Earth, where everything has its own directive on how to survive. Outside the window, I can see the leaves of an oak tree that watches over me, protecting me from too much brightness when I need the dark to heal. Squirrels chase each other through her branches, and I try to identify the different birds I hear calling to each other by their distinctive songs. There are so many ways to be alive and love and work, they all tell me. I am not one of them, though, no . . . I have yet to discover what I am.

And I am going to have to heal and move out again into the world to find out.

~

I am still bedridden up here in the Margaret Fuller room, reading book after book. My head, stomach, and throat feel better, but I am still weak and my broken heart is excruciating. My appetite has started to stir, and the past two days I've eaten all my gruel, which I keep wishing Jessica would bring to me with concern about my recovery, or care enough to poison and put me out of my misery.

Now Martha is in here, throwing open the window, pulling the covers off me, telling me I better die or get out of here and live, because time isn't waiting for me.

She and Young Martha are preparing for a journey. While the house is being demolished and rebuilt, Mary Greeley will be staying in the Austrian spa that Dr. Vincent endorses. His words are now gospel to the Greeleys. There is a large Baquet there designed by Mesmer himself, where Mary will make a full recovery to a health she "never before believed was possible." She will need to make a long trip to get there, and Martha and her daughter will accompany her and Baby Charlotte to ensure the child has the care she needs.

"A mother-and-daughter adventure for us all," Martha says with enough salt to kill a lake. "Now, get up and start packing. You're going to have to catch a train."

"But I am still sick," I say, tears watering my cheeks.

"Now, you stop that," she says, patting my cheek five hairs short of a slap. "Your fever's been gone for days, and you're just whinging about in self-pity. Mr. Greeley's off in the city, writing some big public statement you bullied him into. Wasn't that why you came here? Now, get dressed and come down for breakfast. He left a letter for you."

Fine. If I am to die, I would rather not do it here anyway. I dress and make my way downstairs, feeling like I have eaten a porcupine for how my insides prick with lovelessness, sorrow, and lost illusions.

There is, however, the wonderful smell of biscuits, and while I truly have no appetite, I suppose I can try, for old time's sake, to see if I can get one down.

Martha hands me the letter from Greeley. Some money and a train ticket fall out of it. I have no idea what it says. Truly. I can only make out my name. After that . . . I think that word is "Swisshelm." Maybe she's demanding my return.

Upstairs, I can hear Mary Greeley chirping to Young Martha and Baby Charlotte. "Healing I never believed possible! 'I will, I believe, I heal,' as Dr. Vincent says."

"As Dr. Vincent says," Martha repeats, imitating Mary's voice. "She went into a coma crazy as a jaybird and woke up as nothing but a parrot."

"I cannot read this letter," I say. Despite the fact that I almost died of the flu and am languishing away and will die of a broken heart, I have eaten five biscuits.

"Mr. Greeley's staying in the city near the Rookery for the next six months," Martha says without looking at it. "He's sending you back to Washington, and your article for him is late."

"What about . . ." She never visited, she never checked on me, she never loved me. "Jessica?"

"Well, there's nothing about her in his letter, if that's what you're looking for."

"But where is Jessica?"

Martha fixes me with a withering stare.

"I mean . . . Miss Elliot. Where is Miss Elliot?"

"Mrs. *Vincent* is out in the orchard with Miss Fox."

Chapter 45

"Behold, the *Vincent-Fox* spirit-telegraph!"

Cathie mimics Dr. Vincent's voice and hand gestures, free from irony. I suppose she has already been trained, much like a very talented monkey.

I cannot bear to look at her governess; instead, I keep my eyes fixed on Cathie. The two of them sit outside where I discovered them my first day here, after tearing up my editorial and deciding that I must pivot my attention. When was that? I am disoriented. More time has passed than I can account for. I have been sick for a week, at least. Maybe even two. They both are now wearing thick cloaks. There are no books or lessons or picnic food. It is biting cold this morning, if not yet winter. All the trees have changed color. The sky is slate gray, and the wind is as persistent as my mother's ghost.

"Try it." Cathie stands up to hand me a small rectangular board.

"This is a telegraph?" I am rather disappointed. I expected more from Dr. Vincent. This looks far too simple. It's a thin piece of wood with the alphabet painted on it and a heart-shaped wooden disc that fits neatly under Cathie's hand. "How does this work?"

"It's quite marvelous," she says, laughing at my expression. "Rather than having to go through the whole alphabet and wait for the spirit to knock on a letter, you just put your hands on the disc and let the spirits guide you. Then the rap stops your hand at the right letter. Sit down, Miss Howe. Try it."

"I don't want to," I say, handing back the board.

She sits again, prattling on about how excited she is—they will be going on tour with Dr. Vincent to help him demonstrate how to use the machine and spirit board together. She will continue to receive her lessons from Mrs. Vincent. She says "Mrs. Vincent" with the emphasis of someone who has had it beaten into her.

"Mrs. Vincent," I echo, swallowing my heart to look at her directly. She looks back at me as if seeing me from above some unfathomable sea. We are two people who have never met. We do not even move on this Earth on the same plane. "That was a very speedy marriage," I say.

"We are passionately in love, the doctor and I, so I insisted we get married quickly so it could reach its appropriate culmination." Whatever cruelty is in the words *passionately in love*, her voice is flat. "I wasn't going to accompany him as his assistant like some dollop of jam."

It must be what he wanted from the moment he saw her. She's the perfect addition for his act. A woman who draws every gaze in the room and adds, as I thought from their first demonstration together, credibility sum Keats—*Beauty is truth, truth beauty.* I wonder how quickly after Mary awakened it took for her to fall into Dr. Vincent's arms. Perhaps it happened before that, all my jealous imaginings justified. My stomach clenches, my face hot. It still hurts. I am not well. I won't think of her name. I can't think of her hands or her mouth or the whisper of her breath.

Tap . . . Tap . . . Tap. Cathie's hands move, and as the disc stops on a letter, it makes a light sound. It's probably much easier on her toes than thumping a wood floor.

"Cathie, I thought you wanted to go back to your mother?" I say to her.

"I do," she says. "I miss her so much. I want to cry every time I think about how long it's been since I last saw her, and how long it will be until I see her again."

"Yes, of course, we all want our mothers," the governess says, alarmed, the first look of life behind her eyes. "But it's important, when we have a gift, to use it to help the world. That's what the spirits want from you."

"Do they?" I press on, eager to earn more of *Mrs. Vincent's* alarm. May she look downright anguished. "If so, remember, Miss Lind cautioned you to beware those who would abuse your instrument."

My memory of the séance has taken on the quality of a vivid nightmare. As much as I had thought I figured out how Cathie was making the knocking, I now am unsure of my hypothesis. It seems impossible she could make all those sounds with just her foot. The spirits understood Swedish. The instruments played, and I could see enough to note that there were no fingers touching the strings of the violin. I felt something touch my shoulder. Whether these happenings are real or imagined, I am frightened for Cathie. The spirits, as Miss Lind said, do *disturb*.

Tap. Tap. Cathie's hands move on the board, and she begins to hum a happy tune that I don't know.

"Cathie is free to do whatever she wishes." The governess doesn't reward me with continued alarm. She simply turns her head from us both. "Above all, my husband values one's will."

"I don't think you should go on tour with Dr. Vincent," I say to Cathie. "Even if he did steal your governess."

"I wish to go with them." If I have said something offensive or incendiary, it is only Cathie who seems concerned. She is suddenly anxious and pleading with her governess, as if the turn of her head away from us both is too much to bear. "I want to go on tour with Dr. and Mrs. Vincent, I very much want to go, I would be miserable to not go." *The lady doth protest too much.* She grabs the hand of her governess. "You will let me come with you, won't you?"

"Of course you may come with us, for as long as you choose to do so," the governess says, as if she is granting a favor. "And I am certain my husband will wish to meet your mother and receive her blessing. Perhaps we can make a plan to see her sooner rather than later."

Cathie hugs her, a willful but devoted pupil. The governess soothes and coos, the beloved but firm teacher. They seem far better practiced in their routine than ever before. It continues longer than I can bear. I need to leave. I came out here without a cloak or gloves, and it's so cold, that wind.

"You could come with us, Miss Howe," Cathie says. "Wouldn't that be wonderful? Please, come with us!"

I expect the governess to protest. But she doesn't. Instead, she looks directly at me with hope in her eyes. That which I thought was dead inside me beats her wings. For a moment I see Jessica once again, *my* Jessica, the way I had imagined her.

"You could write marvelous stories from the tour," Cathie says. "Mr. Greeley would publish them all. He will publish anything for Dr. Vincent. Please, come with us, Miss Howe. We would have so much fun!"

"It would be lovely," Jessica says, opening her palm in a gesture of invitation. I recall her premonition. The backs of our hands, wrinkled, together. Maybe different from the way she had thought, but together still. She is making an offer, after all this, for me to come with her. It is a hand wanting to pull me up to her. "I know my husband is fond of her."

No. It will not pull me up. It is a hand waiting to pull me under. Of course Dr. Vincent would be more than happy to add another to his menagerie of captivity. Mrs. Vincent would be pleasantly distracted by me if I could forget what I have learned about her and adore her as before. Cathie . . . Oh, what will become of her? She needs someone to help her, to save her from all these people who use her to ease their own pain. Or to get what they want.

"Ask the spirit board, Miss Howe," Cathie says. "Ask: Should I go on tour with the Dr. and Mrs. Vincent and the famous Cathie Fox?"

I pick up the board, noting the quality of the wood, the shine of the polish, the careful calligraphy of the letters. Upon reexamination, it is not so simple after all. It is something quite striking.

"Now," Cathie says, "ask the spirits to help you."

"Which ones?" I say. "There are so many spirits. Surely they can't all have my best interest at heart."

"True," she says. "Why don't you ask your mother?"

I suppose I might as well. The wind today is the same type as when Cathie saw her over my shoulder, bringing me back bits of my heartfelt words, *a fight for her very soul*. My mother is here, if I believe in that sort of thing. I want to believe it, for this moment. So I do.

"Mother, what should I do?" I ask.

I place my hands on the little heart-shaped disc.

A to B to C . . . A tap stops it on *G*.

It is amazing, I must admit. My hands seem guided, like it is not me who is moving them.

Click-tap.

"O."

Click-tap. What a satisfying little sound it makes. My hands are moving again before I can stop them, a harder sound on the board on the letter *H*. It must be a force within me; I do not think it is otherwise, but still, it is insistent on the message.

"GO HOME."

Chapter 46

It is a long and nasty journey home. My ride out to New York at least had the benefit of novelty and purpose. This cramped, smelly, sleepless ride back to Washington, weak and nursing my broken heart, is a level of purgatory.

There have been a few incidents of violence among passengers. I have shown a level of restraint that is out of character, since I could easily have inserted myself into these situations. Greeley's editorial against the Compromise was published yesterday. A fight broke out after the stop in Boston, when a man, proudly proclaiming Horace Greeley's "radical" opinion as his own, badgered a man from Macon into fisti-cuffs. I did not attempt to join in. Horace Greeley's opinion is not *my* own. While Greeley now sees many of the issues with the Compromise, I still consider his viewpoint as myopic as far as equality is concerned. The editorial I will write for *The North Star* will show just how middling Greeley's "radical" position truly is.

First, however, I need to write this story on Cathie Fox. Ink flows with long phrases about imagination, belief, equality, eternity, free will. My pen scratches the parchment with paragraphs about grief, illusion, oppression. I've decided I am going to title this piece, "The Knocking." At least for now.

The knocking has followed me. I mean, not just the concept but the actual sound.

The sound reminds me that I can't just close the chapter on Cathie. That her destiny and mine are intertwined. I just don't know how, exactly.

"On one hand," I am about to write, but I blot out ~~hand~~ and put in *foot*, for mine is tapping. On one foot, perhaps it is just me making these raps. But it doesn't account for the other sounds I hear that I know I am not making. Like a constant rhythm. Perhaps it is my mother trying to get my attention.

The train stops, jolting the pot of ink I had thought was secure.

In stopping its trajectory, I catch it midair. I cannot congratulate myself, for now I have a big spot of ink right in the center of my chest. That I have now ruined my only professional dress . . . I don't even know what to do. I don't care so much about the stares I will endure for the remainder of my train ride, but replacing it will be a time and expense I don't think Lady Jane can spare and—I am so angry with myself. Here we are at a stop in some stupid city, I don't even know which one, and this would be the perfect time to get some good writing done without all the bumps of the moving train. Instead I am blotting ink from my front and holding back tears like a child.

"Hello," a woman's voice says. "Would you mind if I sit next to you?"

I look up to see someone with a scrubbed-clean face that reminds me of Young Martha's. She looks older than me, not by much.

I grunt, sliding my trunk that has been fashioned as a writing desk, moving my pots and quills and parchment. Not that she has asked for this level of restructuring, this little mouse of a thing.

"Thank you for being so accommodating," she says. "I have been told many times that a woman should not ride unaccompanied. I felt perhaps we could be each other's accompaniment."

How many days have I been on this train? Too many, for I have forgotten how to make an appropriate reply and merely nod, grunting a barnyard-animal type of assent.

We introduce ourselves, using our names and little awkward handshakes. Her first name is Millie. She makes no comment about mine consisting only of vowels.

"You are a writer?" she asks, noting the parchment.

"Yes," I say. I point to the blot on my chest. "And a sloppy one."

"It's a badge of honor," she says with conviction. "I'm proud for you."

I sniff back my sorrow and put on a brave face.

"What type of things do you write?"

"Editorials," I say, without qualification of publication history. "And investigative reports. I am not certain which, yet, this one will be. I write for newspapers."

"Oh, good for you!" Millie seems as proud as a parent. "And good for all of our sex. I am delighted to hear it. What is this editorial or investigative report about?"

"Have you heard of Cathie Fox? She knocks, she channels, she séances."

"Oh, yes," she says, eyes wide and shining. "What a fascinating subject."

We speak a bit about Cathie, but it quickly turns into a discussion about the realm of spirits and how different cultures think about that which animates life. Millie, my new companion, has knowledge about ancient civilizations. She asks me what I know about spirit-writing, as it is called. I don't know enough to say much of anything, but to ask how it is done.

"Well," she says, leaning in close as if it is confidential, "one must quiet the mind, use a process to invoke a spirit, and ask them to write with one's hand, and voilà!" She practically yells out that last French word. "Apologies," she whispers. "I certainly didn't mean to say that so loud."

"So have you tried it?" I ask. It seems as dangerous and thrilling as walking out naked to worship the moon.

"Yes," she says. "I am a poet, you see, but I was struggling with finding inspiration. I thought how wonderful it would be if I could have a conversation with Sappho—do you know her?"

"I can't say that I do."

"She is the first widely recognized female poet. From the sixth century BC. Her poems only survive as fragments, but here is one of my favorites. 'Like the sweet apple which reddens upon the topmost bough, / Atop on the topmost twig—which the pluckers forgot, somehow— / Forget it not, nay; but got it not, for none could get it till now.'"

Well, I am charmed. My first impression of this woman was that she looked rather ordinary. When she recites poetry, her face reflects the goddess.

"I tried my hand at spirit-writing," Millie continues. "There is something to it. Perhaps the words themselves are a type of connection, a telegraph through time."

"I have thought of something similar myself. Maybe all writing is 'spirit' writing. Isn't all reading 'spirit' reading?"

"Indeed!" she says. "What else are these thoughts, moving through the past to become present. It's just as it says in the Gospel of John, 'In the beginning was the Word.'"

The train lunges, and we fall into each other and then back out again, giggling like children.

The nasty, terrible, interminable purgatory of this ride has been so quickly transmutated.

"What a coincidence to have just met you," she says.

"There are some that say there are no coincidences," I reply.

"Then why have such a lovely word for it?" she says. "Although perhaps *serendipity* is better. Which do you prefer?"

I like them both with increasing affection, especially as we discuss the subtle differences.

We talk words, poems, stories. I tell her what I noticed about geometry in the face of a sunflower, she tells me what she learned about love from the night sky. Time seems to both stand still and pass in an instant.

Whether by coincidence or serendipity, Summerland or a child's game of snaps, it's the simple truth—there is no greater comfort in heaven or earth than being in the presence of a kindred spirit.

AFTERWORD

Since the first moment I read about the Fox sisters, I was inspired to write about them. I began my journey, appropriately enough, by going to a psychic and asking her to contact them. The psychic told me that the departed sisters were willing to work with me. They even showed her a shovel as a signal for me to start digging. In planning this novel, I dug through a long list of biographies, memoirs, letters, and academic texts from both the time period and more current sources. Some of these are included below, but not all.

Ann Braude's *Radical Spirits* (1989), Nancy Rubin Stuart's *The Reluctant Spiritualist: The Life of Maggie Fox* (2005), and Barbara Weisberg's *Talking to the Dead: Kate and Maggie Fox and the Rise of Spiritualism* (2004) are a mighty trilogy in modern understanding of the Fox sisters' impact on culture, religion, and activism. Their bibliographies guided me onward.

I used some of Horace Greeley's own words from his autobiography *Recollections of a Busy Life* (1868). I got an original copy from a rare book seller, complete with the illustrated plates of his houses and whiffable old book smell. Margaret Ferrand Thorp's book, *Female Persuasion: Six Strong-Minded Women* (1949), led me to Jane Swisshelm and the quote, "I think it is a sin to be polite in these times." Margaret Fuller and Jane Swisshelm are generally noted to be the first two American female news correspondents, both employed by Horace Greeley. Edith Ann Howe is purely my invention.

Like E. A., reading Frederick Douglass's *Narrative of a Life* (1845) lit a fire in my heart. I have read nothing from that time period that can touch it as far as its enduring emotional and literary excellence. David W. Blight's *Frederick Douglass: Prophet of Freedom* (2018) helped me to understand Douglass's touring schedule with William Lloyd Garrison.

All Garrison's words that he speaks from the pulpit of the Broadway Tabernacle Church are culled from his actual speech, "No Compromise with Slavery: An Address Delivered in the Broadway Tabernacle" (1854). Douglass's speech from the pulpit contains his own words taken from a speech he gave in Lynn, Massachusetts, "The Blood of the Slave on the Skirts of the Northern People" (1848), with the exception of the very end of the speech. I am grateful to the Frederick Douglass Papers Project and the Library of Congress for the collection of these speeches.

I am particularly indebted to Barbara Goldsmith's *Other Powers: The Age of Suffrage, Spiritualism, and the Scandalous Victoria Woodhull* (1999) for solving the mystery of Mary Cheney Greeley's character for me. I used Goldsmith's research on quotes attributed to Mary Greeley and her son, Arthur "Pickie" Greeley, as part of imagined dialogue and spirits channeled. Mary's abuse, neglect, and mental illness were referenced more obliquely in other works. Goldsmith does not shy away from describing Mary's hellish reality that others, like her husband, shut behind closed private doors.

The University of Rochester has an online archive of letters sent to Amy and Issac Post, including two letters from Cathie Fox. Seeing these and her handwriting from her time at the Greeley estate was meaningful to me in imagining her as a real child and not just as the subject of so many books. In biographies and texts, "Catherine," "Katie," "Cathie," and "Kate" are all used for the same person. Mostly commonly she is called Katie or Kate Fox, but after reading her letters, Cathie was the name/spelling that I most connected with for the character of this book. It is from her own letters that Cathie's quote, "I hate her"—referring to Mary Greeley—is taken, as well as her writing of the "marvelous" things the spirits were doing, including touching everyone on the shoulder and playing instruments during a seance.

"Camptown Races," "Nellie Bly, Ah!" "May the Red Rose Live Always," and "American Taxation" are songs and poems of the times. Sappho's poem, "One Girl," was accessed online through The Poetry Foundation and was translated by Dante Gabriel Rossetti.

I most gratefully acknowledge the profound public good that is the library system where I live in Massachusetts. I think it's Benjamin Franklin who is credited with starting the first library system in America. There is nothing in this country that has done me so much personal good throughout my life than the public libraries. Bless the librarians and bibliophiles.

I made a few pilgrimages to put myself in the actual spaces this story takes place, whatever is left of them.

I began writing this book in earnest in Lily Dale, the spiritualist center in upstate New York, where a museum boasts the trunk of Charles Rosna. They have a wonderful library filled with books on every woo-woo concept you could wish for, and the entire hamlet is filled with mediums. On my way there, I stopped by the location of the Hydesville house, where a marker around the foundation rests. A dead bird in front of the glass was a sad reminder of the lack of bird-friendly windows—and also a sad irony in terms of her proximity to the sign, THERE IS NO DEATH. The actual Hydesville house was moved to Lily Dale in the early 1900s, but has since burned to the ground.

The Greeley estate of this book is a hodgepodge home nightmare that never existed, but a house in the woods he called Castle Doldrum/ Doleful did. There is a Horace Greeley house in Chappaqua, New York, where the family moved in 1864. You can visit that place, and the wonderful volunteers who maintain it can show you around. If you expect ghosts, you will be disappointed.

All of this digging helped me find ideas for settings, events, dialogue, characters, and the timeline of the story. However, even when I use actual quotes from the historical figures or refer to historical events, I make no claim to historical accuracy or even passing fidelity to facts.

I do, however, claim a deep fidelity to the spirit of Cathie Fox, and hope that this book honors her.

I want to believe in spirits . . . and so I do.

ACKNOWLEDGMENTS

I am so grateful for the following people, who have helped me bring this book to life.

My incredible agent, Priya Doraswamy. The wonderful Laura Van der Veer, who believes in this book and the next to come. The expertise and encouragement of Alison Castleman, Megan McKeever, Karah Nichols, Jo O'Neill, Rosanna Brockley, and the whole Little A team. Ryan Lewis, my awesome film/TV manager.

Louise Dale, who believed in art as a way to save the world. John Skipp, a champion of my work and one of my dearest friends. Carolynne Dale Levine, Francesca Lia Block, Chris Kelso, Courtney Sutton, Kameron Runyan, Eric Siegel, Susanna Brown, Jesse Nickerson, Debra Curtin, Josh Malerman, Ariel Kiley, Rabbi David Werb, and my BFF Natasha Levinger. My mother, who taught me to doubt, and my father, who taught me to believe. Emily Trask, who helps me be social. My partner Ezra, who helps with everything.

My friends in the South Shore Preparatory Meeting and all those who, with conscience and commitment, show up to work for peace and equality.

ABOUT THE AUTHOR

Photo © 2018 Ashley Inguanta

Laura Lee Bahr is the author of the novels *Who Is the Liar*, *Haunt*, winner of the Wonderland Book Award for Best Novel of 2011; and *Long-Form Religious Porn*; and the short story collection *Angel Meat*, a Wonderland Book Award winner for Best Collection 2017. Her short stories have been featured in over a dozen literary magazines and anthologies, including *Ghost Parachute*, *Tragedy Queens*, Francesca Lia Block's *Lit Angels*, and the Noir Volume of Nicholas Winding Refn's byNWR.com. Her filmography includes writing/directing the feature film *Boned*, winner of Best Micro-budget Feature, Toronto Independent Film Festival. She was awarded the spring 2018 writer-in-residence at the Kerouac House in Orlando, Florida. For more information, visit www.lauraleebahr.com.